STRIAN

VIKING GLORY BOOK FOUR

CELESTE BARCLAY

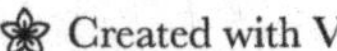 Created with Vellum

To all the women who forge their own path without reservation or regret, may you continue to march to the beat of your own drum.

SUBSCRIBE TO CELESTE'S NEWSLETTER

Subscribe to Celeste's bimonthly newsletter to receive exclusive insider perks.

Subscribe Now

VIKING GLORY

Leif
Freya
Tyra & Bjorn
Strian
Lean & Ivar

Lorna + Rangvald Thorsson
Lena + Ivar Sorenson
Erik Rangvaldson
Freya Ivarsdottir
Leif Ivarsson
Sigrid Torbensdottir
Reinhold Erikson
Thorsen Leifson & Ilka Leifsdottir
Bjorn (Cousin)
Tyra (Friend)
Strian (Friend)
Gressa Jorgensdottir

ONE

Strian looked over his shoulder at the woman rowing just two benches behind him. Other Norsemen surrounded her, but she appeared out of place and alone. Despite trying to remain focused on navigating his ship towards the fjord just beyond his home, Strian Eindrideson failed to overcome the temptation to look back at Gressa time and again.

Gressa Jorgensdóttir refused to lift her gaze from the shoulder blades of the people seated in front of her. She followed the rhythm of the other rowers as her oar dipped and slid first through the water then in the air before returning to the water. She could feel Strian's eyes on her even though she had not looked up in hours. She refused. She refused to acknowledge him, and she refused to acknowledge her own feelings, or rather the ones he stirred in her. She forced her mind to focus on the motions needed to keep her oar synchronized with the other rowers. She would not allow herself to think about how her hands, blistered and raw, ached from rowing for hours after not having touched an oar in years. She would not think about how her stomach rumbled from refusing anything but the most meager amounts of food; one of the few rebellious acts available to her. She would not think about how once again fate forced an abrupt sacrifice of the life she had. She would not think about Strian. There was far more for her not to think about than what she was willing to entertain, but her attempts to force her mind away from the painful topics only made them linger in the forefront of her mind even more. Gressa caught herself before she shook her head.

Strian gave up all attempts at ignoring Gressa the second day aboard his ship. It was an exercise in futility to pretend she did not exist. He had never been able to ignore her, and ten years of separation had not changed that. Gressa stood out from the rest with her heart-shaped face, dark brown hair, and deep blue eyes with their almond shape, giving proof to her Sami heritage. None of her clothes resembled the ones he remembered. Gone were the conical rolled toes on her boots or the beading at the hems of her wrists and collar that she wore at home. The more subdued forest colors of a Welsh bowman replaced her Sami clothing. Her clothes had always made her stand out, first as a Sami and now as a Welshwoman. But Strian knew the clothes did not matter. His memories clutched to the images of Gressa when she was undressed. He snapped his eyes back to the water and slammed the door shut on those memories. They had haunted him ever since he last saw Gressa, and now they caused a painful knot to squeeze his heart.

"Captain, Tyra's given the signal that we are only five knots from the entrance to the fjord. We will be home soon." Strian nodded once to his first mate and followed the man to the stern where he took the rudder from one of his oarsmen.

Now that Strian was behind Gressa, it was easier

for him to watch her. It was not so obvious when she was in his line of sight as he navigated the ice and sandbars. He had been sailing in and out of his homestead's natural harbor since he was a child. He could spare some of his attention and continue to watch Gressa. The linen shirt she wore stuck to her sweaty body, and he could see the muscles ripple through her back and shoulders as she continued to row. He watched her head twist slightly to the side as though she might look back at him. He knew she was aware he watched her, but he had caught her staring at him just as many times.

Strian guided his longboat into the harbor and docked beside Bjorn's and Tyra's boats. He avoided Freya because their falling out just before they left Scotland remained unresolved. Strian knew Freya felt guilty for their argument, and he did not enjoy being at odds with one of his oldest friends, but he would not overlook her high handedness as their leader or her unwillingness to hear why he wanted to remain in Scotland. Strian approached Gressa and waited until she noticed him. It was only a matter of a heartbeat before she looked up at him.

"Stay next to me," Strian whispered. When Gressa looked ready to object, Strian raised an eyebrow in warning. "It's been ten years."

Gressa sucked in a breath and looked at the place where she had grown up.

"Everything looks different but it still all looks the same," she breathed.

"You're right about that. Much is different, but the people are the same."

"Then you should have left me in Scotland," Gressa hissed. "They won't want me now any more than they did before I left."

"Is that why you hid? Is that why you didn't try to

find me?" Strian's deep voice rumbled in his chest, and Gressa could feel it as he leaned against her shoulder. He intended his words for only her ears.

"Does it matter?" She knew those were the words that would push Strian away, giving her space to think, but she had not anticipated the depth of hurt she would see when she looked at him. He reeled back from her.

"Why would you ask that? Of course, it matters. You still haven't told me what happened when we got separated."

"And I don't intend to." Gressa's mind filled with images of the battle they fought side by side then the injury that nearly killed her. She remembered being near death and calling out for Strian, but he never came. This brought back memories of the past ten years she had spent building a life in Wales.

"You will explain one of these days. If you won't volunteer the information to me, then Jarl Ivar will demand it. You still wear your fealty ring at your wrist. I've seen it several times." Strian did not wait for her answer before grasping her upper arm and pulling her towards the gangplank that was lowered to the dock. His hold was not so tight that Gressa could not have broken away, but she did not want to. Try as she might, she still longed for any contact with Strian that she could manage. Her pride railed at him maneuvering her about like livestock, but every other part of her longed for their bodies to touch.

"What will you do with me?"

"I told you before we left, I changed my mind. You are not a thrall. I said it in anger and hurt," the last word coming out more of a mumble. "I couldn't have made you one in truth, and there is no point in pretending. You are a free woman just as you were before."

"Being a thrall would be better," Gressa grumbled.

"And why is that?" Strian's curiosity got the better of him. He could not imagine Gressa ever accepting being a slave.

"I would be safer."

"What do you mean? You are returning to our people. You grew up here, and everyone knows your family."

"Exactly. Everyone knows I'm half Sami."

Gressa glared at Strian waiting for him to understand. She wanted to tap her toes with impatience as she waited for him to piece it together, but it did not seem to get any clearer to Strian the longer she waited.

"It was bad enough that my father captured my mother and made her his concubine, but when she died giving birth to me, and I wasn't a boy, it made me completely useless in his eyes. You know all of this. You heard him."

"I do, but I don't see how that has to do with your safety. You're home."

Gressa balled her fists and wanted to lash out at him for being so dimwitted.

"This isn't my home. How many times must I tell you that my home and my people are in Wales? My father never wanted me, and neither do any of these Norsemen. To them, I'm tainted. I'm more Sami than Norse. In Wales, none of that mattered. You should have left me where you found me." Gressa felt the burn of tears behind her eyes, but she refused to allow any to fall.

Strian leaned forward, nearly bending in half to look into her eyes.

"You are home. You will be safe. And you are not going back to Wales!" He was nearly yelling by the time he finished.

"Then my death will be on your hands because I promise you, I was safer in Wales. Damn it, I was safer fighting in Scotland."

"With Gr--" Strian did not have a chance to finish because it was their turn to disembark, and he could see Jarl Ivar and Frú Lena approaching. They had already greeted the others, and now it was his turn. He tugged Gressa along beside him until they were both on the dock.

"Strian, it is good---" Ivar's eyes widened as he took in the slender figure standing next to Strian. "Gressa?"

"Yes, Jarl Ivar. It's me." Gressa raised her chin, and the defiance was clear to everyone.

"We thought you were dead. I made Strian--- I mean, I forced--- Dear gods, child. I'm sorry. I should have listened to Strian." Almighty jarl's loss of words frightened Gressa more than any threat he might have lobbed. "Dear gods. Strian--"

Ivar Sorensen's shock was garnering attention that made both Strian and Gressa uncomfortable. The man was just as tall and as well muscled as Strian, who was more than twenty years his junior. It was disconcerting to see their leader so befuddled, and his face had lost all its usual ruddy color.

"Gressa," Lena intervened. "It fills my heart with happiness to see you return. Life has not been as sunny without you."

Coming from anyone else, Gressa would have felt Lena's words were a barb, but she had known the woman her entire life. She was the only one in the homestead who had been willing to attend her birth, and even though Gressa's mother did not survive the delivery, it was Lena who ensured Gressa had a place within their tribe. Lena brought Gressa into the jarl's longhouse when it was obvious that her own father would not provide for her. When the older woman opened her arms, it was the invitation she needed. Gressa lurched forward and allowed Lena to enfold her in an embrace that felt like home.

Strian watched as Gressa willingly allowed Lena to hold her, and the jealousy and pain from being excluded burned a gaping hole in his heart. Gressa had not welcomed him as she did Lena.

"I think you have much to tell us," Lena smiled as the two women backed apart.

"She has nothing to say that any of us want to hear," called out Freya as she walked past. "She is a traitor, and she would have made Strian one, too. We should have left her where we found her. As Grímr's woman."

Freya's last three words, "as Grímr's woman," had the exact intended effect. Strian pulled Gressa behind him and put his hand on his sword hilt. He challenged anyone to speak or come near him or Gressa. The crowd on the dock morphed from excited to vengeful with those three words.

"Come to the longhouse. I think you have much to explain," Ivar boomed. His lack of anger reassured Strian, but as Gressa clung to the back of his fur cloak, he knew she was unconvinced of her safety. As Strian looked around, he was certain she was right to fear the others.

"Jarl," Caution drove Strian's choice of words. "There is plenty to tell and plenty to hear, but the others can do just as good a job as I can. Besides, Tyra and Bjorn are to marry tomorrow. I heard the announcement before I even left my ship. I think it would be better if we didn't appear in the great hall."

"Nonsense. That will only make it look like you have something to hide." Ivar murmured. "Nothing will happen to Gressa. Anyone foolish enough to try, will answer to me."

The others left Strian on the dock with Gressa still clinging to him. He reached behind him and gently pulled her to stand beside him.

"He's wrong, Strian. I know it. You shouldn't have brought me here. I'm not safe." Gressa looked around and saw that they were alone at last. She let the tears fall that she had been swallowing for days.

Strian wrapped his arms around her loosely, and when she did not shy away, he pulled her to his chest. She burrowed into the familiar warmth and sobbed. She had fought her own will and Strian's for the past fortnight, and exhaustion overcame her she was exhausted. She knew she would regret accepting this comfort, but she needed it as much as she needed her next breath. Strian ran his hands over her hair as his other arm wrapped around her waist, and his thumb drew circles on her ribs.

"You may not want it, you may not accept, you may not even believe you need it, but you will always have my protection, Gressa. Always." Strian kissed the crown of her head, and he felt her tense before her entire body went lax. He was quick to catch her before she dropped to the ground. "Gressa?"

She made a soft sound like a wounded animal then her eyes fluttered open.

"Gressa, you've eaten so little since I found you. You insisted upon taking your turn at the oar, and you don't have enough clothes for this far north. You will make yourself ill." Strian paused for a moment as a thought came to him. "Is that what you're trying to do? Are you trying to make yourself sick enough to die? Do you want away from me that badly?"

Gressa looked tiny as she curled further into the warmth of Strian's body. She tried to shake her head, but the effort was too much.

"No. I love you." Those were the last words she spoke before she succumbed to blackness.

Strian looked around, but there was no one else on the dock. He lifted Gressa into his arms and walked to his longhouse.

TWO

S trian struggled to open the door with Gressa still in his arms, but he pushed against the wood until it gave way. He walked into the place he had called home for most of his life. He had been born in this home, and he had lived there with his parents until they were both dead. There had been several years when he lived with his aunt and uncle, but their house was never home. Even when his aunt and uncle were still alive, he always came back to this building when he needed to feel connected to his family. Since his uncle's death, he had returned to his parents' home. His aunt and cousins were already dead, and his uncle's shame blighted that longhouse. Here, he could still hear the voices of the people he loved and missed most. He walked across the center room until he came to the doorway that led to his chamber. He looked down at Gressa, her eyes closed and the blue veins shining through translucent skin, then pushed open the door. He pulled back the covers to his bed as best he could before laying Gressa on the mattress. He pulled her boots off and pulled the covers over her. He went to the chest at the foot of the bed and pulled out more blankets. There was one left at the bottom. It was a blanket he thought of often but refused to look at or touch. It had lived at the bottom of the chest since he returned from a raid ten years ago without his father or his wife.

Strian looked at Gressa once more and remembered the smile on Gressa's face when she presented the blanket to him as a gift. He ran his fingers over the stitches that represented them coming together as one. He had no more time to reminisce because Gressa called out to him.

"Strian?" Gressa's eyes were closed, and her voice craggy as though she had not used it in days. "Strian, don't leave! I'm over here! Don't go. Don't leave me. Why can't you hear me?"

Strian realized she was dreaming. Or rather, she was having a nightmare of the day fate separated them.

"Strian!" Her scream turned into a whimper as her fingers combed through the air grasping nothing.

"Gressa, I'm here. I'm not going anywhere. I can hear you." Strian sat on the edge of the bed, holding her hand. She relaxed as the pressure of his hand on hers registered, but she did not say another word.

Strian let her sleep as his mind ventured to the same place that caused Gressa's nightmare, the day war separated them. The day he lost his wife.

"Stay close to me, Strian. When I run out of arrows, then you can move ahead. Let me pick off as many as I can before you have to fight."

Strian looked down at the little pixie face set in stone. His wife of three months was not joking. Gressa intended to protect him from the battle that was about to begin. She was just as fierce as any of the other shieldmaidens. She had the same skill and strength as Tyra and Freya, but unlike the other two women, she had something worth defending. Strian knew she would fight to the death to protect him just as he would do the same for her.

His tribe had been tracking a band of neighboring Norsemen for close to a month after they raided his tribe's home. Strian and Tyra both lost their mothers in that raid, and Lena had almost died while trying to hide the other women. Gressa and Strian, along with Leif, Freya, Tyra, and Bjorn, had been with their fathers on a fishing trip when neighbors to the south overran their homestead, killing any and every one they saw.

"Strian, are you even listening to me?" Gressa pinched his forearm. "Stay behind me. You are a much bigger target than I am. Wait until there are few arrows flying before you charge forward."

Strian wrapped his large hands around Gressa's trim waist and lifted her until she was eye level with him. He gave her a firm peck before putting her back on the ground with a spank to her backside.

"I remember it was me who pledged to protect you. Don't be reckless, Gressa."

She pinched his arm again before rising on her toes and kissing his chin, the highest part of him she could reach since he was a foot taller than her.

"I would say the same to you. Just because you're bigger than most warriors doesn't make you any less mortal. You aren't one of the gods, even if you look like one." She grinned as she slapped his backside for good measure.

They heard the call go up from Ivar and Eindride, Strian's father. They moved into their position in the shield wall and waited for the order to move forward. It was only moments later that the first arrows bounced off their shields. Strian kept his shield locked with those at his shoulders, only pulling back long enough for Gressa to poke her bow and arrow through. The band of warriors moved as one with the shield wall unbroken, creating openings for archers to shoot at their enemy. They made steady progress, and Gressa would soon run out of arrows before the first chink in the shield wall fell. It was like a domino effect after that. One warrior after another screamed out in pain and tumbled to the ground, some to writhe in agony as others turned to stone.

"The shield wall won't hold much longer. Gressa, get behind me when it does. Shoot over my shoulder when you can, but otherwise stay down!" Strian had to yell to be heard over the cacophony of battle sounds even though Gressa was only inches away from him.

"All right."

They continued to advance, and Strian could hear his father's voice from further down the line, booming like thunder. The shield wall gave way, and the melee began in truth. Warriors from both tribes clashed as they wielded their shields as weapons just as they did knives and swords. Blood splattered across Strian's chest as he used his long reach to block anyone who might try to get past him and get to his bride.

"Strian, to the right."

Strian twisted in time for Gressa to release an arrow into the neck of a man he had not even seen approaching them.

"Thank you."

"You can make it up to me tonight. With that thing you do with your tongue."

"You're thinking about that right now?" Strian chuckled even though they were amid a gruesome scene.

"I need something to look forward to." Gressa teased as she threw her knife into the eye of a man who prepared to charge them.

"I will gladly offer that if you don't fall asleep again while I make love to you. It's rather insulting."

"That happened only once. And it had been a long day of riding and then fighting. It wasn't a reflection upon your skills."

Strian's snort turned into a grunt as he lunged forward and brought his blade across his enemy's ribs. The fighting became too intense to continue talking. Strian would regret for the rest of his life that he had not tried harder to keep talking to Gressa. He might have discovered she was missing far sooner.

Gressa tripped over a body with sightless eyes as she tried

to keep up with Strian. A fight with another shieldmaiden, who wielded a sword and an axe, forced her to fall behind. She was a fierce opponent but held too high an opinion of herself if she believed she did not need a shield. Gressa hacked and slashed until her opponent lay waiting for a Valkyrie to carry her to Odin. By the time Gressa could look around for Strian, she could not spot him. She scanned the battlefield, but he was nowhere in sight. She controlled the panic that wanted to take hold as fear flooded her. She was not scared about her own safety but that of Strian. She rushed forward toward other members of her tribe, but she still could not find her husband. She was nearly to where Freya and Tyra fought alongside one another, but fire ripped through her back and into her thigh. She staggered several steps until her leg went numb, and her entire body felt as though it disappeared from beneath her neck. Gressa pitched forward and landed with a thud, her head ringing with the vibration and the sounds of the ongoing battle around her. She looked around, but when she sensed someone stepping over her, she shut her eyes and remained motionless. Later, she would look back and realize pretending to be dead was what kept her from dying. Whoever felled her assumed they had killed her too, because they left her where she lay.

Gressa laid in the same spot, blood pooling around her, for what felt like hours. The battle shifted away from her, and the sun moved across the sky. She forced herself into action and dragged her uncooperative body behind her as she crawled on her elbows until she met the tree line and could hide. It was several hours later that she heard a voice she recognized.

"Gressa!" The voice screamed over and over.

"I'm here." She could not muster more than a whisper. No one, not even her, could hear her as she tried to lift her arm. Most of the bleeding had slowed, but she was too weak to do more.

"Gressa! Where are you?" Strian's despair was palpable, and her heart ached to cause him such pain when she was so close.

"Strian, we must go."

Gressa twisted her head to see Bjorn running towards her. She tried to call out to him, but no sound came from her mouth.

"Strian, we've searched for hours. No one has seen Gressa. They may have taken her."

"All the more reason to search for her. Bjorn, I'm not leaving without my wife. Go without me. But I will not leave without her."

"You have little choice. Ivar is ordering us all back to the boats."

"No."

"What do you mean, 'no'?" Bjorn was incredulous. "You can't say no to the jarl's order."

"I can, and I am. I already found my father's body. Without Gressa, what do I have to return to? Nothing. I am not leaving without her."

Gressa watched as Strian changed directions and started to walk towards where she hid in the bushes. She reached out her hand and called to him.

"Bjorn, shh. What was that? I'm sure that was Gressa calling me."

Gressa held her breath before trying to yell as loudly as she could, but it was more a whimper than a bellow.

"There it is again. I know I heard my name."

"I didn't hear anything. Come on, Strian. We must go. Ivar won't wait much longer."

"And I told you, I'm not going anywhere without her."

Gressa watched in horror as Strian drew his sword against his best friend, and in turn Bjorn pulled out his knife. They circled one another, but before the fight could begin, it ended. Leif and Ivar lunged forward and caught Strian's arms as Bjorn, joined by Strian's uncle Einar, caught his legs. He twisted and writhed, head butting Leif more than once, but he was no match for the four large warriors. They bound him and dragged him away.

"I curse each one of you. I will never forgive you for this. She is alive and nearby. I know it, and you're abandoning her. May the gods curse each of you. I won't leave my wife."

Those were the last words Gressa heard from Strian even though his howls carried through the air. Anyone who had not seen Strian being restrained would have thought it was an engaged wolf baying at the moon.

Exhaustion had a choke hold on Gressa as the last dregs of energy evaporated along with her hopes of rescue. She regretted thinking the trees would offer her safety. Instead, they were her undoing. She closed her eyes and gave into the craving to sleep.

"Here's one," a whiny tone filled Gressa's ears as her eyes fluttered open. She snapped them shut when pain surged through her back and leg. She gagged as the excruciating tingling and burning rippled from her wounds into every inch of her.

"This one is alive. Barely. I saw her fight. She's worth keeping. She'll bring plenty of money if she survives."

Rough hands grabbed Gressa's hair and lifted her head from the ground.

"Yes, this is the one I saw, too. Remarkable archer and would be good with a sword if she paid more attention to those around her. I was the one to cut her down. I claim her as my thrall."

Gressa watched a middle-aged woman walk around her until the older woman's toes slipped under her shoulder. Gressa could not swallow the groan when the other woman used her foot to push her onto her back. Gressa was in agony as her wound hit the ground. Any thoughts of responding were gone when blackness swallowed her once more.

Gressa had never been seasick, but she was sure she would be as her stomach pitched one direction then the next. She struggled to open her eyes as they felt crusted shut. Her tongue slid along her salty lips, and Gressa knew she was on a boat.

Various thoughts fluttered through her head, but the two

loudest were that she did not know whose boat she was on or where it was headed.

"Mae hi'n effro." A man's voice floated to her. She searched her memory for the words she heard, but there were barely any memories to begin with, let alone ones in a foreign language.

"Who are you?" Another voice asked in her own Norse tongue.

"Gressa," She mumbled.

"Gressa what?"

She refused to give any more information until she knew who held her captive and where she was going.

"Gressa what?" The voice repeated. After a long pause, a sigh followed. "You can make this easy for yourself or you can dig your own grave. I already know you are one of Ivar's people, but you aren't really Norse, are you?"

Gressa bit her tongue. She refused to say or do anything. The owner of the voice came into focus. It was the same middle-aged woman who had found her on the battlefield.

"You recognize me. Very well. You remember that I claimed you as my thrall?" Again, the voice waited, but Gressa did nothing. "I decided it's worth more to sell you than keep you as my slave. I just have to keep you alive."

"Sell me back then," Gressa managed to choke out.

"Back? To Ivar? To that husband who nearly got himself killed trying to abandon his people for his Sami bride?"

Gressa lifted her head at the woman's last comment.

"Oh, yes. We watched from the bushes. Not only was your husband bound and dragged to his jarl's ship, he jumped overboard the moment they untied him. He was trying to get back to you. Last any of us saw him, they lashed him then shackled to the mast."

Gressa stifled the sobs that fought to escape her throat. She looked away from the older woman as she pictured Strian fighting not only their jarl, but his uncle and his best friends. Fighting them to get to her. She prayed to Frigg and Freya that he would do nothing to get himself killed. She shifted slightly, *but this time she could not suppress the sound that escaped as her wound shot blazing pain to the very tips of her toes and fingers.*

"I wouldn't move around so much if you don't want to bleed to death. You won't do me much good dead."

"Where are you taking me?"

"You shall see when you arrive." The woman bent over her and ripped apart the vest and tunic she wore. A bucket of water seemed to appear out of nowhere, and the woman dumped the saltwater over Gressa's wounds. It felt like a thousand pin-pricks dancing across the serrated skin of her back and leg. Before she caught her breath, the searing pain intensified as Gressa caught a whiff of syra, a fermented wine, as she poured it onto the wound. It was believed to have healing prop-erties, but Gressa could not get past the putrid odor.

"I must stitch this." The middle-aged woman, whose name Gressa still did not know, took a needle and thread from a pouch tied at her waist. Gressa had no way of knowing if the woman knew what she was doing, but she trusted her. She hated to admit it, but it was obvious the woman was a sea-soned warrior. Gressa was certain her wounds would not be the first the woman had sewn. Her would-be healer yanked the belt from Gressa's waist.

"Here." Gressa took the leather and bit down on it before rolling back onto her stomach.

It took the woman over an hour to stitch Gressa's back and leg, and by the time she finished, Gressa had a raging fever and was unconscious.

The next time Gressa awoke was when the boat bumped into something and lurched to one side. She lifted her head to see they were docked, and it was the dock that they had knocked against. Gressa had no idea where she was, how long she had been asleep, or what would happen next.

"I see our invalid has rejoined the living." The words came from a voice she did not recognize. "You've been battling a fever

for a week and barely been awake. I doubt you remember any of it."

Gressa tested out shaking her head. There was a dull ache in her skull that matched the ache that seemed bone deep in her back. She tried moving her injured leg, and relief flooded her when she could flex her foot. She had feared she would lose the leg.

"Where are we?"

"Your new home. Wales."

Strian sat beside Gressa until she awoke. He had a pitcher of water and a tray that held cheese, bread, and an apple waiting for her.

"Water," Gressa croaked.

Strian helped prop her up as she sipped the cool liquid.

"How long have I been asleep?"

"The rest of the day and into the night. I would say it's an hour or two after midnight. Would you like something to eat?"

"The apple, please." She reached for it, but her hand remained empty. She watched Strian peel then cut the apple just as she had always preferred. He did not appear to give much thought to his actions, as though it was still a habit. He passed the wedges to her and waited in silence as she ate.

"What happens now?" She asked around the bite of apple she had taken.

"I'm guessing you would like to bathe and have fresh clothes."

Gressa's brow creased as she was uncertain if Strian was being purposely evasive. She looked into his gray eyes; never having forgotten how they were so translucent that they appeared almost silver. It matched his sun-bleached hair. He wore it longer now than when they had been a young couple of seventeen and nineteen. Her fingers itched to comb through the tresses just as she had done countless times while he courted her and then during their all too brief marriage. She forced her mind to return to the present.

"It's the middle of the night. I can't go to the bathhouse at this hour."

"If you want the steam and then the cold-water dunk, then I will take you and stand guard outside, but if you'd prefer to stay here, then I still have the tub I could fill."

Gressa's cheeks flamed red as a vivid memory of them making love in the tub on their wedding night and then several more times when his parents socialized at the jarl's home.

"Why are you being so solicitous?"

Strian chose to ignore her, instead moving to a chest that sat in a corner. He lifted the lid and pulled out several pieces of clothing. Gressa gaped as he laid out the beautifully stitched knee-length tunic and the wide leg pants worn under the tunic.

"You kept my clothes?" she murmured.

"Of course. I assumed you would need them again one day." Strian returned with a pair of her Sami rolled toe slippers.

"But it's been ten years."

"I haven't forgotten," Strian's voice was tight as he forced out those three words.

Gressa filled her lungs until they hurt, knowing she should not start this discussion now, but her curiosity would go unsatisfied until she had her answers.

"Why don't you have a wife?"

Strian's eyes narrowed to slits.

"I do have a wife."

Gressa considered playing ignorant but decided better.

"A companion then?"

"I pledged my fidelity to my wife."

At that, Gressa snorted.

"You as much as admitted when we were at Castle Varrich that you'd been with other women."

"You assumed that. I never said I had."

"You accused me of having been with other men." Gressa snapped her mouth shut wishing she could retrieve the words that hung in the air.

"A shame only one of us was right." Strian turned to walk out of the room, but Gressa tumbled forward as she tried to rip the sheets out of her way. She grabbed Strian's arm and pulled none too gently.

"I explained that. I explained I had no choice. He didn't bed me." Gressa looked away, too ashamed to meet his eyes. "He made me do something else. On my knees." The last part came out as only a whisper.

"There was always a choice, Gressa. You chose to remain with the Welsh. You chose to travel with the other archers. And you chose to warm Grímr's bed. They are not your people."

"They are."

Strian caught Gressa's hand as she swung at his cheek.

"They are not. Tell me. How many other women came with you?"

"None," Gressa's forehead crinkled. "None are experienced fighters like I am. There are many who can shoot, but none who have fought like I have."

"And it was vital that you go? I saw other Welsh

archers as good as you. Why would your prince send you as the only woman?" Strian paused for effect. "I can tell you why he sent a beautiful woman to an evil man. You were either part of the payment or they meant you to be an enticement." Strian leaned forward. "Unless you are a spy. Did you fuck him so you could take information back to your precious prince? Is that who you are bedding?"

Gressa wailed in anger as her knee came up and struck Strian's groin. When he bent over double, she brought her fists down as one and struck the side of his neck.

"I'm not a whore," she screamed. "And you have a foul mouth these days."

She was not sure if she was angry at Strian's insinuation or because he spoke aloud what she had deduced weeks ago. It was one thing to hear her own mind chide her, but to hear Strian voice the second greatest betrayal of her life was more than she could bear.

Strian pushed his shoulder into her middle causing her to fall backwards, but he cradled her head before she landed. He covered her body with his and groaned as she writhed and struggled beneath him. His bollocks hurt from the combination of her striking him there and the growing arousal from having her beneath him.

"Yield," he ground out.

"Never," she spat.

"I'm sorry."

Gressa froze. She had not expected those being his next words.

"For what part?"

"All of it."

Gressa's heart broke as she saw the pain in Strian's eyes. It was there whenever he looked at her. She had seen it disappear when he spoke to his friends and then flood back in when he saw her.

"The past is the past," she whispered. "But I am not a spy nor was I the prince's mistress. His wife is my friend. I realized he wasn't mine weeks ago. You're right. I'm sure that's why he sent me, but I hate hearing it said aloud. It makes it real, and I can't deny it."

Strian stood and pulled her to her feet.

"I wish they hadn't manipulated and used you. You don't deserve it. Do you think your friend, the prince's wife, knew you were being sent?"

"Of course, she did. We said our goodbyes."

"And she didn't warn you? Neither of you figured it out? Or did she know all along and said nothing?"

Gressa eyes widened then slammed shut. She shook her head, and when she opened them, tears streamed from them.

"She and the prince have a good marriage. She counsels him on most things. It was her idea," Gressa choked out.

"Then who else do you have to return to? Grímr?"

Gressa bit her tongue before she said things she could not take back.

"I told you I made that choice rather than wait for him to force me. I told you I did it because he threatened to kill you. You specifically. He may have wanted Ivar, Freya, and Leif dead to claim this homestead, but he wanted you dead for the sheer pleasure of watching the life slip away from you."

"Why would I matter that much to him? I don't believe you." Strian shook his head as he looked into the fathomless blue eyes he once thought he could drown in.

"It had always been your uncle Einear's plan to kill you just as he did your father along with his wife and children. But it was his ineptitude, or at least that's what Grímr believes, that ruined his plans. Grímr had been content to let his brother Hakin and your uncle do all the dirty work. But it was you and Leif, Freya, Tyra, and Bjorn who burned his homestead. It was Freya and Erik who discovered his wife's slave trade. That discovery cost Grímr financially. It may have been Inga's treachery that led to her own brother killing her. I know Rangvald had no other choice." Gressa rushed to explain what she had learned, hoping that sharing the information would prove she was not there as a spy. What spy would give away so much?

"I still don't see how any of this has to do with me. I wasn't with Freya and her husband when they went scouting. I wasn't the one to kill his bastard son. Freya was the one who caused Hakin to bleed to death. I have merely been a silent warrior through all of this."

"You have to know that Grímr's mind is warped. It doesn't think like a normal person's. He believes that you are one of Ivar's favorites just like Tyra and Bjorn are. Ivar has always treated the three of you more like his own children than just tribe members. He wants to capture and torture you in front of the others. When I overheard two of his sons talking about all of this, I had to find out what he planned. You deduced why they sent me as the only woman before I did. Maybe I fulfilled the Welsh prince's plans, but I didn't do it for the prince's alliance with Grímr."

"Then why did you? If you really hadn't been with another man since me, why choose Grímr?"

Gressa threw her hands up in the air.

"He gave me the choice of coming willingly or by force. Was that ever really a choice?"

"And you just happened to learn all this information about your enemy. How do I know you're not really on Grímr's side and you're not filling my ears with lies?" Strian pulled the door open and then slammed it shut behind him.

"Because I love you," Gressa whispered to an empty room.

FOUR

Strian did not know what to do with himself. He was hurt and furious. Furious that any man might force Gressa to service him. Hurt that she had agreed. Furious at himself for being hurt when the only other option for Grímr to rape Gressa. It hurt him that she had not tried to escape or done more to turn Grímr off. And furious that she would compromise herself to protect him when he should have been protecting her all along.

He picked up a piece of crockery from his table and smashed it into the fireplace. He was tempted to go on a rampage through his home, but he knew that would solve nothing, and he would only regret later destroying things that had been his parents' and his while Gressa lived there. He also did not want to frighten her.

Strian built up the fire and pulled the tub before the hearth. He slipped out of his home with four buckets and a yoke. He made his way to the well and filled one bucket after another before trudging home where he heated each bucket before dumping the water into the tub. When he finished, he walked to his chamber door, the room that was once more occupied by his wife, but this time without him. He knocked twice.

"There is a bath before the hearth. I will wait in my parents' chamber."

He did not wait for an answer before he walked to the next door down and shut himself into the room that had once been his parents' sleeping chamber. He had not been in it for years, rather keeping it shut up and ignored. The painful memories flooded back to him, first of him as a child climbing into bed with his parents when thunder frightened him then the image of finding his mother on that same bed, brutalized and with her throat slit. He could not take another step forward, but he would not invade Gressa's privacy.

Strian was unprepared for the door to bump into his back. He turned around to see Gressa peeking in on him, her eyes wide as saucers.

"Strian," her voice broke. "You don't have to wait in here. I never meant for you to hide in your own home, and certainly not---" She waved her hand at the room, unable to finish.

"It's fine," the words slipping out from between clenched teeth.

"No, it's not." Gressa pushed the door open further and took Strian's hand. She tugged, and he followed without resistance. "Thank you for my bath. I won't take long, so hopefully there will still be some warm water left for you."

The vacant expression on Strian's face unnerved Gressa. It was as though he had seen a ghost.

"Strian?"

"It's fine," he repeated.

Gressa did not know what to do. She had caused his pain ever since they had been reunited.

"One day that was supposed to be our chamber, and our children would have had mine." Strian spoke to thin air as though Gressa was not truly there. He did not look at her before he walked to the front door where he paused long enough to warn her to bar the door and open it for no one but him. He did not say where he was going or when he would return.

Gressa stripped out of her filthy clothes, regretting that Strian had put her in his bed on clean sheets. She stepped into the tub and slid under the water before sitting up and reaching for the bar of soap. She was quick to wash her hair then scrub her body. The water was already growing cold, and she had goosebumps. After she dried herself, she scrubbed her clothes in the murky water. She was relieved that Strian would not be using the water that she had left a shade of brown before she even dunked her clothes in. She assumed he would not be using the water. She had no idea if he would return that night. She slipped back into his chamber and had just finished dressing when there was a knock on the door.

She crept towards it and called out, "Who is it?"

"Gressa, it's me." Strian's monotone voice responded.

She quickly lifted the bar and let Strian in. He did not look at her, instead going straight to the tub. He scooped a bucket of water from the tub and went outside to toss it out. Gressa watched him do it a second time before rushing to grab her own bucket of water. When the tub was empty, Strian returned it to its spot out of the way then laid down on the ground before the fire, his back turned to her.

FIVE

Gressa spent a fitful rest of the night unable to get uncomfortable, mainly because her mind would not quieten. She had never imagined she would be reunited with Strian let alone him finding out what she had done to try to ensure his safety. She had convinced herself that he would never learn of it, and since he would be none the wiser, he would be even safer. Guilt consumed her as she thought about breaking the pledge she had made to Strian all those years ago and for the betrayal she was sure he felt. But a part of her could not bring herself feel remorse. There was nothing she was not willing to do to protect him. She was relieved she had not had to share a bed with Grímr, but she would have. She would have sold her body to *Hel* if it would save Strian.

Strian woke just as the sun's first rays poked over the horizon. He was stiff from sleeping on the floor, but he was surprisingly warm even though the fire had died. He realized that during the middle of the night, Gressa had brought two blankets out and covered him. He looked towards the door to his chamber and scrambled to his feet when he saw it wide open. There was no way Gressa would have slept with it like that. She knew it made it too easy for an enemy to slip in and kill her in her sleep. He looked around in a panic.

She fled.

That one thought was all he had time for as something or someone banged into the door of his longhouse. Gressa awkwardly pushed the door open, her arms filled with a basket that held eggs and some vegetables, and she carried firewood as well. Strian crossed the room in a few long strides and lifted everything from her arms. Where Gressa's cheeks were stained pink from the exertion and crisp morning air, Strian's were ash white. Gressa reached out without thinking and put the back of her hand on his forehead then cheeks.

"Are you not feeling well?" She studied him before she understood. "You thought I ran."

Gressa backed away and turned her back to him, stung by his assumption. She gathered the eggs and reached for a bowl to crack them into, but she did not make it before strong hands gripped her waist and pulled her back against a wall of muscle. Strian inhaled the fresh scent of her clean hair. He had slipped into the bathhouse the night before, but he was sure he did not smell as tempting as she did. He kissed her temple as his hands slid over her belly, pausing before wrapping around her. She did not resist, the comfort feeling so familiar. Strian felt her give in and lean against him, but it was not enough. He turned her and lifted her chin, his mouth descending before either of them realized they both hungered for a kiss. Gressa opened her mouth before their lips met and welcomed Strian's invading tongue. They dueled as the kiss intensified. Gressa's hands roamed over Strian's body. He was well-built and handsome when they married, but he was still young at the time. Now his body was one of a fully-grown man. His shoulders were broader and felt as though they could carry the weight of ten men. His chest and stomach were chiseled, and she moaned at the feel of the muscles rippling in his back and the firmness of his backside.

Strian was starved for contact with the only woman he had ever loved, and the only woman he had desired since he was nineteen. Gressa had not been the first woman he coupled with. He had gained his experience with some of the most beautiful women in their tribe, having put forth little effort to gain their attention. But Strian would never forget the day he noticed Gressa had gone from a spindly girl to a well-developed woman. There had been no others since. He had allowed his friends to think he had moved on from Gressa. Their attempts to distract him had upset him, but he realized carrying on a charade was the best way to appease them.

He lifted the hem of her tunic and brushed his fingers against her satiny skin, eliciting a deep rumble from his chest. The sound amplified Gressa's own need to be skin to skin. She tugged at his tunic until she could slide her fingernails along the notches of muscle on his stomach. Strian's lips burned a scalding trail to her ear where his tongue grazed the whorl of her ear before nipping her earlobe. Gressa felt desire pool at the bottom of her belly as his iron length pressed against her mound. She rocked her hips as her hands moved to grip his buttocks. She pressed his hips forward to grind against hers.

Reason and sense crashed into Strian's mind, and he pulled away. He was sure Gressa would regret this, and he did not want her to believe he took advantage of her.

"We have to stop. We can't do this," he panted.

Gressa whimpered as the unspent lust ached within her core. She clung to Strian as her body began to tremble. Strian watched the confusion wash over her and need still shown in her eyes. He felt like a cad for making them both so aroused and then breaking off what he started. He did not know if walking away now, before they got more carried away, would be better or if he should bring her to release and risk her wrath after. When she whimpered again, his mind was made up.

"Shh, little one. I know. I feel the same. I will make the ache go away." Gressa's look of relief did little to convince him this was the right choice, but his hand dipped within the waist of her pants, and his fingers worked their way to her sheath. Her dew coated his fingers as he slid two into her. Memories of making love to her and what she enjoyed flooded him. His other hand traveled to find her breast under her tunic.

"Strian," she moaned. The sound of his name from her voice made him leak within his leather pants.

He pressed a third finger into her as her hips rocked, and she tried to gain the friction she needed. He kneaded her plump breast before pinching her nipple hard. It was all she needed to fall over the cliff, her climax surging through her as she threw her head back, eyes squeezed closed. A moment later, she yanked the front of his tunic and strained to meet his mouth. The kiss was brief but powerful and possessive. Strian drew his hands away to pull her against his body, but she had other plans. Her nimble fingers were already unfastening his belt, then she pushed his pants over his hips and dropped to her knees. She stroked him twice before her mouth encased his cock. Strian could not control his need to thrust, and she did not draw back, but rather sucked harder. Her moan vibrated against his cock, and he was sure this would be over before he could savor it. He looked down at her as she moved her lips over him, eyes still closed.

An image formed in Strian's mind, and it was the last thing he wanted to see. He pictured Gressa doing the same thing to Grímr. His arousal evaporated in an instant. He pushed back on Gressa's shoulders and pulled away.

"No."

"What? I thought you enjoyed this."

"I do, and you know that."

"Then why not let me pleasure you as you did me?"

"Because I know you had recent practice."

Gressa gasped and fell backwards, the power of his words feeling like a punch.

"I can't believe you said that," she whispered. "I can't believe you were thinking about that."

She looked up at Strian as tears streamed down her cheeks.

"You're going to punish me. Punish us for that." She rose to her feet. "You should have listened to me. I never should have come here. Not with you."

She spun around and stormed out of the long-house, and all Strian could do was stare at the door. His physical discomfort paled in comparison to his heart's. It ached for thinking of Gressa with another man, for the hurt he caused, and for the damage he had done to their tenuous truce.

SIX

G ressa was not sure where she was headed until she opened the door to the jarl's longhouse kitchens. She regretted it immediately. Every woman froze and stared at her, stared at her Sami clothing. She had not intended to leave Strian's home dressed in the clothes of her mother's people. She had stormed out without thinking. Now she regretted coming to a place where she would already be unwanted. She scanned the faces but did not see Lena, Freya, or Tyra. She remembered in an instant that they would be preparing for Tyra's wedding.

She looked at the hostile faces, none with so much as a welcoming smile or nod. They did not want her there, and in truth, she did not want to be there. But she was. She squared her shoulders and lifted her chin. She refused to back down. She entered the kitchens and went directly to Olga, the chief cook.

"Put me to work. Please." Gressa's tone was soft, but it carried throughout the silent kitchen.

Olga scrutinized everything from the top of her head to the tip of her shoes. She did not appear disappointed and jerked her head in the fire's direction.

"Turn the spit."

Gressa knew better than to say anything, even if the job was reserved for older boys who were still too young to train. She nodded and moved to the fireplace. It was not long before perspiration dripped from her nose and dribbled between her breasts and shoulder blades. The work was not strenuous after years of training as a shieldmaiden, but it was demeaning and hot. The only upside was she was out of the way of the rest of the women, so they pretended to ignore her. She sensed as much as saw many of them looking at her.

The morning creeped into midday, and Gressa's clothes stuck to her sticky skin. The refreshed feeling from the bath the night before was a distant memory as she continued to crank the handle that spun the meat.

"Sami." Gressa wanted to cringe. Despite the clothes she wore, she had never really identified with her mother's people. The only day she had was when she'd worn one of her mother's gowns to her wedding. The rest of the time, she loathed the ignominy that came with the title. They had called her it countless times over the years, but she had a sudden realization that either Strian or Freya and Tyra had always been nearby to defend her or lend silent support. She felt very much alone in every sense.

"Yes, Olga." She turned to face the bristly cook. Gressa had known the woman her entire life and had often helped Lena in the kitchens. The cook now sneered at her like she was an unwanted foreigner. She supposed she was in many ways.

"Take these slop buckets to the swine."

Yet another task that should have been given to an older boy. It took little effort to deduce that Olga wanted to humiliate her in the kitchens and outside. She nodded once before picking up two buckets and heading to the door. She stepped into the crisp air and realized the task was a blessing in disguise. It was later in the day than she realized, having been given a hunk of dry bread and a mug of ale for her noon meal. She breathed in the fresh air while she trudged to the pig pen. The hogs oinked and jostled one another when they smelled their meal coming. They splattered mud on the bottom of Gressa's embroidered pants. Gressa grimaced but continued to pour the slop into the trough.

"What have we here?"

Gressa refused to acknowledge the woman's voice. She was sure it was Soma, a woman Strian had been with before he began courting her. She had been one of the most beautiful women Gressa had ever seen. She had no interest in seeing the enchantress that never forgave her for luring Strian away.

"Are you ignoring me? A thrall ignoring a free woman? I'll have you whipped."

"I'm not a thrall. I am as free as you are." She turned her head enough for her words to be clear. "You can ask Strian."

The woman grunted before Gressa lurched forward from a powerful shove. Gressa stumbled but twisted in time to grab one of the arms that pushed her. She and Soma landed with a splash. Before she could get her bearing, someone lifted Gressa out of the mud. She thought that person had come to her aid, but instead, a ringing slap sent her head reeling back. The new woman's other hand was in Gressa's hair, tugging backwards. Gressa struggled to see who her new attacker was and recognized Magga, another woman from Strian's past.

The sound of their scuffle carried, and a crowd began to form. Women from the kitchens came to join the onlookers. They were already aware the fight involved Gressa and had brought rotten food to throw at her. Gressa forced herself to shut out the onlookers and focus on the two attackers. She brought her hand down in a knife slice and connected with Magga's inner elbow. Her reflexes made her release Gressa's hair and opened her to Gressa's fist slamming into the underside of her chin. Magga staggered backwards, but Gressa was already throwing her weight against Magga only to have Soma land on top of both of them. The women rolled around the sty, fists flying, and fingers bent like talons. Gressa managed to twist Soma off her back as she straddled Magga. She threw one fist after another while jabbing her elbows into Soma who tried to pull her off Magga. Gressa jerked her head back and cracked Soma's nose. She wrapped Gressa's hair around her hand and put a knife to her throat.

"No one wanted you here before you disappeared, and we're all far better off without you here again." Soma hissed.

Soma pulled Gressa to her feet and away from the other woman. Magga seized the opportunity to drive her fist into Gressa's stomach.

Gressa had all she was willing to take for the sake of not looking guilty for fighting. Her foot lashed out and landed in Magga's sternum. She pushed as hard as she could, hoping to break her breastbone. Magga fell to her knees holding her chest, gasping. Soma's blade had already torn a fine line along Gressa's skin. Gressa reached over her shoulders and estimated where Soma's eyes were. She thrust her thumbs into them, gouging them until Soma released her hold. Gressa wasted no time swiping Soma's knees out from under her. When she landed on the ground, Gressa picked her head up and smashed it against the ground twice.

Two more women Gressa did not recognize joined in the fight to replace the injured Soma and

Magga. Gressa was prepared when they launched themselves at her and sidestepped their attack so they collided into one another.

"What in Odin's name is going on here?" bellowed Ivar as he approached with Strian, Rangvald, Erik, Leif, and Bjorn.

None of the women spoke.

"Very well. It doesn't take much to understand what happened. I take it you," he swept his arm in a wide arc to encompass the women who now huddled together, "thought to welcome Gressa home by mauling her. Damn it, the woman has been gone for ten years. How could she have wronged any of you, let alone so many? She's been here all of twelve hours!"

Ivar finished with a roar as he made his way to where Gressa stood staring at him, her gaze shifting to Strian often. She did not know how to interpret the look on his face. There was a dangerous anger percolating, but Gressa was not sure who they directed it at.

Strian was the first of the men to catch sight of the fight. He recognized Gressa immediately. If her clothing had not given her away, her dark brown hair would have. He had pointed to the growing crowd and dashed to help Gressa. It was Erik and Leif who kept him from intervening.

"If you rescue her now, you will only make it worse. They will accuse her of weakness, of being your concubine, of stealing you away from the eligible women who have tried to catch your attention. If you butt in, you will seal her fate."

Strian stared at Leif as he spoke. He could not believe his best friend wanted him to ignore the danger his wife faced. One word broke through the fog.

"She can't be my concubine if she's already my wife," Strian spat.

"You may think that, but neither Gressa nor the other women recognize that anymore." Bjorn cut in.

"Look. Ivar is going to intervene," Rangvald nudged Strian.

The depth of his exhale of relief left his body feeling hollow. He pushed through the crowd that now had both women and men ogling and gossiping. He made his way to Gressa but did not reach out for her. He was not sure how she would react.

Gressa looked at Strian and wanted to burst into tears of relief that he had finally come to her side. She had seen him standing with the other men as the fight finished. She did not understand how he could watch her being assaulted. The rejection fueled her anger and strength as she took on the women she still did not recognize. Strian coming to her as soon as Ivar ended the fight gave her some relief.

Strian extended his hand to her and waited a moment before saying, "I think you'll need a bath before we go to the wedding. We haven't much time."

Gressa swallowed her gasp as she placed her hand in Strian's. He helped her balance as the mud tried to swallow her shoes. They walked hand in hand in silence to the bathhouse.

"I don't have any clothes," Gressa murmured. "And I don't want to turn around and go back. It's already too humiliating."

"I sent Freund, Freya's cabin boy, to ask Lena to find clothes for you."

"You already thought of that?"

"As soon as I saw you fighting. Freund was

40

lurking while Bjorn went through the wedding sword ritual. He was very convenient."

Strian pushed the bath house door open and stepped aside. He was prepared to wait outside until Gressa finished. She bit her bottom lip as she looked at the room filled with five large tubs. She looked forward to soaking in one of the tubs, but she had a more immediate concern. She looked over her shoulder at Strian.

"I need your help." She watched as his nostrils flared, but he remained silent. "I can't get these clothes off on my own. My ribs hurt too much."

Strian straightened at the mention of an injury. Gressa had never voluntarily confessed to being in pain. Not in all the years he had known her, and he had seen her injured more than once. Strian scooped her into her arms, and she squeaked as he carried her inside before setting her down on one of the wooden benches. He added a ladleful of water to the smoldering rocks and waited for the steam to rise. Once he was satisfied, he turned on the tap that would fill the tub with water from the natural hot spring that ran below the building. He returned to Gressa who stood. He eased her back to the bench and went down on one knee to peel away her shoes. He watched her face as his hands skimmed her ankles. When she did not pull away, he ran a fingernail along the sole. Her foot twitched, but she did not move again. Instead she gazed at him, their eyes locked. They both remembered a time when Strian did much the same thing except it was to consummate their marriage. He had been gentle and kind to her on their wedding night, just as he was being now. Except they both knew it would not culminate in the same pleasure.

Strian stood and helped ease the tunic over Gressa's head. She hissed as she raised her right arm, and

Strian could see where a livid bruise was already forming. She stood and pushed her pants off her hips. Strian could not keep from staring. Even with the bruises, her body was the most magnificent and seductive sight he had ever beheld. The need to join his body with hers felt as though it was an all-consuming quest. He ran the back of his fingers along her arm until he could feather them over the bruises. He wanted to pull her against him and bury his head in her neck as he branded her with his kisses. Gressa shivered, but it was not from being cold. She felt raw and exposed being undressed while Strian remained in his clothes, but the touch of his fingers on her skin brought her need crashing back to the forefront of her mind.

"They hurt, but I think nothing is broken," she murmured as Strian's scent of pine and musk invaded her senses. She placed a hand over his heart, waiting to feel the steady thud. Her fingers seemed to be on their own quest as she slid them up to his collar and into the hair at his nape. She rose onto her toes and tilted her head in invitation. She would not kiss him, fearing rejection, but she would give him the opportunity to take what she offered.

Strian's arms wrapped around Gressa as he swooped in for the kiss she offered. Their kiss was a firestorm of need, hurt, memories, and familiarity. Gressa pressed her body against Strian as his hold tightened. She was sure he would fuse their body into one if he could; however, there was only one way to do that. She used the hand not tangled in his hair to pull at the laces to his leather pants. Once they were loose, her hand curled around his length. The heat coming from his cock singed her as she stroked him. Her moan was one of pure pleasure, holding him as his tongue filled her mouth. She stroked his tongue with her own in the same rhythm that her hand pleasured him. She found the position frustrating and awkward with Strian's pants still over his hips. She released his hair long enough to use both hands to push his pants low enough to reveal his muscular backside. Her fingers bit into the taut flesh as her other hand resumed its mission.

Strian was sure his vision would be blurred if he could have kept his eyes open long enough to see. The feel of Gressa's hand on him was bringing him to release far faster than he wanted. A small voice niggled at the back of his mind warning him that she would regret this later. It screamed that he should stop before they went too far. But his heart and his body were not strong enough to deny the craving that grew. He wanted to be fully reunited with his wife. He wanted what they once had, and he knew her body, if not her heart, wanted the same.

"I need more," they both whispered.

A lopsided smile on Strian's face took Gressa's breath away. She had dreamed of that smile night after night while they were apart. It was one she knew he reserved only for her. He lifted her so she could wrap her legs around his waist before walking to the nearby wall. Her back pressed against it as he slid into her.

Both of them froze, enjoying the sensation of their bodies becoming one, but it was not long before need overcame them. They moved in unison as only a couple familiar with one another can. It may have been ten years since they last made love, but their erotic dance picked up where they left off. Gressa squeezed her legs each time Strian thrust into her, tilting her hips to meet him.

"I won't break," she whispered as he lips scorched the skin along her neck.

"I don't want this to end," he admitted. He waited for her to come to her senses, but instead, she lifted his chin to kiss him. Love, desire, need, and acceptance flowed between them in that single kiss.

Gressa could not get close enough as she clung to Strian. Each surge of his sword into her sheath made her body quiver. Her mind had blocked out just how good making love to Strian felt. It had been one of the many compromises she made with herself to survive their separation, but now her body taunted her as it remembered how satisfying it was to join with Strian. She moved in ways she knew he enjoyed, and her soft mewls of pleasure drove him to pound his length into her over and over until she cried out his name.

"Strian! Oh, gods!"

Strian returned his lips to the sensitive skin behind her ear as his seed filled her.

"Gressa," reverence filled his whisper, but she did not hear it over the pounding in her head.

"You didn't pull out," she choked.

Strian leaned back far enough to look in her eyes.

"Of course not. I never pulled out of you."

"That was when I was your wife."

Strian felt his mind freeze at the same time his heart broke. It was a long moment before he could find words.

"You are my wife. Still. I didn't pull out because I have never stopped thinking of you like that. It didn't even cross my mind that I might need to."

"And now what? What if you've gotten me with child?"

"Then we will finally have the family we already planned for."

Strian watched as a look of sheer agony flashed in Gressa's eyes before she let go and tried to push him away.

They both groaned as Strian's cock slipped free, and Strian's glare told Gressa he knew what that sound meant. She missed their connection just as much as he did. She pushed past him to the tub that was now overflowing. She rushed to turn off the water and hopped in before Strian could say anything. She sat with her back turned to him as she scrubbed her body with soap that sat on a nearby tray.

Strian was in shock. There was no other way to describe it. It shocked him He was shocked that they had made love. He was shocked at how it felt like no time had passed since they were last together, that making love to Gressa was still the most earth-shattering experience he had ever had. He was shocked at her reaction, and he was shocked at how deeply it reopened the wound that never fully healed when his friends and jarl forced him to leave without her.

He stood mute as she washed her hair, sliding back under the water to rinse the suds from it. She did not look at him as she stepped from the tub and grabbed a drying cloth before walking to the door that led to the cold-water pool. Her head tilted, as though she might look at him, but she pushed the door open.

As she passed into the part of the bathhouse where she would take a plunge into an icy bath, someone knocked at the door. Strian broke free of his stupor and pulled his pants back into place before opening the door a crack. Freund stood there will a stack of clean clothes.

"Frú Lena gave these to me."

Strian looked at the neatly folded gown along with a chemise, hose, and slippers, but he saw nothing.

"Thank you," he murmured before closing the door.

He turned around in time to see Gressa step back into the steam room. She had a drying cloth wrapped around her and was eyeing the stack of clothing he held. They were at an impasse.

Gressa took a few tentative steps forward before Strian moved towards her. He handed her the clothes, but he could not let go before he tried to set things right.

"Gressa, I can't force you to remain my wife. You have every right to leave this marriage if you want, and I wouldn't want you to feel trapped with me. But know that I will never turn you away. There will never be another."

Strian spun around and left the bath house before he humiliated himself further by bursting into tears. Gressa watched him go. She even ran to the door before she remembered she did not have any clothes on. She did not want him to go, but she was not sure if she could stay.

SEVEN

Gressa watched Tyra and Bjorn's wedding, but it was not her childhood friends she saw standing before the altar. She saw herself with Strian. They had been so young when they married, but she had been so certain that they would have a long and happy life together. Instead, they had only married a few months before war separated them, and the enemy took her as a thrall. As the ceremony continued, Gressa's mind wandered back to when she first arrived in Wales.

"You would do well to make a good first impression," her still nameless captor told her. Gressa looked around as she took in the settlement, she supposed was her new home. She watched as a well-dressed couple approached, and people moved out of their way as they passed.

When the couple stood before her, the woman yanked on her arm.

"Bow," she hissed.

"Magda, I see you've brought us quite a few new servants. Even pretty ones," a woman's lilting tones made Gressa look up. Standing so close, Gressa noticed the woman's unblemished skin was like cream, her blue eyes were the hue of sapphires,

and her hair was even darker than Gressa's. The woman was beautiful in a way Gressa had never seen before. The woman turned to the man standing beside her, but they spoke in a language she did not recognize. When they finished speaking, the woman turned to Gressa. "What are you called?"

The two women relied on Magda to translate.

"Gressa."

Gressa received an elbow in her still sore ribs.

"That's 'my lady' to you. You're in the presence of the prince and princess." Gressa had not noticed her male captor now stood on her other side. She wondered why it would matter if the couple could not understand her.

"She is new to our land. Do not punish her. She will learn soon enough." Gressa did not miss the edge that had crept into the princess's voice, and Magda reinforced it as she murmured beside Gressa. When she glanced up, she noticed the princess was not looking at her but at her husband, who in turn, was staring at Gressa will unmistakable lust.

The woman pushed her down the board until she stepped on a wooden dock. Gressa stumbled off the ship, her leg and back wounds still causing excruciating pain that she attempted to hide. As she stepped foot on the dock, the world began to close in as her periphery turned black. She swayed and tried to take a deep breath, but the world tilted. She managed two steps towards the royal couple before the harbor and people faded to black.

Gressa remained ill will a raging fever for a fortnight, and it was another six weeks before she was on her feet and able to walk more than the distance across her chamber. During that time, she learned as much Welsh as she could, wanting to understand what happened around her and what people said about her. Gressa's first meal in the prince and princess's great hall was exhausting. Walking to the hall and the noise were tiring to her body, but the attempts to be polite when people stared at her, along with not understanding the all of the language, frazzled her nerves. She was glad to escape. The *prince's covetous looks made the entire experience one she wanted to avoid for as long as possible.*

Gressa intended to stay as far from the royal couple as she could, but it was only a fortnight later that the prince summoned her to his private chambers. It filled Gressa with trepidation entering the room that held an enormous bed, and the only other occupant was the prince.

"Gressa, it pleases me that you came so quickly." The prince, Dafydd ap Llywelyn, was a handsome man in his early twenties. Gressa had already learned that he purported to love his wife, but she was pregnant and would not welcome him into her bed. "As you can imagine, I have been lonely these past weeks with Princess Enfys being unable to keep me company."

Gressa stepped back against the door. She wanted nothing to do with the man, nor any other man, but she feared what her rejection would mean for her safety.

"I sympathize with the princess and how unwell she feels. I suffer the same malady each morning, and even well into the afternoon." Gressa had not told another soul that she was expecting, having only had it confirmed by a midwife that morning. She had been feeling ill for weeks but assumed it was her injuries. As her body recovered, she could not explain why she felt weak and nauseous until she counted back to the last time she had her courses. It had been before she married Strian. Now, she prayed it would be enough to discourage the prince. She watched his expression as it passed from surprise, to disgust, to anger. She slid her palm onto the door handle in case she had to run.

"And who would be the lucky father? You have not been here very long. How could you know already?" Dafydd sneered.

"The father is my husband." Gressa did not want to give him more information, and she was not sure how much information would keep her safe.

"Husband? You never mentioned you were married."

"I was never asked." She watched the anger on his face grow and added, "Your Highness."

"And where would this husband of yours be? Did he not protect you from becoming a thrall? That doesn't seem like much of a husband to me."

Gressa's mind raced as she tried to devise a way to escape without infuriating the prince further. She was beginning to see a temper that truly frightened her. Even her father's ranting and raging did not convey such a danger.

"My husband searched for me, but I was too weak to call out to him. He fought our jarl and other men, but they outnumbered him."

"That seems a weak excuse. If he loved you, he would not have given in so easily."

Gressa recognized the manipulation for what it was. Dafydd wanted to sow the seeds of doubt, so he could undoubtedly be the one to come to her rescue. She just prayed it was Strian who came instead.

Dafydd inched forward as though he were approaching a skittish mare. He offered her a smile that others might believe was sincere and charming, but the hardness in his eyes put Gressa on edge even more. The nervousness made her stomach churn, and in turn, made her feel nauseous. Her hand covered her mouth as she tried to choke down the bile rising in her throat. The burn only made her body want to cast up her accounts even more. She tried to shake her head as the prince continued to inch forward.

"Your Highness, I'm not feeling---" Gressa could not squeeze out any more words before she darted to the chamber pot and threw up.

"Woman!" The prince's enraged face only made Gressa heave for a second time. "Get out! Do not show yourself again in my presence."

Gressa wiped her mouth with her sleeve and bolted for the door the prince now held open. She did not stop running until she reached the tiny chamber they had assigned her. Once there,

"Gressa. Gressa." Strian watched the faraway look in
Gressa's eyes as she faced the altar where Bjorn and
Tyra had been standing only moments ago as they
pledged their love and fidelity. "Gressa?"

Strian gave her a little nudge and was grateful
that she looked at him, even if her eyes were misty.

"What's wrong?" Strian whispered.

Gressa shook her head but did not offer an expla-
nation. Strian continued to watch her as she seemed
to come back from wherever her mind took her. She
was beautiful in the deep blue gown Lena lent her. It
was a perfect match for her eyes, and Strian suspected Lena had done that on purpose. Gressa's long
dark hair cascaded over her shoulders and back. She
looked so much like the young woman he had married all those years ago, before the same altar. Strian
had wondered if she was remembering as he had,
but the flash of fear and pain made him question
whether she was thinking of their wedding, and if
she was, why it caused her fear and pain.

"Tell me, Gressa," he beseeched. "You're fright-
ening me."

Gressa snorted at Strian's admission, knowing
little frightened him, but his expression showed he
was not exaggerating.

"You don't need to worry about me anymore,
Strian. I'm not your responsibility."

"Yes, you are."

"Strian, I released you from the bonds of marriage years ago, even if you didn't know."

Strian staggered back.

"You really did give up on us, on me."

Gressa would have done anything to retract her words as she watched the same anguish cloud Strian's eyes as when they discovered Strian's mother dead, violated and murdered in his parents' chamber.

"I didn't give up so much as accepted fate and reality."

"You believe we were fated to never have a happy marriage? A marriage at all?"

"That's what fate has shown us."

"And if we were wrong, and fate has brought us together because that's where we belong?"

"Ten years is a long time for fate to make up its mind."

"That's only because you weren't around to see Tyra and Bjorn," Strian muttered.

"What?"

"Nothing. It's just that it took Tyra and Bjorn just as long to admit their feelings and marry. Clearly, fate believed they belonged together and made it so."

Gressa turned away and walked towards the jarl's longhouse where the wedding celebrations were already under way. Strian followed but did not speak, too lost in his own thoughts.

When they arrived at the longhouse, Strian reached to take Gressa's hand to lead her to the high table where he saw they had left two seats for them. Their fingers grazed one another, but Gressa was moving in the opposite direction. She weaved through the crowd until she arrived at the door to the kitchens. She lifted a heavy tray from a young girl. She moved towards the first table where she placed bowl after bowl of food. She neared the end of the table when Strian, who still stood in the doorway, watched a man throw his bowl of skouse at Gressa's chest. The meat stew splattered the neck and skirts of her gown, but it soaked the linen across her breasts. The saturated material left little to the imagination. She scrambled to lean forward to pick up the bowl and in the process pull her tunic away from her breasts. Her new position created a host of lewd comments, and one man stood up behind her, grasped her hips, and pretended to thrust into her.

Strian plowed through the crowd, shoving anyone in his path. When he came to the last table that stood between him and Gressa's assaulter, he leaped onto the bench then stepped over the table before launching himself at the offending man. Strian pummeled the offender as they landed on the ground, tipping over a bench. Strian saddled his opponent, raining down blow after blow. It was not long before the man's face was mangled and unrecognizable.

Strian stood, looking around for Gressa and finding her backed into a corner by five women. One had her hair wrapped around her fists. Two other women pulled at her gown, attempting to strip her while the last two screamed obscenities and threats, accusing her of seducing the men. Strian stepped over his now dead opponent to go to Gressa, but Freya was already on her way. She barreled through three of the women and landed a punch squarely in the woman's jaw who held Gressa's hair. She was not through; she punched the two shrews by the time Strian made it to the second fight. He pressed his way between the women, refusing to lay a hand on any of them for fear of being accused of something later.

Gressa watched Freya come to her rescue in stunned silence. The woman had barely spoken to her since Strian found Gressa in Scotland. She argued with Strian when he wanted to stay behind with Gressa, and she blamed Gressa for ruining Strian's life. But now, Freya fought as though no time had passed, and they were loyal friends. Strian stepped forward and lifted his arms, but she flew into them before they were to his waist. Gressa buried her face against his chest as she grabbed fistfuls of his tunic as though frightened he might disappear.

The brawl was over just as quickly as it began. Freya turned to the couple and sneered at Gressa.

"Don't think this means I forgive you for abandoning Strian and don't think this means I like you. No woman should have a man touch her in such a way. That's the only reason I defended you." Freya spun on her heel and marched back to her chair beside her husband.

Strian brushed hair from Gressa's face and examined it for any damage.

"Can't we leave?" Gressa whispered.

"Under the circumstances, I think Ivar and the others would understand if we excused ourselves without asking."

Strian led Gressa to the door, neither looking anywhere but straight ahead. When they stepped outside, Strian pulled Gressa against him and backed her against the wall. His lips crashed into hers with no finesse. It was raw passion born of fear and relief. It was need that he could not put into words. Gressa matched his ferocity as she tugged at his tunic as though he could get closer even with their clothes in the way.

"Gressa." His voice a tortured moan.

Gressa welcomed his tongue into her mouth as they tangled and stroked before she sucked softly. The sensation made Strian rock his hips forward until his hard length rubbed against her mons. Gressa squirmed trying to find a position that would ease the growing ache in her belly. They both knew there was only one way to satisfy a need like this, but they both knew they were in the wrong location for such intimacy. They broke apart, staring into one another's eyes, each wondering what the other was thinking.

Strian took Gressa's hand once more and stepped away from the wall. They turned to walk towards Strian's home, but they only made it a dozen steps before Gressa stepped toward a building a few over from Strian's home.

"Where are you going?" Strian had a sneaking suspicion.

"To the servants' quarters."

"You don't need to live there."

"I do. You brought me here as a thrall, and while you may have made me a free woman, I am still a servant."

Strian stared at her as though she was a puzzle to be solved.

"You aren't a servant. You are a wife and a shield maiden. Your home is with me, and you belong in the training yard with the other women."

"I might be one but not the other."

Strian swiped a hand through his hair before scrubbing his face with it.

"You want to go to sleep, unprotected, in the exact same building as the women who just attacked you. Is that what I'm supposed to understand? Because that is both crazy and stupid."

Gressa clenched her teeth and hissed, "I may be crazy, and I may be stupid. I might even still be a shield maiden, but I am not your wife. I'm not your problem. You don't get to dictate to me. When will you understand that?"

"When you can tell me you don't love me."

EIGHT

G ressa felt as though Strian knocked the air from her. Strian had played his hand well and knew it. Gressa would not lie to him, and she knew she had already admitted it twice. It was the truth, but it did not change the circumstances in which they found themselves. At least, it did not in Gressa's mind.

"Gressa, I will continue to sleep by the hearth and you in the chamber. I will not touch you unless you ask me to, and I won't pressure you. But you aren't safe sleeping anywhere else."

"If my safety is in such danger, then let me go."

"I would feel the same way about Bjorn or Leif. I would offer the same to Tyra or Freya. Even if you never agree to be my wife again, I will never turn you out to fend for yourself. If for no other reason than our past. You were my family."

Gressa stood without moving or speaking for so long Strian was convinced she would turn him down. But she saw the sensibility in Strian's offer, and she knew her resolve was running out. Even in her own mind, the reasons to push Strian away were thinning to strands she could not grasp. Continuing to argue with Strian about their living arrangements was only a matter of pride. She knew she would give in to all

Strian's demands if she agreed to live with him. She wanted to, but as much as a life with Strian called to her, her home in Wales called just as loudly. She could not plant roots here that had already been severed. She needed to return to Wales. Perhaps, if she could repair some damage to her relationship with Strian, he might let her go. As soon as the thought crossed her mind, she knew it was ludicrous. Strian would never voluntarily let her go, so she hoped she could convince him to travel with her even if she refused to admit to her reasons.

"I will accept your offer under those conditions, but only those." She cocked an eyebrow in defiance, her pride still holding her hostage.

"Very well. But there is one more thing. Gressa, I can't overlook the danger you are in. And it exists only because I insisted you return here. Perhaps I should have let you remain in Scotland to return with the other warriors to Wales. But I could not see reason. I could only see the woman I have loved for half my life, the woman who was my wife. Gressa, for your safety, please consider letting the others believe we've reconciled, let others believe we are still married. You will have the protection of my name. You will always have the protection of my sword, but this will keep anyone from questioning you."

"Strian, that asks too much. You would have us lie to everyone? And if, no when because it's inevitable, they discover we've been deceiving them, then what?"

"Why would anyone know? What we do or don't do in our home is our business. If we can stand to be cordial to one another in public, then what is there to question? It would allow you to train again which is when you would spend the most time in public. You wouldn't even be training with me."

"And when we dine with the others?"

"We are newly reconciled. Much like newlyweds, why would we want to leave the privacy of our home?"

"So, you would have everyone think you're fucking me like rabbits?" Gressa's temper flared at the notion that others would think she was little more than a bed slave even if Strian called her his wife.

"I would have them think I am making love to my wife. A wife everyone knows I have grieved for. A wife everyone knows I never recovered from losing. A wife more beautiful than any other woman in this tribe. Who would blame me?"

Gressa looked around and noticed for the first time that they were drawing attention from the few people milling about and those leaving the evening meal. She saw the suspicious expressions. She noticed a handful of women glaring at her, and she knew it was because Strian had staked his very public claim by coming to her defense. His anger had not surprised her, not even his violence that killed the other man in front of the entire tribe. He had always been protective of her. She realized now, though, there would be others who did not view their reconciliation with as much eagerness as Strian did. While there were several other handsome men in the tribe, women had always considered Strian the most attractive. She knew from the women he had bedded before her. They had been equally good looking, and they had said more than one unkind word when Strian chose her over the others before they wed. She recognized these looks of envy and covetousness. While Strian believed he might protect her from everyone in the tribe who wished her harm, she knew his protection would only extend to the men. Their relationship, whatever it might be, would fuel the fire of the women's hatred and put her in more danger.

"The women would blame me."

Strian followed her gaze to the women who observed them, and he knew she was right. He had heard the hateful things these same women had said when they were barely more than girls and Strian pursued Gressa. He had been moved to action when the five women cornered Gressa, and it had only been Freya's intervention that kept him from violence towards them. He took her hand and led her to the side of a nearby building where no one could watch them. He was unconvinced that she would return to their longhouse.

"Good thing for you, you have Freya's protection."

Gressa snorted at that.

"You heard her. I can't count on being so lucky a second time."

"If not her, then Tyra."

Gressa looked at him as though he were a simpleton.

"You expect to see Tyra any time soon? She will be holed up with Bjorn as they celebrate their honeymoon."

"Are you making these excuses because you don't agree with my offer?"

"I'm not making excuses, Strian," her frustration clear in her tone. "I'm pointing out reality. You didn't think very far ahead of bedding me again when you forced me to return to a village where no one ever wanted me."

Strian opened his mouth to counter her, but he would only be lying if he tried to placate her. Her Sami heritage and her father's rejection had made her a cast off for most of her life. It had only been Freya and Tyra's friendship then his pursuit that made others accept her. He had not thought of any of this when he found Gressa at the Ross keep in Scotland. When he recognized the eyes he had spent hours gazing into, and then pressed his body against the one he would recognize anywhere, he had only thought of how he had pined for her. When she refused to return, his pride had reared its ugly head and insisted he not give in. When Freya leveraged her position as the jarl's representative on their mission, he assumed it was only her protectiveness of a lifelong friend. While they were sailing, he had only planned for making her feel welcome in their home. He had failed miserably to consider reality.

"You're right that I didn't think clearly, or truly didn't think at all about how others would respond. I could only think of the life we were supposed to have. The life I have envied all of my friends for having now. They moved on while I continue to cling to the past. I focused on the relief that you were alive. Thoughts of a future with you as my wife filled my mind while conflicting unending love and hurt that you rejected me filled my heart. Pride and need won out, Gressa, and for that I realize I have wronged you. But I can't bring myself to apologize even if I should. I'm not sorry to have you near me again. It's all I've dreamed of for ten years."

Gressa tilted her head back and gazed at the twinkling stars. They had spent many nights lying on a blanket looking into the night sky when they were courting. They slept with the window covering open because they would fall asleep in one another's arms as they watched the stars shine into their chamber. Gressa inhaled, stretching her lungs before looking back at Strian. She knew she was the only person he had ever shared his feelings with. He was confessing emotions he would deny to anyone else. He deserved her honesty, even if she could not tell her entire tale.

"Strian, I dreamed of you every night for the last ten years. The only time I did not was when I exhausted myself training, trying to avoid those dreams. They were a mixture of memories, things we had planned, and what our life might have been." She swallowed the lump forming in her throat. "I'm trying to bear the guilt of making you think I no longer want you, want to be your wife, but I can't. The burden is too heavy."

Gressa's head was still tilted back, unable to face Strian as she made her own confessions.

"Life has been unkind to us, cheating us of what we deserved, but while time has not made me love you any less, it has changed everything around us. We can't go back to when we were younger. We can't pick up where we left off, regardless of whether we both wish we could. Ten years in Wales is nearly as long as I lived here. It changed me. I may live in your house, and I may train with our tribe, but my home is in Wales. That is where I belong now. That is where my heart remains." She finally looked at Strian and wished she had not. His crushed expression was one she would never forget.

"Why?" he croaked.

"Because I can't make a life somewhere where only one person accepts me. I can't depend on you for everything. I will only become a burden to you, and I will be miserable facing each day knowing that everyone in my life hates me and resents my return."

Strian recognized the truth in her argument even if his heart railed against it.

"Gressa, stay in our home, er, my house for now. I will arrange for us to travel to Wales."

Gressa was sure she had not heard Strian.

"You'll let me return?"

"If that is the only place where you're happy, then that is where we shall be?"

Gressa tilted her head and looked at him sideways as she worked through what he said.

"We?"

"If being here instead of Wales is what keeps you from accepting me, then what's keeping me here? I have no family left. Ivar has plenty of other warriors to fight for him." Strian shrugged.

"But your life is here."

"My life was meant to be with you."

"You would give up everything you know to live in a land where you don't speak the language and don't know a soul besides me?"

"Weren't you forced to do the exact same thing? Besides, I don't believe you are any safer there than you are here."

Gressa's brow furrowed, but she could not deny this truth either.

"Dafydd sent me to fight for Grímr, and I was the only woman. I suspected the same thing that you did: Dafydd offered me to Grímr for more than my archery skills. I just hadn't considered Enfys would betray me the way she did. We did not start out as friends, but I thought she had become my closest ally and confidant."

Gressa's heart pinched as she once more had to accept that her best friend was aware, may have even suggested that, her husband give her to Grímr more as a bed slave than as a warrior.

"I don't understand how you could have become friends with a princess when you arrived as a thrall."

Gressa shook her head. She once again could not divulge the entire reason, but she could share most of it.

"We had much in common even though we didn't start off on a good foot." Gressa bit her bottom lip as she considered her wording. "When I arrived Enfys was pregnant and refused to share her bed with Dafydd. Once my injuries healed, he tried to make me his mistress. I tried everything to make myself unappealing to him, and I suppose he decided

I wasn't worth the effort. I no longer piqued his curiosity. Enfys knew of Dafydd's lust, and she punished me for it often, but I was there when she delivered her son. It was a difficult birth, and both mother and son nearly died. I had been serving as the midwife's assistant rather than a servant in their home—Enfys refused to look at me, let alone welcome me into her home. I suggested a mixture of herbs that helped Enfys when she would not stop bleeding right after the delivery. I also was the one who realized something was blocking the infant's throat, keeping him from breathing. Enfys was grateful for my wherewithal, and I believed she had accepted that I was not trying to lure Dafydd from her and had forgiven me. She insisted that I become her personal attendant. We grew close spending much of our days together, and we confided in one another about many things. I told her of you, and she knew I never moved past being taken. She sympathized and said she wished there were a way for me to return, if only more Norsemen traveled to Wales. I never saw the two slave traders who left me in Wales, so I gave up hope that they might bring me back. It was several years before I accepted that I would never leave Wales. Now I wonder if Enfys ever forgave me or if she manipulated me the entire time."

Gressa closed her eyes as bitterness and sadness washed over her. She had tried to make the best life she could, and no one in Wales knew of or cared about her Sammi lineage. She felt accepted and even wanted there. More than one man had tried to court her, but she had refused all of them. She refused the men who offered her companionship with no strings. While she may have accepted that it now meant she was to spend her life in Wales, she never accepted the idea that distance ended her marriage.

She startled as Strian wrapped her in his embrace. She soaked in Strian's pine and musk scent, something she remembered so vividly that she could smell it in her dreams. In his arms, she was truly home. Truly safe and welcomed. She was where she most wanted to be. But she could not overcome the truth that she could not live every day in his arms. Their embrace would end, and she would once again be at the mercy of the tribe members.

"Are you serious that you would live in Wales?"

"If that is where you want to be even knowing now what you do about the prince and princess, then that is where I want to be. If you lead, I will follow."

"It's that simple?"

"Perhaps between us it is. I expect disagreement and refusal from the others, but Ivar loves Lena more than his own life. He would do anything to protect Leif and Freya. He will understand why I must go with you. He would not keep me again from my wife and the family we might have. He has expressed his guilt and remorse for forcing me to sail away. Many times, in fact."

Gressa was in awe of Strian's blind faith in her. He knew nothing of the life he was willing to accept, all for her sake. He trusted her implicitly. He could tell her he loved her every day, all day, for the rest of their lives, and it would not carry the same weight as his promise to her now.

"I love you, Gressa."

Gressa cupped his jaw and strained on her toes to reach his lips.

"I love you, Strian."

Their previous kisses had been wrought from passion, grief, need, and comfort. This kiss was different. It was the promise of a new beginning. It held hope and love in its languid caresses. Strian ran his hands up and down Gressa's back as she tangled her fingers in his hair.

"Take me home, Strian," she murmured against his lips. "Make love to me as your wife."

Strian's heart skipped a beat as he peered into her eyes, looking for any signs of regret or uncertainty. All he saw was the same expression she wore the first time they kissed, and once more the first time they kissed as man and wife. Strian swept her into his arms, much like he had on their wedding day, and she giggled against his throat as she kissed the rough skin all the way to the spot behind his ear that she knew aroused him. She kissed along the prickly jaw that had a day's worth of stubble. He was one of the few men Gressa knew who shaved daily, and she was thankful for it. Neither said a word as Strian carried her to the door of their longhouse. She leaned to push the handle, and Strian used his foot to open it. He kicked it closed behind him and wasted no time walking to the chamber they once shared. Before placing her back on her feet, he grazed his lips against hers.

Together they undressed. Once they stood bare, Strian moved behind Gressa, but she tried to twist away. She was sure he had glimpsed her scars when they were in the bathhouse, but she was embarrassed to let him see them now.

"Don't hide from me," Strian whispered before kissing along one shoulder before his lips traveled up her nape and down the other shoulder. His calloused fingertips feathered along her spine before pressing against the scar that ran from just below her left underarm to her right hip. He could tell it had been a deep wound and whoever stitched it had done so to keep her alive without care for appearance. It was jagged, leaving an angry line of puckered skin. Strian took one step back and tilted his head to see the scar that ran across the back of both thighs. The right side had been worse.

"Strian," she beseeched, trying to remain still rather than twisting away from him.

"Don't hide from me," he repeated. "Wear this scar as a testimony to your strength and bravery. Don't think of it as marring your skin, for your beauty has always been perfect to me. Nothing about that has changed."

Strian pressed his arousal against her, sliding between the cheeks of her backside. When Gressa moaned and leaned back against him, Strian knew how he would make love to his wife. He moved them closer to the bed and guided Gressa to lean forward, bearing her weight on her forearms as he slipped inside her. His groan matched hers as the pleasure of joining their bodies coursed through them. Strian wrapped his body around Gressa's, their fingers entwining on the bed. Once more Strian kissed Gressa's shoulders while rocking his hips into her. He was not ready to thrust yet, and Gressa was content to feel their bodies move as one. Strian released her left hand and leaned back to kiss along the top of her scar while his right hand moved to find the rosebud hidden among her petals.

"Strian, please," she begged, and Strian knew they both needed something more.

He slid all of his length from her before surging back in, his hips colliding with the flesh of her bottom. He watched the ripple of her skin each time he thrust into her. His need was building faster than his mind could control. He continued to kiss Gressa's scar as she hung her head, panting from the fire building within her belly.

As erotic as the scene was, Strian felt something was missing. It did not feel complete.

"I need to look at you," Gressa paused from

rocking her hips back to meet each of Strian's thrusts. Her need was the one thing Strian knew was missing. He pulled out of her before she turned and kissed him. He lifted her, and she wrapped her legs around him. Slipping into her, he returned to the place he most wanted to be as he climbed onto the bed. Gressa marveled at his strength as he maneuvered them on the center of the mattress before easing her down.

Gressa's eyelids were heavy, and as much as she wanted to gaze at Strian, the sensations overtaking her body were more than her mind could manage. She tilted her head back as her body followed the rhythm Strian's set. Her nails bit into his shoulders as she lifted her hips to accept Strian's cock. The passion that had always fired between they quickly replaced the gentleness of their last kiss outside. Strian was the only man Gressa had ever been with, and not once had she wondered about bedding another man. Strian had always been all she wanted. She knew anyone else would be a disappointment.

Strian listened to Gressa's soft noises as he watched the cords of her throat tighten as she strained against him, her eyes closed in ecstasy. His memory had kept him company over the years. It was images like this that his mind conjured when he relieved his need with his own hand, but nothing compared to the feel of being within the only woman he had ever loved. Once he discovered Gressa as a young woman, no other woman appealed to him. He could have been with any number of women since he last saw Gressa, he had even let others think he had, but there was no one who could outshine his memories of Gressa.

Strian's chest and shoulders strained as he pistoned his rod into her channel. Gressa forced her eyes open, knowing she was missing a view of Strian that had always been unparalleled in her mind. She watched the muscles ripple through his chest as he held himself over her. The sight of his muscles in his stomach flexing with each tilt of his hips made her need grow.

"Gods, Gressa. What you do to me," Strian panted.

Gressa pressed on his shoulders, urging him to bring his weight down on her. Strian acquiesced, and they pressed together, noses rubbing for a moment before pleasure coursed through them both. Strian tried to pull away, but Gressa's nails once more bit into his shoulders.

"Stay."

It was the one word Strian longed to hear. Gressa was willing to take the chance of getting pregnant. He knew that meant she would not leave him. He kissed her neck as his seed flowed into Gressa, her legs entwined with his and her arms wrapped around him. She clung to him just as he clung to her, and for the first time in ten years, they both felt like they were where they belonged.

NINE

A pounding on the door woke Strian. He looked down at Gressa who slept tucked against his chest. They had made love throughout the night until the early rays of dawn greeted them, and they both grew too exhausted to remain awake. Now the sun streamed into the chamber, alerting Strian to the time. It had to be the middle of the morning, well past when he should have been in the training yard.

Gressa shifted and opened her eyes but snapped them shut as the brightness startled her.

"Are you going to get that? It sounds like they don't plan to leave."

"I'm willing to wait them out. I have no intention of either of us leaving this bed today."

Gressa rolled over to look at him. She slid her hand along his belly up his chest to his shoulder. Strian leaned forward and kissed her as she slid her leg over his hip. Both were content to forget whoever continued to hammer on the door. It was only when they heard it slam that they pulled apart. Strian had just covered Gressa in time when Leif burst into their chamber.

Leif froze as he took in the scene of clothes strewn around the room and the couple in bed.

"I'm sorry. I didn't realize. I would have---" Leif stuttered and backed out of the room.

Strian gave Gressa peck on her nose before leaving their bed. He moved to the door, but Gressa gasped.

"Aren't you going to put some pants on? At least wrap a blanket around you?"

"No."

"Strian!"

"I have every intention of letting Leif know I plan to return to my wife. The man can't keep his hands off his own wife. She was pregnant within a moon of their marriage. He'll understand."

"Still--"

Strian was through the door before she could finish her thought. He pulled the door closed and crossed his arms as he glared at Leif, who in turn laughed.

"There's nothing funny about barging in on a man with his wife. A wife who was content to laze the day away in bed with her husband. Speak."

Leif continued to laugh, able to tell Strian had plans for the morning, and they didn't involve anyone but Gressa.

"We were wondering where you were."

"I think your sister sent you to rescue me. Who couldn't guess what I would be doing with Gressa in our home? Especially after the scene I made last night. I thought it was rather obvious to everyone I still consider her my wife."

"Freya's nagging might have had a little to do with it, but we *all* still thought you would make it to the training field. This isn't a time to grow lax."

Strian glared at Leif as he insinuated Strian shirked his duties.

"Have you already been to Tyra and Bjorn's door? Are they in the fields?"

Leif's brow furrowed.

"Of course not. They're newlyweds."

"And just what do you think we feel like? It was our first real night together as husband and wife. It's been ten years since I've had my wife in my home." Strian growled. "Go tell your sister and all the other busybodies, that we will emerge when we're ready and not before. If that's in a day or a week, that's no one's business but ours."

Leif opened his mouth to say something, but Strian was faster.

"I may have let you think I've been with other women, but I haven't touched a woman since the last time I made love to Gressa. It was easier to let you think I moved on than hear you nagging that I should. Leave, Leif, before I throw my best friend out of my home."

Leif nodded.

"We suspected as much, but as you said it, was easier to think you moved on." He turned towards the door but paused before opening it. "Be sure to let the poor woman come up for air long enough to have a proper meal. She's thinner than I remember."

Strian grunted, but he knew he had gained his friend's approval, and his off-hand remark was the closest thing to a kind sentiment that they would share.

Gressa scurried to duck back under the covers when she heard the front door shut. She had crept out of bed when she heard Leif's voice because she could not hear what they said until she stood close to the door. She managed to arrange the covers and close her eyes just before Strian opened the chamber door.

Strian took in the sight of Gressa's hair strewn across his pillow, and her shoulder peeking out from under the blanket. He slipped into bed and pulled her against his chest.

"You don't need to pretend. I'm sure you were listening at the door." His fingers found her nipples as he talked. He toyed with them until Gressa pressed her hips back against his still hard length.

"How did you know?"

"Because as much as we have changed, we are both still the same. You've always been too curious, especially if you think it concerns you."

"And it did."

"Yes, in part."

Strian rubbed his finger over the beaded nipple before pinching. He was unprepared for Gressa's lusty response. She rolled towards him, pushing him against the mattress before straddling him. She guided his length and moaned as her body swallowed his cock.

"If you're going to claim we're like newlyweds, then we should act the part."

Strian could not remember what he had been about to say as he watched Gressa's breasts sway as her hips undulated above him. He sat up and once more pulled Gressa's body against his, wanting them to fuse together. Gressa tightened her embrace as they moved as one. She let her head fall back as Strian nudged, making room for his scorching lips to trail kisses up to her ear.

"I want to make love to you until neither of us can see straight, until starvation forces us to stop. But the only hunger I feel now is for your body against mine. The only place I want to be is inside you."

Gressa listened to Strian's words and felt the ache in belly grower stronger and somehow deeper. She wanted what he did, and she wanted to hear more.

"Does it feel good?"

"Gods, do you even have to ask?"

"I'd like to know," her tone hesitant, proving she needed some reassurance after their years of separation.

Strian dug his fingers into her backside as he pressed her harder against his length. As much as he liked the intimacy of their position, he wanted, no needed, to show her the intensity of his desire. He twisted until Gressa laid on the bed. His thrusts increased in speed and force.

"I want to be deep inside of you until you scream my name. I want to watch your nipples tighten as you climax with me so deep I feel like I can touch your heart. I want to show you how much I love you as much as I lust for the feel of you squeezing my cock until I can't stop my need for release. I want to make love to you, and I want to fuck you. I want everything."

Gressa's arousal blocked out everything but Strian's words and the feel of him. He said everything she needed to hear, and she trusted him enough to know his words were sincere. These were not the words of a man who merely sought pleasure. They were the words of a man who loved her more deeply than she might have understood if she did not feel the same for him.

"I want to see your face as you come apart in me, a look no one can share. It's mine, and mine alone, knowing I did that to you. I want to hold you deep inside me until your need consumes you. A need that we create with only each other. Strian, we've made love all night. Now I want you to fuck me."

Strian needed no further prompting. His thrusts were deep, hard, and fast. He might have worried that he would hurt her if he did not remember how much she liked this. She had always met his lust pound for pound, inch for inch. She was the only one who ever had, but then, she was the only one who had ever aroused him to such measures. She lifted her hips in time with his movements, and she begged for more with her moans and the strength of her grip on his buttocks. He was only too happy to comply.

Gressa's body responded to Strian's urgency with an ache that bordered on pain. The mixture of pleasure and pain had her begging for more. She watched as Strian's control slipped further and further until there was none left. She had lost hers the moment he rolled them over. She knew her fingers would leave marks on Strian, and she wanted to. She had hidden her possessiveness and jealousy when they were younger, but she had always enjoyed seeing the small bruises, not because she enjoyed hurting him, but rather knowing she put them there, knowing no other woman had. Strian had understood without ever remarking on them.

"Are you claiming me once more?" Strian smiled despite the exertion. "I wish to do the same."

Strian pushed up on his forearms and squeezed her breast mercilessly, garnering yet another moan of pleasure. He suckled as her nails raked down his back. He pulled back and kissed the puckered and red flesh before pressing his lips to her just above her nipple. He sucked until he was sure he would leave a mark. He repeated the love bites several times before switching to the other breast. As he covered her skin with small bruises, Gressa could no longer hold back. The physical and emotional pleasure was more than her body could withstand, and she climaxed with a loud scream that finished in a moan.

"Strian!"

Strian no longer needed to wait, his release overtaking him as he listened to his name being called from her lips, his own lips filled once more with her breast.

They collapsed breathless, Strian rolling to his

side to keep from crushing her. He pulled her hip, urging her to face him.

"You're mine, Gressa. I won't ever let you go again. I will follow until we meet again at Odin's feasting hall."

"You promise?"

"With my life."

"And I will find the strength and the way to always come back to you. I don't know that I could survive another separation. I need you."

"Do you know how much I have longed to hear you say that ever since I found you? Do you know how I've ached to know you feel the same as I do?"

Strian brushed hair away from her damp temple as tears slipped from Gressa's eyes.

"My love," she choked out. "I'm sorry. I'm so sorry for turning you away the weeks we traveled. I'm sorry for pushing you away since we have been home. I never imagined you would leave this tribe."

Gressa held her breath, waiting to hear Strian say he had changed his mind. Her watery eyes looked at him before she continued.

"I don't know if you'll be happy in Wales, but I know you won't be shunned."

"My home will always be where I can fall asleep with you in my arms."

The tears fell faster as Gressa's heart expanded to absorb Strian's pledge, but they also fell faster for the secret she could not share. As full as her heart was, it shattered with the misery of not being able to tell Strian everything from the past ten years. So instead of letting her mind linger, she infused her love into their kiss. It was long after that, that they fell asleep once more, exhausted but fulfilled.

TEN

Strian and Gressa remained secluded in their love den for three more days. During that time, they shared how their lives had evolved since the battle that left Gressa behind. She told him she had seen and heard him calling for her, but that she had been too weak for him to hear. She told him more about her friendship with Princess Enfys, or at least what she thought had been a friendship.

"Enfys listened when I spoke of you. She comforted me often during the years when I thought I couldn't go on and that the heartache would break me. I spoke of our childhood together and our courtship. She knew things about us that no one but you would know. I believed I would never see you again, so I divulged those secrets believing they would never go further than her ears. The more I think about how I came to be with Grímr, the more I realize her betrayal. She must have shared those private conversations with Dafydd because there is no other way Grímr could have known what you mean to me. He never would have known that threats to your life would be the only thing that could manipulate me and force me to, to---" Gressa could not continue, the shame of having put her mouth on any part of Grímr, let alone his manhood, made her nauseous.

"Gressa, I don't consider what you did infidelity. Not anymore now that I understand. You thought you were protecting me. I understand because I would've done anything if I'd been in your place. Please don't feel ashamed. I don't enjoy thinking of it, but I can't explain how loved I feel knowing you still put me first." Strian caressed her back as they sat facing one another, Gressa's legs resting near his hips. He lifted her until she could take his sword into her sheath. They sat, joined, for a long moment just enjoying the connection.

"I still regret it. I regret ever trusting Enfys and Dafydd. I believed she had forgiven me for Dafydd's pursuit those first weeks I was there. I thought Dafydd had moved on to find other women while Enfys bore him four more children. One, if not both of them, deceived me."

"That is the truth but sending you to Grímr is what made us find one another. I can't overlook that blessing."

"But I--" Gressa sucked in her lips, making her mouth a taut line.

"I know. I know you never intended to let me find you."

Gressa shut her eyes, unable to look at Strian as he spoke the truth. He kissed her neck before smattering kisses on each cheek, her forehead, then her nose before reaching her lips. His thumb pressed to release her bottom lip from her teeth. The kiss was slow, building the fire in their bellies once again urging them to rock against one another.

"Gressa, I know there is something you are still holding back, even after these days alone talking of the past. I won't force you to share your secret, but I wish you would trust me."

Gressa's eyes flew open.

"I do trust you. It's why I never tried to escape ever since you found me. I still believe I'll be safer once we're in Wales, but I trust you."

Strian lifted and lowered Gressa as her inner muscles clung to his cock. His body cried out for him to stop talking and make love to her, but his mind was not at rest.

"There's still a secret though. I'm a patient man, and I won't break from whatever you're hiding. I won't deny that it hurts, but it seems it's your secret to keep."

"You can overlook it? Or at least live with it?"

"Yes. I suspect you are trying to protect me just as you always have."

"I am, Strian. I'll never stop trying to protect you."

Fire fueled their kiss, and the time for talking had ended. Their motionless joining had been a fusion of their souls as much as their movements now were a fusion of their hearts.

They finally left their longhouse, Gressa having agreed it was once more her home, and ventured out to the training field. Strian had returned Gressa's bow and arrows before they set sail from Scotland and then her sword while they remained secluded. Tyra had found the sword on the field after the battle and given it to Strian. He had kept it tucked away in his parents' chamber, knowing it was a place he did not have to see it. He could not bear parting with it, but the sight of it had caused more pain.

As they approached the others, Strian squeezed the hand he held. Gressa continued to look straight ahead but returned the squeeze.

Tyra and Bjorn had returned to the fields just

that morning after celebrating their own union for the past three days. Freya scowled at Gressa but said nothing instead turning to whisper to her husband Erik. Leif stood silently, but his gaze caught and followed his wife Sigrid as she left a storage building and returned to the jarl's longhouse.

"It's good to see you out here," Tyra smiled warmly. "I've missed training with you."

Tyra's comments garnered a grunt from Freya, but Freya turned back to Gressa. She studied Gressa, and when Gressa did not flinch, Freya nodded.

"I would have a word with you, Gressa," Freya said.

"Very well." Gressa agreed without breaking her eye contact with her former friend.

The two women stepped away as Erik and Strian tensed, watching their wives walk away together.

"Freya won't do anything to harm Gressa," Tyra reassured. "She only wanted to protect you, and you frightened her when you said you wanted to remain in Scotland."

Strian looked over his shoulder at Tyra and knew she was right. The argument that ensued when Strian said he wanted to remain in Scotland after finding Gressa had been a bitter one, and it was the only time in any of their lives that Freya used her rank as the jarl's daughter and leader of their expedition. Strian could only imagine Freya's, and everyone else's reaction, when he told them he and Gressa would leave for a new home in Wales. He turned back to watch his wife and his friend speak. There were no raised voices or punches thrown, so he considered that a win.

"Gressa, I know I owe you an apology for what I said and how I acted at the Ross keep, but I won't apologize for wanting to protect Strian. I can't imagine what you endured being injured and stolen away, but I do remember what happened to Strian. He barely spoke the first six months we were back. He trained harder than I had ever seen, thinking we would return to Scotland soon and that he could search for you. We didn't for several years, and resentment began to fester within Strian. He was short tempered and drank too much, rarely leaving your home. The one-year anniversary of your disappearance frightened all of us. He disappeared, too. He was gone for two moons. He'd gone into the mountains and built a hut where he hunted and grieved. The second year was as bad as the first, but he was willing to join us for meals in my parents' home. By the third year, we thought he had resigned himself to you never returning. We went raiding in Scotland that year. Everywhere we went he asked about you, hoping someone might have a hint to where you were. No one ever knew, not on any of the raids after that when he interrogated anyone we captured. Each time we returned home, he would lock himself in your home for a moon. So, maybe now you can understand why I wanted to protect him. I truly don't believe he would survive losing you again. I fear he would let go of everything, believing he has no more reason to live. Searching for you gave him purpose even if it tore him apart."

Gressa listened to everything Freya said without interruption. She found herself holding her breath as the story progressed. These were things Strian never admitted in their many conversations over the past three days. She understood why he had not, but now knowing the truth convinced her even more that keeping her secret was worth it.

"Thank you for telling me, Freya," Gressa's voice

cracked as she spoke. "He didn't tell me any of this, as I'm sure you guessed since we're speaking now."

Gressa looked over at Strian, knowing he worried about her. She smiled before turning back to Freya.

"When I saw his father, Ivar, Leif, and Bjorn carry him away, I was sure there would be no reason to go on. I accepted that I would die where I lay. Needless to say, it was a shock when I awoke on the deck of a boat, having stitched me to prepare me for being sold as a slave. The man and woman, who I suppose saved me, saw Strian jump from the boat and try to swim back to me. I knew then that I had to fight to stay alive. I wanted to find some way, anyway, to get back to him. I was fevered and bedridden for two moons once I arrived in Wales and was too indisposed to travel for several months after. I listened to those around me who said they would never sail to a land filled with Norsemen. I listened to those who told me I would die trying to cross Britain and Scotland as a Norse woman alone. I listened and grew more defeated each time someone told me it was impossible. I would have tried running away, but I was bound to Wales whether or not I liked it." Gressa was in danger of letting her secret slip, but if she would ever tell it, Strian had to be the first to know. "I also knew I was safer in Wales because no one knew what it meant to be half Sami. They accepted me because I was a trained warrior and a better archer than even their most well-known. There was not a day that went by that I didn't think of Strian. Something always brought forth a memory, and it was agony those first years as the memories tried to consume me. I finally learned to live with them, but I never moved on from Strian. Never."

Freya's eyebrows shot up, and Gressa knew what Freya was thinking.

"Grímr threatened Strian's life. He threatened to

find Strian and torture him while he was content to just kill you and the others. He knew who Strian was to me, and I wasn't willing to risk his threats being proven true."

"That must have been awful for you," Freya's words understated the disgust and loathing Gressa had felt towards Grímr and herself.

"You will never know just how right you are." Gressa once again glanced at Strian before continuing. "Freya, you might understand now that you're married, but there is nothing I won't do to keep Strian safe. It's all I've tried to do since I was seventeen and he started to pay attention to me."

Freya nodded and did something that no one expected and caused their friends to collectively gasp. She pulled Gressa in for a tight embrace and held her as she whispered.

"I've missed you more than you could ever know. Neither Tyra nor I were the same after you disappeared. I didn't want to get close to anyone because I couldn't stand feeling the pain I did after you went missing. I am glad you're home, and I have been ever since Strian brought you to us, but I just couldn't move past the hurt Strian endured. Or mine as well. You were my sister even if we weren't born of the same parents."

Gressa returned Freya embrace, holding her as though she might slip away.

"I've never met anyone else like you. I missed how we used to sneak into one another's rooms at night to gossip about the boys. I missed how you always made sure I belonged. I just missed you."

The two women hugged for another moment before turning to walk arm in arm back to their friends. Freya slid into Erik's arms, needing the comfort of her husband after such a raw conversation. Gressa buried her face in Strian's chest as he stroked her back and kissed her crown. She inhaled his scent and felt her mind settle.

"You two reconciled, or it looked that way," Strian murmured.

"We did."

The group walked to the training fields, but before anyone could begin sparring, a commotion at the gates to the homestead drew everyone's attention. Five men on horseback galloped through the gates with three men, wrists bound, being dragged behind them. The riders reined in when they reached the training fields. Ivar and Rangvald, Erik's father and Ivar's ally, walked forward from where they had been sparring together. Ivar wiped his brow as the men dismounted, and they pulled the three captives forward and presented them to Ivar.

Strian blocked Gressa's view, but when she heard Welsh being spoken among the prisoners, she pushed past Strian. She gasped before she could bite back the sound. Strian looked down at Gressa as the color drained from her face. His eyes darted to the three men before looking down at Gressa. As she stood staring at the men, she bit her lower lip to where Strian wondered if she would draw blood. Her reaction made Strian question who these men were to Gressa, and jealousy began to take root in his mind. He wrapped his hand around her upper arm and pulled her against his side.

"Explain," he bit out.

Gressa looked up at him in surprise, but his glare told her more than his words would. She looked around before tilting her head towards the back of the crowd that was forming. Strian's suspicious expression only made Gressa's stomach churn as dread had already seized her when she recognized the men.

When they reached the back of the crowd, and Gressa was sure no one could hear them, she gestured for Strian to stand closer as they both looked back at the crowd. They both attempted to make it appear as though they were watching the scene unfold rather than having a private conversation.

"Strian, this isn't good. I know those men."

"I gathered as much," Strian cut in. "Who are they to you, and why are they here? Are they trying to rescue you? Do you belong to one of them? Does one of them miss you in his bed?"

Strian's last question tore through Gressa's heart. She pivoted and drove her fist into Strian's stomach before her other landed on his chin.

"I can't believe you'd accuse me of that. I thought you believed me and that you were done accusing me. So much for a marriage if you assume the worst of me the moment something tests us. I'm no man's whore. Not even yours."

Gressa spun on her heel and pushed through the crowd before Strian could catch her. She moved until she stood once more at the front. One man caught sight of her and called out her name. She wished she could wither into the ground. She had not intended for anyone to know she was acquainted with the men. Her rush to get away from Strian and her own curiosity would now be her undoing.

"Ydych chi'n iach?" the man closest to her asked if she was well.

"Rydw i gyda fy ngŵr o'r diwedd." Gressa forced herself to keep from smiling as she explained she was with her husband at last. She knew the others would misunderstand her smile, and while she was angry at Strian for his accusations, it did not change the fact that she was happy to be with him.

"Who are these men?" Ivar demanded as he looked between the captives and Gressa.

"The one speaking is Rowan, Prince Dafydd's youngest brother and captain of the prince's archers. The other two are both bowmen. The one with the longer hair is Afan, and the other is Afon. They are twins even though they don't look much alike."

"So, they're friends of yours since you're an archer, too." Ivar's eyes narrowed.

"Hardly. The twins are Princess Enfys's older brothers. I've discovered the prince and princess betrayed me when they sent me with these men to fight for Grímr."

"Don't believe her," came a voice from the crowd.

"She's a spy!" another yelled.

"I am not," Gressa spoke evenly. "I know them because they lived in the same village as I did. I was there for ten years; there are few people I didn't know there. I trained with these men, but they are not friends."

"Beth maen nhw'n ei ddweud?" demanded Rowan, wanting to know what was being said in a language none of the men understood.

Gressa ignored him as she turned to Ivar, catching sight of Strian from the corner of her eye. He had returned to the front of the crowd, but he had not come to stand by her. His distance hurt, cutting through her worse than when she realized Dafydd and Enfys's betrayal.

"These men are spies. That's the only reason they are here."

"And you're willing to turn against them as quickly as you were willing to join them." Ivar's tone made the hair on the back of Gressa's neck stand up. She had grown up living in Ivar's home, and he had been the nurturing father figure her own father refused to be. She looked around as the entire crowd seemed to sneer at her. Everyone was convinced of her guilt.

"Quickly? You forced my husband to give up searching for me. You abandoned me. What was I supposed to do when slavers took me to a foreign land where I knew no one and depended upon strangers to remain alive? I spent ten years thinking I would never see my husband again. I made a home for myself, and they allowed me to train. How could I have known one day that the people I supposed were my friends would trade me to the enemy of people who never wanted me to begin with? You might believe I would betray you, but it's far worse that you think I would betray Strian." Gressa turned to look at the men who strained to catch what she said but had no way of understanding. "These men do not deserve to die, but if it's a choice between them and Strian, then let them rot."

"Roeddech chi'n ffyliaid i sbïo ac idiotiaid am gael eich dal." *You were fools to spy and idiots for getting caught.* Gressa turned her back on the men as she once more addressed Ivar. "You have valuable prisoners. Ransom them to Rowan's other brother, Rhys. He's with Grímr, too. Or don't. I couldn't care less about any of this. You've already decided I'm guilty by association, what do I care what happens to the men who sealed my fate?"

Gressa did not know where to go, but as long as she was not a captive too, she could not stay there. She left the training field and headed toward the forest and the path that would take her to the fjord. Her own husband believed she had lied and been unfaithful. She no longer cared for her safety. She had nothing left. The last person she loved had turned on her.

ELEVEN

Strian stood stunned as he listened to Gressa defend herself. He chided himself for his rash words, knowing he had ruined his marriage by believing the worst rather than coming to Gressa's defense. When she walked away, he followed. He would not let her go alone into the forest when it was obvious Grímr's men were nearby, and he would not wait to apologize and attempt to salvage the tatters of their relationship. He raced to catch up to her when she broke into a run once she was out of sight of the tribe.

"Gressa! Gressa, wait!" Strian called to her as she wound her way among the trees. Hearing his voice only seemed to make her run faster. Her quick pace was no match for Strian's longer legs. He pulled her to a stop. He was prepared for her to strike out again, so seeing the tears streaming down her face undid him. Her crushed expression only made the guilt gnawing at his gut consume all of him. He fell to his knees as he took her hand. His own tears watering his eyes.

"Gressa," his voice coming out a broken plea.

"No, Strian. You sided with them instead of me." She tried to pull her hand free, but Strian's grip was like a manacle. It was the one time he would not let her go when she tried to walk away. Strian bowed his head, and the way his shoulders shook told her he was crying. The only other time she had seen him cry was in the privacy of their home as he grieved for his mother. Her heart wanted to comfort him, but her mind railed against it. Her heart won, and she ran her hand along his hair.

"How could you?" her voice not more than a whisper.

"Because I was afraid," he confessed.

"Afraid? Of what? That I would turn out to be a spy?"

"No." He shook his head. "I was afraid one of them meant more than me, and that I would have to watch you choose someone else."

Gressa understood. She had worried about the same thing their entire voyage. She feared a woman would be waiting for Strian, and that had been a large part of why she resisted. She could not bear watching Strian with someone else. She had battled jealousy and insecurity when they courted and other women flirted with him. She had become possessive when they married even though she tried her best to hide it.

"Strian, look at me." She waited until he lifted his head, but his eyes were slow to meet hers. "I know that feeling. I know that fear because I felt it too the entire time we sailed. I feared what I would find when we arrived. It's one reason I didn't want to come back. I couldn't survive seeing you with someone else."

She shook head before continuing.

"But I didn't accuse you. I didn't forsake you. My resistance came from my fear for my safety. You heard how quick others were to accuse me. Do you think those accusations will be gone by the time we walk back? They will have festered, but me remaining in the crowd wouldn't have done anything to prevent the rumors. Strian, the moment I needed you, you refused me. The weight of that is crushing."

"I'm sorry, so, so, sorry," his voice cracking once more before he cleared his throat. "You are right. I've wronged you as your husband. I pledged to always protect you, and yet, at the first sign of danger, I was a coward."

There was no mistaking the shame and remorse in Strian's voice or in his eyes. Gressa tilted her head back to look at the clouds as she took a deep breath. Life had seemed so fresh and uncomplicated those first three months of their marriage. They had awakened to one another, making love before going to the training field, slipping off during the noon meal for a few minutes alone before they each had other duties to attend. They found each other before the evening meal where they often fed one another, living in a land of love and affection that had no other occupants. They would fall into bed kissing as they worshipped one another's bodies and made love well into the night, only to awaken to the same routine.

Now, life was complicated, and they could never return to that time of bliss. Fate had sealed that for them. They had been apart far longer than they had been a couple. Strian had only courted her for four moons before they married. They had spent less than a year as a couple, but their love still bound them together. It was a part of each of them that was inextricable despite years of separation and now yet another trial.

"Strian, you're not a coward. I don't want to ever hear you say that again. I would kill anyone stupid enough to accuse you of that, so I won't accept it from you. Stand up." She waited as he shuffled to his feet. She grasped both of his hands. "I am angry and hurt still. That won't go away just because you apologized. It will take me a while to calm down, but I told you I understand. But, Strian, you can't go around accusing me any time something complicates or tests our marriage. I can't spend my life with someone who is so willing to believe the worst of me, who doesn't trust me."

"I do trust you. It was my own selfishness that made me lash out. You never gave me reason to believe you aren't worthy of that trust, but I saw how you paled when those men stepped forward. I assumed you were fearful for at least one of their lives. That cut through me like a knife, but Gressa, there's something you refuse to tell me. My mind assumed it had something to do with those men, that you're hiding something that involves one of them. I believe your reason for wanting to return to Wales has to do with them. You can't live your life fearing I believe the worst in you, but I can't spend my life knowing you're hiding something from me."

Strian tried to keep the bitterness from his voice, but her secret sat in the back of his mind, and it had come screaming to life. His remorse fought against his impatience, and this time the latter won.

Gressa closed her eyes but could not keep the tears from falling. There was no other choice but to tell Strian why she needed to return to Wales. There was no chance for them to heal if she did not divulge what she fought to keep hidden. Keeping the secret would not protect Strian from the same pain she lived with daily. It would only drive them apart.

Strian watched as Gressa struggled with the decision to tell him what she continued to hide, and the longer she waited, the more his mind wanted to suspect the worst.

"Stop. Stop being evasive. Stop lying by omission and tell me the damn truth." Strian's voice was wrought with emotion: impatience, fear, and frustration.

Gressa knew Strian's demand was reasonable. She had been lying by omission.

"Our son!" she sobbed.

Strian felt the air whoosh from him, and he let go as dizziness overtook him. He sank to his haunches and shook his head.

"I have a son. We have a son." Hate filled his gaze as he looked up at Gressa. It was the same look he had given her as they stood with the crowd. His guilt morphed into anger as once again he questioned her loyalty. Loyalty he believed had been proven only moments ago. "You stayed there. You didn't do everything in your power to come home. With our son."

Gressa kneeled before him and reached for his face, but he brushed her hands away.

"I was injured then ill for weeks. By the time I was well enough to travel, I was too far along to go anywhere. I told you it was two moons by the time I was well enough to get around. I was already five months pregnant when I realized my condition." She hiccupped as she tried to control her tears. "He's dead, Strian. He was stillborn, but he's buried there. They wouldn't let me give him a Norse funeral. They stole away his chance to go to Helgafjell to live a life like the living among the spirits. They took him away before he could earn his entrance to Valhalla or Fôlkvang. I can't leave him behind if his soul isn't at rest. He will be alone and without our gods."

Gressa turned towards the water and walked to the shore. Strian let her go as what she said permeated his foggy mind. When he made sense of what she said, he ran after her. He caught her around the waist and pulled her into his embrace. She felt the shudders run through him as his tears soaked her shoulder.

"Were you never going to tell me?"

"I don't think so. I couldn't stand seeing you like this. It was one thing to let you believe I caused you pain or doubt. It was another to hurt you with this knowledge. I would have spared you it for I know it all too well. I live with it every day."

They stood holding each other until they knew they could no longer wait to return to the tribe.

"I will take you back to Wales as soon as I can assemble my crew. They can return with my long-boat, and I will pass its ownership to my first mate. But Gressa, do you want to return to the court of Dafydd and Enfys? Do we have to?"

Gressa drew in a deep breath not wanting to think about the reality of returning to Wales. It was no longer as simple as it had seemed. Now she feared what would happen to Strian if she brought a Norse warrior into their midst. She feared his life would depend upon him fighting against his own people. She could not leave their son, but she could not en-danger Strian. The conficting thoughts made her head ache. Even if they did not live in the royal stronghold, they could not escape Dafydd and Enfys knowing she had returned. Her return would signal her escape from Grímr's forces; forces she had been specifically sent to join. There was no where they could live that was close to their son's grave without being close to the couple that betrayed her. Gressa shook her head before answering.

"I don't know. I won't return to their service, and I fear for your safety, but my heart demands I return to our son as much as it insists I protect you. I don't know that I can do both."

"What if you let me worry about protecting myself?"

"Never." Gressa's visceral reaction was unwavering and immediate.

Strian could not fight the smile that wanted to break through. He looked at his wife who stood a foot shorter than him and who weighed slightly more than half his weight. She was a fierce warrior in her own right, but it seemed almost humorous that she was his protector.

"Then what do you propose?"

Gressa swallowed before offering her solution.

"We bring him home."

"You would have us exhume his bones and bring them here? I thought you did not want to remain here. I thought you believed Wales is your home."

"What other way is there? You aren't safe in Wales, and I can't leave him."

"There's your safety here to consider."

"I'm your wife and we are once again living as a married couple. That should ensure my safety as long you don't get yourself killed."

Strian shook his head.

"No."

Gressa's brow crinkled as she tried to understand which part he was against.

"Gressa, I will be more useful as a warrior in Wales than you are remaining here. I was a fool not to consider that before I dragged you back here, but now I know the risk. That's why I agreed to go to Wales with you in the first place. If we disturb his bones, then the gods may not choose him for Helgafjell."

"Do you think the gods would overlook he was but a babe when he died? Would they punish us for wanting to ensure we buried him among our people and our gods?" Gressa countered.

"I don't know. None of these choices feel right.

What about your mother's people? Would they accept us?"

"Of course not. I've never even met them. A half Norse woman with her Norse husband and a dead baby doesn't strike me as people who will receive an invitation to live among them."

"Can we not find somewhere else in Wales to live that is beyond Dafydd's reach?"

"Perhaps. There are other principalities, but I don't think you'd be any safer. I blended in because of my darker hair. Your blond hair is a beacon that screams you're Norse."

"Not all of our people have such light hair. I'm sure the Welsh have seen other Norsemen with dark hair. They cannot assume every blond man is there to raid and pillage."

"No. Only the ones who don't speak their language."

"You learned it. So can I."

"It took me years of living there before I sounded like a native. It's not an easy one to learn. It's not one I could teach you in the time it takes to sail there."

"Then we are at an impasse."

"What if we sail there, but only I go ashore? I gather his remains and return to the ship without you or any of the others stepping foot on Welsh land."

"Absolutely not. You were sold to them as a slave and given to Grímr as one. I don't doubt for a minute that they could enslave you again given half a chance."

Gressa turned back to face the water as her shoulders hunched, and she wrapped her arms around her middle.

"Then the only choices are for me to return without you, or we leave him there."

Strian slid his arms around her waist and leaned

his body against hers as though he could be a shield from the world's cruelty.

"Must we decide today? There is too much to consider to make our decision now. Let us think about it more before we choose."

Gressa nodded her head but continued to look out at the water that could carry them back to their son.

"What was his name?"

"Strian. Strian Striansson."

TWELVE

Both Strian and Gressa were weary as they walked back to the homestead. Neither wanted to talk, and neither wanted to face the tribe's accusations. They steered towards their longhouse, but the crowd remained in the center of the village. They could not make it to their home without being seen. Strian felt Gressa tense as they passed through the gates and people noticed their return.

"There she is. Why would she have run if she did not want to escape her guilt?" A man called out.

"Strian returns with his thrall. He's captured her once again," a woman's voice rose from the buzzing of the crowd.

It was obvious that Strian was not returning with a captive as they walked with their arms wrapped around each other. Strian pulled her so close to his side, it felt as though he would meld them into one.

"Don't listen to them. Ivar knows you're not a traitor, and so do those who matter. They won't allow these accusations to continue."

"If you believe that, then you did not see or hear Ivar when he accused me of being friends with those men."

"He won't turn his back on you. You were like a second daughter to him. He and Lena raised you. He knows you wouldn't betray us."

"If you say so."

Gressa was far from convinced, and Strian's optimism and naivety only made her more wary. They walked until they reached Ivar and their friends. While Leif and the others bore looks of sympathy and worry, Ivar's was a storm cloud.

"Why did you run if you aren't guilty?"

"Why would I stay when I am being accused?"

"To assert your innocence," Ivar growled.

"Innocence everyone has already decided doesn't exist. Besides, I didn't run. I walked."

"Gressa," Strian hissed. Everyone knew of Ivar's temper. The last thing Strian wanted was for Ivar to release it upon Gressa. Then he could not protect her.

"You better confess all that you know," Ivar threatened.

"I already did. I told you who those men are. I suggested you ransom them or kill them at your choice. I told you I choose Strian over those men."

"Perhaps you choose Strian so you can continue to spy," Rangvald offered. The other clan leader had stood observing the scene before and after Gressa and Strian disappeared into the woods.

"Father," Erik challenged.

Rangvald shrugged but did not retract his words.

"And who was I supposed to report to? Do you think I could slip off to meet with Grímr's men when they were so easily captured? Do you think I would guarantee my own death? Or do you think I would steal a longboat to sail on my own?"

"You lived among their people for nearly as long as you lived among us." Ivar asserted.

"And they gave me as much choice to leave as they gave me to move there."

"From what I saw, you were anything but relieved to reunite with your husband," Rangvald stated.

"I had my reasons."

"Yes. You're a traitor!" A faceless voice bellowed.

"She is not." Strian's tone was as smooth and strong as a slab of marble. "She is my wife. I'm aware of her intentions, and I understand why she did not return. She had her reasons, and these accusations are reason enough on their own for her not to want to return."

Strian's gaze swept across the gathering. Taller than most, he looked around him at people he had known his entire life.

"When we discovered my uncle Eirnar's perfidy, how he coveted Lena, how he sired Rangvald's sister's children and that Inga plotted against her own tribe with him, how he sold our secrets to Hakin and Grímr, and how he killed his own brother, none of you accused me of being a traitor. You did not question my loyalty because of my relation to Einar. But now you stand before me and accuse my wife. No one gave her a choice about where she goes or who she answers to. Our enemy sold her as a thrall in Wales but released as a free woman. She was ordered to serve our enemy but did not try to escape me. She had reason to fear returning here, and you clearly justified those worries. But I still claim her as my wife, and we live as a married couple would. We have proven that in the three days we spent in the privacy of our home. You have no reason and no right to accuse her. She did not lie or refuse to tell us who those men are. She even accepted their death rather than turn against this tribe. What more do you want?"

Strian's voice carried, the resolve and anger evident to everyone. He turned his gaze to Ivar, disregarding Ivar's position as jarl and his vow of fealty.

"You can stand here accusing a woman you raised. A woman you trained to fight and taught loyalty. Yet you think she would turn against us. That makes me wonder how well you did as a father to her if you're convinced she is honorless."

"Strian," Gressa tugged on his arm as her eyes widened to saucers. Questioning their jarl and posing his own accusations could see Strian dead.

"You overstep, Strian. You will keep your head only because I have known you since you were born, and I raised Gressa as though she were my own. But time changes people just as it can change their alliances. She is your responsibility now. If I'm wrong to trust you, and you're wrong to trust her, it's not just her life that will be forfeit."

Ivar's threat lingered in the air as he and Rangvald left the crowd. The moment the two jarls left, the crowd surged towards Gressa. Strian and his friends only had seconds to draw their weapons and circle Gressa for her protection.

"You will not touch this woman," Leif's voice was low but carried the authority that came from being first in line for the jarldom. "My father has not condemned her, and neither will you. She is Strian's wife and is under his protection. If that is not enough, she is under mine as the heir to this jarldom. She is under Freya's, the daughter of our jarl, and her husband Erik's, son of our ally. She has Tyra's, captain of our fleet, and Bjorn's, the captain of our forces. You will not harm her without facing our wrath. Which one of you would stand against any of us, denounce our authority? Test any of us, and you will die."

"Anyone who attempts to make her look guilty or makes any further accusations will be treated as a person without honor and will find themselves tied to the níðstöng. The shaming pole shall become your new home." The tribe members knew Freya's warning carried a greater promise of death than anyone else's among the jarl's leaders. She was intensely loyal and slow to forgive, making her someone others rarely crossed. "Leave now. Return to your homes or your duties. We will see those who linger as lazy and shirking their responsibilities. They will find themselves shoveling shite from the cesspit."

No one waited to determine whether Freya's warning was a hollow promise. Once everyone scattered, Strian lowered his sword. The others followed suit. Strian pulled Gressa into his arms and held her, anxious over her exchange with Ivar and his tribe members' threats.

"I'm all right," Gressa murmured as she ran her hand over Strian's heart.

"Just let me hold you until my fear goes away. I need to feel you safe against me," Strian's breath brushed her ear as he whispered.

Gressa wound her arms around his waist, content to be held after the draining morning. Their friends gave the couple their privacy as they turned away.

"We can't let her be alone now," Tyra kept her voice quiet. "Someone will attack her if they see her by herself."

"You're right, but she'll refuse our help. She'll feel as much a captive as those Welshmen." Freya nodded her head towards the níðstöng, the tall wooden pole made from a tree trunk where they shackled prisoners or accused while awaiting their fate.

"I don't have a solution, but I will ask Sigrid if she has seen anything," Leif offered. Leif's wife, Sigrid, was renowned for her gift of second sight. So much so that Hakin, Grímr's older brother, had her kidnapped early in the ongoing battle. "Perhaps she's had a vision or can cast the runes."

Erik and Bjorn stood quietly, neither having anything to add to the conversation, but they were in agreement that their friend's wife needed more protection than the woman would willingly accept.

THIRTEEN

Gressa knew her friends were handing her off one after another, rarely leaving her alone. She appreciated the time to reconnect and rebuild what had been an unbreakable friendship when they were children. But after three weeks she was tired of being followed everywhere, feeling once more like a thrall than a shield maiden and a free woman. She had tried to bring it up with Strian, but his look of worry then resolve made her abandon hope that he would agree to dismissing her guard. Gressa was honest with herself and knew they were right to protect her, even if the over protectiveness chafed. She saw the looks directed at her and even caught some of the whispers.

It came to a head one afternoon as she walked with Freya and Tyra to the kitchens. She joined the other two in the kitchens after their training in the morning. She worked alongside other women from their tribe, but the women kept their distance as though they would catch an illness from being too close. Tyra and Freya huddled around her, pretending there was not an expanding rift between Gressa and the other women of the tribe. They shielded her from anyone who might insult her, but

Gressa was growing claustrophobic from their constant attention. When they needed more eggs for the bread dough, she dashed out before Freya or Tyra could stop her.

"I'll fetch them," Gressa leaped at the chance to volunteer. She looked to Freya and Tyra as they exchanged a look, deciding who would be her chaperone. "I'll be gone only a moment."

Gressa grabbed a basket as she bolted for the door that led outside. She basked in the freedom she lost a month earlier when the Welshmen arrived and her life once more tilted on its axis. She did not dally as she made her way to the chicken coop. She was bent over, reaching for eggs under the roosting hens when voices that were much too near reached her.

"Her bodyguards seem to have abandoned her. It was only a matter of time before they grew fed up of playing nursemaid to the Laplander."

Gressa recognized the men's voices as one that belonged to boys she had avoided as a child. She did not bristle from the pejorative name for her mother's people, but she did from their proximity. She inched her fingers toward the knife sheathed at the front of her belt. She drew it, prepared for the inevitable attack. She had it clutched in her hand when strong hands bit into her waist and dragged her backwards. A hand clamped over her mouth as an arm that felt like an iron chain wrapped around her chest, pinning her arms to her side. She kept the knife pointing down, hoping to conceal it until she had the opportunity to use it on her captors rather than them using it on her. Despite having a hand over her mouth, her head was unrestrained. She threw it back with as much force as her neck could muster. It crashed into the man's nose, cracking it with a crunching sound. Rather than release her, the man's fingers bit into her cheek. She tried to snap her teeth but could only reach the edge of his hand, no flesh within reach to bite down upon. A second man stepped in front of her, attempting to gather her legs. He made the mistake of stepping in line with them. She threw her upper body's weight backwards as she kicked her booted foot into the man's groin. Her foot landed in its desired destination, but it only gave the second captor the chance to grab her ankle as he pulled her other foot from the ground. She writhed and twisted as she tried to break free.

A third man appeared from beyond Gressa's peripheral vision, landing his fist in her exposed middle. She slashed out with her knife and tore through the man's forearm. He reeled back, and Gressa twisted her wrist to stab his throat. Blood geysered from the attacker's neck, spraying Gressa and the other two assailants. The warm fluid hit her face, galvanizing her into further action. She threw her head back once more contacting the man's already broken nose. His grasp loosened as he howled in pain. With a little freedom to move her arms, she felt for the sensitive flesh beneath his wrist and dug her nails in as she pinched, hoping to break the skin. Her teeth sank into the fleshy side of the man's hand until she tasted blood. He dropped his hold on her, and as her body crashed against the ground, she released a blood-curdling scream. She scrambled on the ground trying to twist away from the man who held her legs. She tried to kick, but while her legs moved, she could not connect with his body.

"Scream if you want, but no one who cares will hear you, and no one who hates you will come to your rescue." The man dragged her along the ground, small rocks and pebbles abrading her skin despite the tunic she wore. She screamed over and over, but the man did not slow. He pulled her around a storage building before throwing himself onto her, fumbling with the laces of his leather pants. She could feel his arousal pressing against her leg and wanted to be ill. She even tried to conjure vomit she could spew at him.

Once he had his cock free, he set his sights on the laces to Gressa's pants. She tried to bring her knee up between his, but his weight kept her pinned to the ground. When he tried to push her pants from her hips, she sank her hips against the ground, refusing to budge. A hand she had not expected slapped her hard enough to twist her head. She cried out in pain, but she meant her scream more as a distraction than a hope for rescue. She wrestled her arms free and gouged her thumbs into the man's eyes. His hand came around her throat and tightened the deeper she plunged her thumb. She released one eye to push her knuckles against his Adam's apple and windpipe. As he gasped for air just as she did, she used the last bit of strength she had as stars danced in the blackness before her eyes to dig her feet into the ground and thrust upwards as she twisted, hoping to buck her assailant off her. It gained her some leverage, and his body rolled from hers, but not completely. She screamed once more, but a hand grasped her hair and yanked backwards. Gressa groaned as the man whose nose she broke returned to the fight. A knife bit into the skin at Gressa's throat, and pressure convinced her to stop fighting the assault. She would have to wait until she had a better position to defend herself without having her neck sliced.

A feral growl came from behind her before a weight was thrown at the man who fisted her hair, making him flew sideways. The force knocked her over, pinned beneath the weight of two giant men. She gasped for breath as they struggled on top of her. Everything turned to black as she heard Leif and Bjorn yelling.

Strian wrestled the man who dared touch his wife. He had already beaten one man to death for touching her, so he had no qualms of doing it again. He tried to roll off Gressa, seeing her pinned beneath him and the man who had clutched her hair, but his opponent kept pulling them both back onto Gressa. Strian heard more than saw Leif handle the man whose cock still hung free of his pants. Bjorn added his weight and strength to Strian's fight and helped Strian move them off Gressa. Two blonde heads with long braids carried Gressa from the fight. Bjorn backed off once Gressa was free, allowing Strian to finish the fight as was his right. He drove his fist into the man's windpipe, crushing it and forcing the last breath from the man's body. He turned his sights to the man Leif had laying on the ground at knife point. He stood and moved towards the last living attacker, but Freya pushed past him, knife drawn. She swiped it across the attacker's manhood, severing it in one deep cut.

"Tyra can't be the only one with a reputation for cutting off a man's cock." Freya announced as she stepped way, leaving Strian to finish the man with a knife through the eye that had viewed Gressa as a target.

"Strian! You'd better come here," Tyra called out.

Strian ran to where Freya and Tyra had laid Gressa on the grass. There was blood on her throat. Strian feared it was from the cut he could already see on. He slid onto his knees as he arrived at his wife's unmoving body. Gressa's eyes fluttered open as Strian used his sleeve to wipe the blood away. She looked into eyes she had once believed she would stare into every day for the rest of life, eyes she had once feared she would never see again. She reached her hand out and cupped his cheek, running her the pad of her thumb over his stubble.

"It's not mine. Not my blood," she rasped. "I stabbed one of them and broke the other's nose. It's their blood."

"Most of it, but the skin is broken on your throat again. I think this time it may be deep enough for stitches." Strian looked up at Leif and Freya. "Fetch Lena and Sigrid. Have them meet us at my longhouse."

Strian lifted Gressa into his arms before his long strides carried her to their home. Bjorn, Tyra, and Erik who had just joined them, walked behind them. Onlookers whispered as Strian carried Gressa away from the dead bodies strewn across the places where the attack happened. Strian did not stop or look around, knowing what he would see. His singular focus was getting Gressa into the safety of their home to await help from Sigrid and Lena.

FOURTEEN

Bjorn, Tyra, and Erik stood outside the door of Strian and Gressa's home, glaring at the crowd that dared to follow the wounded woman as her husband carried her.

"I see my own people have joined in watching," Erik snarled. "You shame me to see you take pleasure in watching a woman attacked by three men. Not a one of you came to her rescue when we all heard her screams. Not a one of you offered her aid. You disgust me."

Erik crossed his arms as he glared at a crowd comprising tribe members who lived on the homestead and those who fought for Rangvald, having traveled with Erik and Rangvald to Ivar's village.

"We feel the same shame as we look at our own people. We warned you that Gressa was under the protection of those who lead Ivar's forces. You swore fealty to your jarl which means you are to obey those who represent him. Ivar has said more than once in the great hall that we welcome Gressa back into his family as the daughter he and Lena thought they lost just as they had so many of their own blood children. I have never seen such enmity towards one of our own." Bjorn stood with his hands on his hips as he scowled.

"Before anyone is foolish enough to argue Gressa is not one of us because of who her mother was, remember her father captured her mother just as Gressa was after the enemy wounded while she fought our battle. Gressa was raised among us, remained with us and marry one of us. She fought alongside us as soon as she could raid. She nearly died defending our home, our people, and our safety. She has chosen us over and over, yet you still question her loyalty and her right to live among us. You are nothing but fools who would rather gather like a gaggle of hens clucking and spreading rumors. You are a disappointment to the honor we have pledged to live by." Tyra spat at the feet of the group of onlookers.

Lena, Sigrid, and Rangvald's wife Lorna pushed through. While Lena and Sigrid ducked into the longhouse, Lorna remained outside. She scanned the crowd, her upper lip curling.

"Those of you who are my people know how I came to live among you. You arrived in Scotland to slaughter my clan. I watched as you killed my mother, my father, and my last brother. But yet, I trusted Rangvald when he offered me a new life among you when I had nothing left to keep me in Scotland. I, too, was an outsider you ignored and spoke out against, but your jarl chose me as his bride and has remained faithful to me since that day. You have accepted me as your frú, seen me fight alongside you, and trust me. Yet I stand here now, seeing my people complicit in hatred of a young woman who has more right to the Trondelag home than I do. You are a disgrace to our clan, and you offend me as someone who was once an outsider. Gressa grew up on this homestead. She is a

Norse woman just as any standing here. I will be judge and executioner to any of my people who dare stand against her again. I suggest you make yourselves scarce before I seek you out, one by one."

Lorna's tone brooked no disagreement, and the crowd thinned as those who belonged to Rangvald and Lorna's tribe rushed away. Lorna now turned her scorn on Ivar's people who were foolish enough not to escape while Lorna's people hurried away.

"From what I understand, you blame Gressa for being Sami. Did she choose that any more than you did to be Norse or me a Highlander? Did a one of you choose your parents? I know I did not choose mine. The stories I've heard tell of a woman who grew up beloved by her adopted family. A woman who trained hard to earn her title of shield maiden and fought valiantly as she defended your honor and avenged the loss of your people, who included her husband's mother. I've met a woman who would protect her husband, a man twice her size, before giving up. What more can you ask of her? She has bled for you time and again, but that doesn't satisfy you. You would rather hold on to a hatred that makes no sense to feel superior. A smart tribe would have welcomed her home, celebrated her courage and a strong will to survive, and would appreciate the knowledge of an enemy who refuses to be defeated. There is much Gressa can teach us both on and off the battlefield. You are not the people Rangvald and I thought we allied with." Lorna passed one last disgusted look over the crowd before slipping into the longhouse.

"Lena?" Strian whispered as he looked at his wife whose eyes had remained closed since he lifted her into his arms.

"She'll be well soon enough. She's drained from

the fight. Her mind needs time to rest after the fear and the need to survive. Give her time. The cut to her throat is not so deep, and it will heal with the help of the salve I'll leave with you."

Strian looked doubtful but nodded his head.

"Strian," Sigrid's soft voice called for his attention. "She will defeat these suspicions, but you will try to stop the only way she has. You have the power to change that fate that I saw, but you must trust her to know what she's doing."

Strian nodded. He believed every vision Sigrid had since she shared the conversation she had with his dead father while she spirit walked. She had told him things that no one but his father could have known, and she had never met him while he lived. Strian wanted to ask her about further into the future, but he did not dare without divulging a secret Gressa had fought so hard to keep.

"You'll *all* return home." Strian heard the stress Sigrid put on the word "all." He glanced up to see her gentle smile before her slight nod. He stood and kicked off his boots before walking to his side of the bed. He laid down on top of the covers but as close to his wife as he dared.

"Thank you. All of you. Thank you for caring for my wife."

"We didn't just care for her. We care about her," Lena stroked hair away from Gressa's cheek just as a mother would. "Ivar and I may not have been blessed with many children who survived their birth, but Gressa is as much my daughter as Leif and Freya. She is the daughter of my heart. I have tried to let her find her way since she returned. I have tried to honor your right, as her husband, to protect her. But my failure to show our people that she is my daughter, one I grieved over losing just as I did each babe I lost or died in my arms, has allowed people to believe she can be a target. That ends now. She cannot remain a captive here, a bodyguard with her at all times, nor can she live here with a rightful fear of being attacked. I end this now."

Lena leaned over and kissed Gressa's forehead. "Get well, my little flower. I've missed you too much to let you go again."

The women left Strian to care for his wife. He draped his arm over her waist as he kissed her temple. Gressa shifted closer in her sleep, seeking the warmth and safety he provided. While Gressa slept, Strian's mind would not cease replaying the scene he had come upon. He could not suppress the memory of two men pinning Gressa to the ground as one tried to violate her. He was proud of Gressa for the fight she put up, but his head pounded with a deafening cadence as he remonstrated himself for letting her come to harm. His arm tightened around Gressa as he laid his head on his pillow.

"Stop thinking about it," Gressa's murmured. "It was no one's fault but those men, and they got the death they deserved."

"I have failed you over and over, Gressa. I have not been a worthy husband."

Gressa's eyes snapped open as she rolled to face him. She fisted his tunic and pulled with a strength that surprised Strian, the collar biting into his neck.

"Just as I won't tolerate anyone, including you, to say you are a coward, I will not stand for you to think you failed me. I won't have it, so don't ever let those words come out of your mouth again. You have protected more times that I can count. You harp on the handful of times you couldn't but overlook the many more times you have."

"Those handful of times you so casually mention were times that nearly got you killed. You nearly died because of my failure."

Gressa hissed as she pulled harder on his tunic.

"Stop it," she bit out.

Strian could not believe the strength Gressa possessed after being unconscious only minutes ago. Her fierce defense warmed his heart, but his mind was not ready to release his guilt.

"I can't control what you think any more than I can those who wish me ill, but it infuriates me to hear you doubt yourself. It overwhelms me to know I'm the reason for that doubt." Gressa's eyes filled with tears. "Freya told me what you were like after Ivar and the others tied to the mast and forced you to leave me behind. She told me how you lived, how you withdrew for so long. You have lived with guilt and grief long enough. We both have. What life will either of us have, even if it's together, if we can't loosen our hold on the past?"

"It's your future I fear."

Gressa lifted her chin and brushed her lips against Strian's.

"I would be lying if I said I didn't fear it, too. But it can't control us. We can't let it. We already lost so many years of being together, of having a family. I don't want to miss our chances now. I'd rather picture a future filled with children and grandchildren. And for now, I rather enjoy picturing how we try to make those children." She brushed her lips against him again, feathering a kiss on each side of his mouth. "But for now, I want to sleep. I expect you to hold me and not let go until I wake again. Then I want to practice making those babies."

Gressa rolled over and nestled into Strian's body as he spooned her. Her eyes drifted shut, and Strian soon felt her breathing deepened. As he matched his breathing to hers, he slid into slumber, too.

FIFTEEN

The next morning, Ivar summoned them to stand before him. Deep lines were etched between his eyebrows, ones Gressa did not remember from all those years ago. His eyes looked tired and his face drawn. Gressa was nervous as she faced the man she had longed to call father. As a child, she often wondered why Ivar could not have been her true father. Now she feared his love had run out. Ivar looked up as they approached. Before they reached him, he marched forward and pulled Gressa into a tight embrace. She felt him shudder as she wrapped her arms around him. It felt so familiar, just as it had when she was young and hurt by the unkind words of the other children or fell while playing. She half imagined he might pull her onto his lap just as he had when she turned to him for comfort as a child. She wished that he could.

"Gressa, I am ashamed of how I treated you in front of the tribe, of how I could cast doubt on you, and how I have neglected you since your return. It's my fault. All of it. You being left behind only to returning to suspicion and hostility. I've said you are welcome here, but I have not shown it. I have not been the father I pledged to be or the one you deserved." Ivar held her as he made his confession.

"I don't blame you. You had more people than just me to worry about. You may have been, are, my adoptive father, but you are still our jarl. You did what you thought was best. You welcomed me home with the same warmth as you do now. This, this hug and these words, make up for much. Father." Gressa tried out the word and waited for Ivar to recoil, fearing she had gone too far. Instead his hold only tightened.

"You have no idea how I longed to hear you call me that rather than Ivar. I care for you just as I do Freya and Tyra. I harbor guilt that I did not do enough for either you or Tyra. She is like a daughter to me, and I should have made her come to live with us after she lost her parents too, but she was older, and I thought it best she lived with her aunt and uncle."

"Regret is getting us nowhere. The past is done and as it will remain. I'd rather look to a better future."

"You have become quite sage, daughter."

They embraced for a moment longer before they pulled apart, and Gressa returned to Strian's side as their friends joined them.

"Gressa, we need your knowledge of the Welsh. The men don't speak any Norse, or at least have not let on if they do. We can't learn anything from them. You're the only one who speaks both languages." Ivar paused as he seemed to consider his thoughts before sharing them. "Rangvald and I need to know as much about how the Welsh fight as we can. It seems Grímr has abandoned his search for Scottish mercenaries and is relying on the Welsh bowmen. We've had reports that attackers have killed sentries near the borders on both my land and Rangvald's.

We believe they are trying to weaken our defenses to make it easier to attack either this homestead or Rangvald's. Once again, you are the only one with that knowledge."

Gressa's gaze did not waiver once as she looked into Ivar's eyes while he explained the situation.

"There were two hundred Welsh footmen and archers who traveled with Grímr. After the battle at the Ross keep, I would say you killed only a quarter of the force. The few men who made it over the wall and then the archers who rode into the bailey. Grímr purposely held back many of the foot warriors in case the battle tide turned against him and he needed to retreat to plan for the next one. He has at least a hundred but likely a hundred and fifty men still with him." Gressa finally looked around the group after watching Rangvald and Lorna join them. They sat in chairs beside Ivar's and Lena's, showing their elevated status. "I didn't hear of any specific plans beyond the battle at the Scottish keep. He was unprepared for your allies to arrive. He thought you would show up and was prepared to fight, but he did not expect a second wave of fighters to arrive. I suspect he once more used his son who bears an unlikely resemblance to him even though I heard he was a bastard sired by another man. He makes his son pretend to be him, so he can move around during battles without anyone being able to keep up with two men who appear the same but are going in different directions. He has no qualms about retreating and fleeing, leaving his son to be captured or killed in his place."

"That bluidy well explains why we can never catch the bastard," Lorna grumbled, her brogue trying to inch into her voice.

"I was not with Grímr's forces very long, and I don't know what he negotiated with Dafydd,"

Gressa lips drew in and pursed as she thought of just what the two men had negotiated for her to be the only woman sent to Grímr's aid. "I can only guess based on the Welsh tactics I learned. Their archers are better than any others, anywhere. Grímr will most likely try to lure your forces into the woods near here. Then he'll have the bowmen pick off your warriors one by one until Grímr's men can overrun you and sack the homestead. Once he's brought the tribe to its knees, he will either destroy the holding or leave his sons in charge before moving onto Rangvald's. One thing I did hear was he's no longer interested in capturing and possessing the extra land. He wants each of you dead more than the power. He figures the power and land will come naturally after he slaughters all of you."

Gressa felt Strian's grip on her waist tighten as he gave her a reassuring squeeze. He must have known how to she dreaded looking around the group.

"Do you know when he plans this attack?" Rangvald spoke up for the first time.

"It has to be soon. The weather will change and be too unpredictable. Now that you have royal prisoners, Grímr will have a hard time getting the Welsh to cooperate. You could ransom the men to Rhys like I said the day you captured them, but you should exchange them for Grímr. He has no value to Rhys, and I doubt Dafydd ever thought he would gain much from his alliance after he was paid."

"Do you think you can get those men to talk?" Lena's eyes showed the concern she felt for Gressa.

"I don't know. I told them I was happy to finally return to my husband. They will know where my loyalty lies."

"Lie to them." Strian broke in. "Tell them you had to say that in front of everyone. Tell them you had to trick me into thinking you want to stay to keep yourself alive. Ask them how you can escape."

Gressa shook her head vehemently.

"No. Whether or not anyone else understands what I'm saying, I will never let them think I want to return to Grímr's aid. They know---" she trailed off.

"Then let them think you want to return to Dafydd and Enfys. They don't know you're aware of the couple's betrayal. They might speak more if they think you're naive or ignorant of the truth."

Gressa could see the reasoning to that, but one last concern refused to let go.

"And when the tribe members see me talking to them? They will all believe I am what they accused me of. They will surely go after me, and I'm not convinced any, even all of, you can protect me from an angry mob."

"We will have the prisoners brought here where you can speak privately, or at least they will believe that, and we can guard you with us hidden nearby." Freya offered the only solution that could work.

"Fine, but not without my sword." She had once believed Rowan, Afan, and Afon were her friends, but now she questioned whether anyone in the ten years she lived in Wales had ever been her friend.

Gressa and Strian stood together alone as they waited for Freya to retrieve Gressa's sword and for guards to bring the Welshmen. Strian's hands rested on her shoulders as he peered into her eyes. He saw resolve and determination as she bristled with anxious anticipation.

"I will stay with you if you want," Strian offered.

"I wish you could, but how am I supposed to convince them I want to escape you if you're hovering over me."

"You can tell them you tire of my possessiveness, proven by my presence, and that you lied about being happy to be with me to protect yourself. They know I won't understand, so they'll believe you." A flash of doubt crossed Gressa's face, and Strian knew what worried her. "I know you'll be pretending. I won't question you again. I trust that you want me to be your husband, and anything you say is to convince them to tell you Grímr's plans. Say what you must, whatever that is. I know you're coming home with me."

Gressa strained to kiss him, but it was cut short when they heard people outside the chamber where the jarl conducted business. With no plan for him to remain present, Strian darted to stand behind a boulder carved into the face of Odin. He glanced over to see the door leading to the great hall was ajar, meaning Tyra and Freya were nearby. Leif and Bjorn led the prisoners into the room before standing by the door through which they passed. Ivar and Rangvald had agreed their own presence would not make the captives very talkative.

"Ydych chi'n iach?" Gressa begar. by asking if they were well. The men only nodded their response.

"Rydyn ni ar ein pennau ein hunain heblaw am y ddau a ddaeth â chi yma ac nid ydyn nhw'n deall." Gressa continued as Strian listened to a language filled with strange sounds. Gressa had told him her plan was to assure the men from the very beginning that no one would understand their conversation even those who stood guard.

The three men looked around before nodding again to Gressa.

"Why're you here? Did you intend to get caught?" Gressa continued her questions.

"They sent us to spy, and Rhys wants to know where you are." Rowan spoke of his brother.

"Are you all afraid that I will share Grímr's secret plans?"

"What secrets? We all know he's a madman, but Dafydd accepted his coins and jewels, so we must play like his puppets," Afon grumbled.

"You never answered whether you intended to get caught. Did you want to enter the homestead so you could see for yourselves what you faced?" Gressa tried to keep them on topic without pushing too hard, too fast.

"Rowan told you Rhys worries about you," Afan answered as though that was enough to explain everything. When Gressa's expression remained blank, Afan grumbled. "You know he intends to make you his wife. He thought you had finally gotten past mooning over some man you'd never see again, that you were moving on if you were willing to fight against your own people."

"Who said I was willing? Dafydd? Enfys? They sold me to Grímr just like they bought me from those slave traders. No one gave me a choice." She paused before she defended herself too well. "But I have a choice now. I can't leave here with you if you get yourselves killed as spies. I've suggested they ransom you to Rhys."

Rowan laughed but it was hollow. "The only ransom he'd be willing to pay is for you, and the cost will be in his bed."

"What about what you said when you first saw us? You said you were happy to be with your husband." Afon demanded.

"What was I supposed to say in front of the crowd? I didn't want any of you to react the wrong way if I said I wanted to run away with you."

"But it's not like you could have summoned us to

this meeting. Someone ordered you here." Afon looked at her suspiciously.

"Of course, I was, but they don't know what we're saying. They will believe whatever I tell them, truth or lie. But I'm not willing to risk my life for you or Rhys or anyone else if I don't know that it's worth it. Did you intend to get caught?"

The three men looked at one another before Rowan answered.

"Yes. We'd been spying since before you even arrived. We nearly rescued you when you ran to the water, but your husband followed you. You looked awfully cozy for someone who wants to leave her husband."

"I wouldn't be able to go anywhere, do anything, *learn* anything if they thought I would leave."

"But you warm his bed when you refused Grímr and continue to refuse Rhys." Rowan countered.

"What is a wife supposed to do? I need him to trust me enough to let me out of his sight."

"Or perhaps you like where you are, and all of this is lies." Afon narrowed his eyes as though she would spill her secrets if he glared at her.

"Whether I want to go or stay won't matter if I don't know where I need to take you to escape. If we're caught, you'll die for spying, and they'll kill me for being a traitor."

"It's been a long time since you lived here, how will you know where to go?"

"I grew up here. I played in those woods as a child then hunted in them as woman," *and made love to my husband there* she nearly added. "I know my way around. Tell me where we need to go and how you got here. I will take us a different way to avoid the sentries that will work twice as hard to keep more spies from getting too close."

Gressa held her breath, hoping her demand was

reasonable rather than suspicious. Rowan trailed his eyes up and down her body, lingering at her breasts and the juncture of her thighs. Gressa's skin crawled, but she did not move.

"Grímr set up camp about an hour and a half's ride south of here."

"It there a mountain that looks like it has three peaks?"

"Yes. How did you know?"

"I told you I grew up here." She did not add that they were on the land of the tribe that had attacked Gressa's people and the same land where she had been stolen away. She had been gone too long to know how matters lay between the tribes and had not thought to ask.

"There is another route there that's shorter, but the terrain is much harsher. Is there snow on the mountain yet?"

"Only a dusting," Afan offered, the only one trying to be pleasant.

"Then we cannot wait. That dusting could turn into a blizzard while the sun shines on the coast. We have to go into the hills on our route."

"How do you propose to set us free?" Afon glared at her, not at all convinced that she could rescue them nor come with them.

"No one will watch you during the dead of night. There is a hidden doorway in the wall surrounding the village. I can release you then we leave by that door. We will have to make our way into the hills as soon as we can, or they will track us."

"You sound as if you already had this plan before we arrived." Rowan's smile made Gressa's stomach curdle. It was more of a leer, and Gressa knew there was no way she could be alone with these three men in the woods unless she wanted them to complete the assault she had already survived.

"I need to know I'm not running away to my own death. You say Rhys awaits my return, but you haven't said anything to convince me that Grímr will win the next battle."

"We intended to get caught. They sent us to watch the comings and goings of the people living in this homestead. Finding you alive and well was just a bonus. Grímr intends to lure Ivar's people out into the woods where we can easily shoot them before he raids the village."

"You meant to get caught before you even knew I was here and could help you?"

"No, we decided that after we saw you arrive on the dock."

Gressa swallowed her gasp. The three men, possibly with others, had been practically inside the village for weeks if they had seen the longboats dock and her disembark.

"You must have a great deal of faith in me," Gressa tested them.

"Not faith. You either serve your purpose-- freeing us then warming Rhys's bed-- or we kill you. It seems rather simple." Rowan once again leered at her.

Gressa's heart pounded as Rowan spoke aloud what she had assumed before their conversation started.

"Very well. It can't be tonight. They'll already suspect what we talked about for so long. They'll expect me to free you. We must wait at least one more night."

"So, you can tell Ivar all that you've learned. I think not." Rowan spoke as the leader of the group. "You take your chances tonight."

"They'll kill you alongside me. Then how will you report back?"

"A risk we must take."

Gressa nodded before looking toward Bjorn and Leif. She jutted her chin towards the men before tilting her head to the door. Bjorn and Leif dragged the men from the chamber as she watched them go. She waited until the door slammed shut before spinning on her heels. Strian was already crossing the room to her, and she raced into his arms. Strian held her against his chest until she calmed enough to share what she had learned.

"They saw us on the docks when we arrived." Gressa trembled, thinking about how close the men had been and wondering what else they had seen if they planned to nab her near the fjord before Strian joined her. "They saw us together in the woods, and I'm not convinced they believe I've been fooling you. My suspicions were correct. They want to lure us into the woods for the archers to fire on before they raid the homestead. They said once they saw me, they intended to be captured, so they could not only get to me but to learn the inside of the village. I told them I could help them escape but we would have to go into the hills to get to Grímr's camp. They're on Jarl Fengr's land."

Gressa waited for the significance to register with Strian. Anger transformed his handsome face into a mask of fury.

"I take it things have not improved with that tribe in the years I've been away."

"Things are calm, but I haven't forgotten what they did to my mother, to Tyra's mother, or any of the others they found here while we fished so close to the shore but just too far to hear their screams."

Gressa held Strian while it was his turn to tremble, but his was born of rage.

"I don't know that Fengr is giving them aid. I suspect he either doesn't know or doesn't care to get involved."

Strian nodded, but Gressa knew his mind still battled the memories the name brought forth.

"Strian, they insist that I rescue them tonight even though I warned them I would be under greater suspicion after our conversation."

"You're not going anywhere with them this night or any other. I heard the name Rhys several times. It was one of the few words I recognized besides Grímr. What were they saying?"

Gressa geared herself as she once more had to share information she would have protected Strian from.

"You know Rowan is Dafydd's brother. But so is Rhys, and he's been pursuing me for years. He's demanded my hand in marriage, both from me and Dafydd. I've been able to ward him off, my grief for you very real and a barrier between me and any man. He's growing tired of waiting, and I feared he would force me to marry him once I returned with the other warriors."

Strian pulled away as he looked down at Gressa. Yet another secret she had kept from him in her mixed-up way of trying to protect him.

"You insisted on returning to Wales before you told me why. You were willing to return there, claiming it was safer all the while knowing a man would be waiting. A man who would insist you marry him. Is that what you wanted?"

Gressa stamped her foot in frustration.

"Of course not. I would have found yet another way of keeping him away. We have been apart a long time and a few weeks aren't enough time to learn all that happened in each other's lives, but I took your promise that you had been faithful as the truth from the beginning. Yet, you question me every time you suspect I looked the wrong way."

"What's happened here to give you any reason to

believe I wanted someone else? Nothing. But every time I think we're on solid ground, another man pops up, and I learn yet another reason that might be why you truly argued for your return."

"Being attacked by two women the first full day I was here was more than enough to make me wonder which women would be jealous of my return. But I believed you, I chose to. I made the commitment to believe you, and it wasn't easy, and you certainly don't make it easy now when you accuse me over and over. You know the one reason why I want to return to Wales. You might also do well to remember that I never asked again once you offered to come with me. Is that the motive of a woman yearning for someone else? Why would I bring you with me if I planned to marry someone else?"

"We have been apart a long time, and you keep secrets that you should have shared with me even if you thought they would hurt me. Your actions are what makes me suspicious. Every time I'm sure you've told me the last hidden truth, something else crops up. It's hard to give blind faith to someone who can't seem to tell the truth."

Gressa reeled back as though Strian struck her. She shook her head as she took several steps away.

"Don't touch me. Don't even come near me." She bolted for the door and yanked it open. "Follow me, and I may very well kill you."

Strian stood dumbfounded as he watched Gressa disappear through the doorway before slamming the door shut.

"You're an even bigger arse than either of us ever were with our wives," Bjorn crowed as he and Leif stepped out of the shadows. Strian had not noticed their return while he argued with Gressa. He looked over his shoulder to where he knew Tyra and Freya had stood watch.

"They've likely gone after her," Leif shook his head, his face filled with pity. "Do you remember when you'd just started to take an interest in Gressa and some of the other young women taunted her? They said the best she could hope for was to be your concubine just as her mother had been her father's. They were ruthless with their cutting remarks to where neither Tyra nor Freya could get the other women to stop, so Freya ran for Lena. You couldn't find her at the evening meal because she wanted to avoid those women. You became so worked up that you tore through my parents' home and kicked her door down when she refused to open it. Bjorn and I chased after you only to find Gressa apologizing to you for getting you so upset with worry. She steered the conversation away from what made her retreat to her chamber. Strian, she's been trying to protect you, rightly or wrongly, since the very beginning. She endured Grímr because she was not willing to take the chance that he would torture you, and I'm sure she knew her compliance was no guarantee, but there is no limit to what she will do to keep you from harm. She didn't tell you about this Rhys man for two reasons. I'm sure it was because she wasn't thinking of him and she didn't trust you not to go berserk and charge off to find the man."

Bjorn clapped a hand on Strian's shoulder before he put in his opinion.

"Our women may be smaller than us, but never doubt they possess the heart of a warrior. I often think our wives are far more ruthless and unforgiving than any man when they believe we're in danger. We may be larger and stronger, even louder, but I don't know that we are any match for our women when they believe we need protecting." Bjorn squeezed Strian's shoulder before adding. "You'd do well to beg her forgiveness and convince yourself to stop questioning her. It always comes back to the same thing: she won't give an inch if she fears that inch will harm you."

Strian knew his friends were right. He could have kicked himself for once again opening his mouth before thinking, for not giving Gressa the benefit of the doubt. Neither of them had given the other cause for suspicion, but Strian's jealousy kept putting a wedge between them. Gressa may have kept things from him, but she believed it was necessary. He accused her because he still had not forgiven fate for stealing so much time from him, time filled with a life Gressa had without him.

SIXTEEN

Strian looked around the village in search of Gressa or at least Freya and Tyra. He found the latter two walking back through the hidden door in the wall. He waited for Gressa to follow them, but when no one appeared, his heart sank, and a cold sweat broke out across his back. He met the women halfway, and their expressions told him more than he wanted. Gressa was gone.

"She just disappeared, Strian. It's like she blew apart in the wind," Tyra's voice wobbled as she spoke.

"We saw her run from your home with her bow and quiver and followed her through the gate. We watched her enter the forest and even kept up with her for a while, but she weaved in and out of the trees, and then was just gone."

"Did you look in the branches?" Strian barked.

"No. We didn't think to."

"You learned nothing about the Welsh then. Their bowmen sit in the trees waiting. She didn't disappear. She outsmarted you both." Strian's words were one accusation after another.

"We weren't the arse who yet again accused our wife of cheating. We weren't the arse who demands everything from her while giving only part of him-self. I'm surprised it took her so long to leave you by choice." Freya snarled. "You reap what you sow."

Freya pushed past Strian, Tyra on her heels glaring at him. Strian knew they were right, but it was of little consequence if he did not find Gressa in time. If their sentry already found three spies, there were bound to be others. He charged through the gate and sprinted into the woods. He looked for any signs of tracks and picked up three sets of footprints small enough to be a woman's. He followed them until two came to an abrupt end, and the third blended in with fallen pine needles. Strian tilted his head back and looked among the branches. He edged past one tree after another until he came to one he was sure sheltered something far larger than a squirrel. He hoisted himself onto the lowest branch and began to climb.

"I warned you not to follow me," Gressa seethed, tempted to kick him from the tree when he was in reach. "I have nothing to say to you that I can't take back."

"Then maybe you'll just listen."

"No." It was a simple but emphatic answer.

"Then we are once again at a stalemate because you may not want to hear what I have to say, but I have no intention of staying quiet."

Strian was unprepared to see Gressa step out on a branch and balance while moving towards the branches of a neighboring tree. She leaped and grasped the limb of the nearby tree before scam-pering through the fir needles and branches. He watched her in awe of her graceful movement through the trees. He remembered she had enjoyed climbing trees when they were younger, but this was a skill she had learned from the Welsh archers. Strian had no choice but to climb down before he could chase after her once more.

"Squirrel," Strian called up to the tree he was sure Gressa rested in. "I was trying to apologize."

"Don't want to hear it," came a voice two trees behind the one Strian stood beneath.

"Well then, I suppose I'll be talking to myself. I'm angry but not at you. I'm angry at fate for stealing ten years from us, for creating one obstacle after another than makes you feel you have to protect me. I'm angry that fate stole that time and forced you to have a life that didn't include me. Every time something comes up that reminds me of what I had taken from me, I lash out. But it's not you I blame or accuse. It's fate. I couldn't blame you if you moved on after ten years of thinking you would never see me again. I wouldn't want you to be alone when you still have so much of your life to live."

"But isn't that exactly what you planned for yourself? To remain alone. Why shouldn't I want the same for you, for you to move one? The real difference is I don't keep accusing you."

"Because you're here with me. There's nothing I can hide when you can see it for yourself."

"If hiding my past were my true motivation, then why would I agree to you coming to Wales with me? Why would I bring you to a place only to leave you for another man?"

"Everything you say is reasonable. I just have a great deal of anger and bitterness to overcome. Fate has no mercy, and I begrudge it for what it's taken from us."

Gressa swung down from the branches where she hid. Strian reached up and caught her as she dropped from the last one. She cupped his cheeks as she rubbed her nose against his.

"I understand. I'm hurt each time you have so

little faith in me, but I'm angry and bitter with fate, too. If it were a person, I would run it through with my sword before hacking it to bits. I wish we could both release those feelings once and for all, but it will take time. But you can't blame me every time you're heartsore. I'm on your side."

"I know. We have come a long way in our reconciliation in a very short amount of time. There are things from our time apart that we must learn about one another, and things that come out may hurt us, but I won't live a life without you ever again." Strian kissed her deeply as she opened to him, her mouth warm satin that his tongue caressed. She sucked lightly, hinting at what she enjoyed doing with his length in her mouth rather than his tongue.

"Take me home, Strian."

Gressa had barely gotten out the words before the hair on her arms stuck straight up. She shoved all her weight against Strian, catching him off guard and off-balance seconds before an arrow embedded in the ground where he had been standing. Gressa whipped her bow off her shoulder and knocked an arrow. She scanned the trees and found her target. She shot off three arrows in quick succession as an arrow flew past her, aimed only at Strian. Her third arrow found a home before a body tumbled from the branches. Gressa did not take the time to see if she recognized her first victim. She launched another series of arrows where she believed their attackers hid. She used her instincts and her experience to find her targets, one after another body falling from the trees until the arrows flying towards her and Strian ceased. Only after waiting several minutes did Gressa look towards Strian, relieved to see him unharmed, then her eyes swung to the bodies that did not move beneath trees close to where she had been hiding herself. She stepped forward with caution and an arrow at the ready. She toed the shoulder of the first man and recognized him as a man who trained with her, but she did not know well. The next body made her heart squeeze as though in a vice. The unseeing eyes seemed to look beyond her until she pressed the lids closed. She murmured a prayer to her gods regardless of whether the man accepted them.

"Who was he to you?" Strian wondered. He was careful not to accuse but to inquire.

"He was a lot like Ivar in many ways. He was the closest thing to a father I had in Wales. He trained all the archers. When he discovered my skills with a bow and arrow, he took me under his wing, allowing me to train with the men. He encouraged me to continue training even when the men scoffed at me, convinced I could never be equal to them. And now I have killed him."

"Before he killed you," Strian's hushed tones still felt as though he screamed in Gressa's ears. "He was shooting at us just as the others were or he would have stopped them."

Gressa shook her head as she looked up at Strian.

"None of them were aiming at me. They were trying to kill you not me. I feel sad for the death of one of my only true friends, yet I cannot overlook that he was willing to murder my husband. They had to have heard us, seen us. They all knew who you were to me. They intended to take me alive to Grímr and Rhys, but they would have killed you had I not had my bow."

Strian opened his arms, and she leaned against his solid frame, using it to hold her up. Exhaustion threatened to overcome her as her two worlds crashed together once more, always necessitating she save Strian's life.

"We should return home. Let me take care of

you after you protected me. Again. I'll run you a hot bath and prepare something for you to eat."

Gressa shook her head against his chest before leaning back.

"We can't. They were too close to the homestead again. We have to find out who else is nearby, how many are close to our people."

It was the first time since returning to the Trondelag that Gressa called the tribe her people. Neither of them missed it, and Strian looked into the distance as he weighed their options. He wanted to carry her home, kicking and screaming if necessary, but he had to honor her right as a shield maiden to defend their tribe.

"You know we are more likely to be captured than to discover anything we can report back."

"You're probably right," Gressa answered as she swung the bow back onto her shoulder after it slid down her arm while Strian embraced her. "But we have a duty."

"But we would be wiser to go back and gather the others to come with us."

"True, but they will have disappeared by then."

"Who?" Strian scanned the trees again, but nothing unusual seemed to lurk in the branches.

"They're not here, but when the men don't return, others will come searching for them. Those are the men I want to find. I think I know who they will send, and if I'm right, we can learn more than any of our spies ever could."

Strian nodded, refusing to question her knowledge of people she believed she belonged to not so long ago. They slipped further into the trees as they traveled in silence, their footsteps as soft as a forest animal's.

. . .

They walked for an hour before Gressa held up her fist. Strian froze mid stride and watched Gressa as she silently pulled an arrow from her bow. She glanced at him and tilted her head slightly away from him, indicating she wanted him to get behind her. He had no intention of hiding behind his petite wife. He returned her gesture with a scowl. Strian was sure Gressa would have huffed if she were not aware of danger. She knocked the arrow and took sliding steps forward not risking stepping on a twig. Once more she tilted her head, but this time she indicated Strian should follow.

It was only moments later that five bowmen dropped from the trees surrounding Strian and Gressa. She released the arrow she had at the ready and felled one of them. Strian drew his sword, but he was no match for an arrow. The archers would kill him before he could get within reach.

"Beth ydych chi eisiau?" Gressa asked them what they wanted. It was clear from their clothing they were Welsh. The length of their bows and their unique arrows confirmed it. Gressa strained to see their faces in the dim light of the forest. She suspected she knew who stood before her.

"Dydych chi ddim yn adnabod eich darpar wr?" One man stepped forward, causing Gressa to step back. She knew the man who asked if she recognized her future husband.

Strian watched as Gressa's body language went from being on alert to rigid and defensive. He could not understand their words, but he understood his wife. He took a step forward, but an arrow landed at his feet as a warning. Gressa whipped her head around and bit out what sounded like an order.

"I recognize my husband just fine. I did the first time we saw each other at the Ross keep."

"So, your Norse man has survived all these years.

I suppose that's him." The man Gressa recognized as Rhys jutted his chin in Strian's direction. "Such as shame you will be a widow and a bride in such a short time, or perhaps it is a blessing that I still want you."

There was no response Gressa could give that would not make the situation worse. She would not lie and give Rhys a false sense of success, but she also could not tell him that she would die before marrying him as it would only encourage a violent reaction from a man she had avoided for years. Gressa had seen him at his most charming when he tried to seduce her, but she had also seen him when he did not know she was present. She had seen him mistreat more than one woman and abuse many slaves assigned to the royal home.

"My husband isn't going anywhere and isn't to have a hair on his head touched. Rhys, you know as long as we are in this country, Grímr will not let you have me. Killing my husband serves no purpose when I'm not yours to take, anyway."

"Obviously we are not letting you get away, so are you turning your husband over as a prisoner?"

"Of course not. He's an informant." Gressa forced herself not to wince at the lie. She disgraced Strian's honor by telling such a falsehood, but she feared it was the only way to keep him alive. "He has already agreed to move back to Wales with me. He is ready to be one of us."

"And why would you tell him he could when you know a man awaits you?"

"And why do you insist upon something that can never happen?"

"It can if he's dead."

"We're going in circles. Take us to the camp, and we will tell you what we know."

Rhys observed her for a long moment before he

nodded his head to the other men. They remained in a circle around the couple as they continued to walk through the trees.

"You'll be furious with the deal I brokered." Gressa spoke out of the side of her mouth. She knew the Welshmen could hear her, but it was not loud enough to sound like a conversation.

"I'm angry that man looks at you like he's ready to strip you bare and bed you in front of me."

"He probably would if he could, but he knows I'd kill him first. You've just met Rhys. The man who's convinced he will marry me."

"Wonderful. Another one of your secrets that comes out at the worst moment."

Gressa looked towards Strian, but she had nothing to say.

"Did you plan for us to show up in Wales where a man is waiting to make you his bride? Did you not think that might complicate things?"

"It was one complication to returning to Dafydd's court. It was one of many. I just didn't name them all."

"Woman, you test my patience beyond all resolve. It's a good thing I love you."

"I still haven't told you the worst part." Gressa tried to infuse her smile with some cheer, but she feared it was more of a grimace. "The only way to keep you alive is to make you sound useful. I told them we intend to return to Wales. Together. I told them you're an informant."

Gressa really did grimace when Strian turned to look at her, his face a thundercloud waiting to release its might.

"Before you say anything, Strian, listen to me. We don't have to tell them anything that is true. They won't know. We have their spies who got the best look at the homestead chained to the pillory post. Dead men don't talk. Besides the spies never mentioned Rangvald. They don't know the combined forces are there. We feed Grímr and Rhys misinformation."

"You've left us with little choice. Neither of us should have been foolish enough to wander so far into the woods or to think we could spy any better than the men our tribe caught. What about Grímr's threats to me? It seems Rhys has relented and won't see me dead by nightfall, but what of Grímr?"

"I don't know." Gressa's stomach churned with fear that the only way to keep Strian might require her to once again sell herself in exchange.

"Don't even consider it. I'll kill myself before I force you to give your favors to that man, any man."

"Don't even consider that either. We'll figure it out. Together."

The curious glances and Rhys's glare warned them that talking any longer would not do them any good.

SEVENTEEN

Gressa and Strian arrived in the camp that supported a mixture of Norsemen, Highland mercenaries, and Welsh bowmen. The flow of conversations created a level of noise that disoriented both of them. Their captors forced them to a stop outside a tent that Gressa recognized as Grímr's. Her stomach churned, and her mouth went dry.

"Grímr?" Strian whispered.

Gressa nodded. They had managed to come to a stop standing close enough that their arms brush together. They linked their pinkies together as they awaited their fate.

A man with a grizzled face and a pronounced limp pushed back the flap and stepped outside. He sized up Strian before his gaze jumped to Gressa. What had been an assessing and defensive expression morphed into a lascivious one. His grin pulled his lips taught over yellowed and broken teeth. He swept his tongue over them as he reached out to grasp Gressa's breast. He squeezed mercilessly. She refused to make a sound, not granting Grímr the pleasure he sought. Strian swallowed the growl that rose in his throat, understanding that coming to Gressa's defense would only put them both in more danger.

"I see the little dove has returned to the coop to nest. I've missed you at night. It's been very lonely without your company." Grímr continued to grope Gressa, but he stared at Strian as he spoke, testing the man's resolve not to intervene. Grímr spoke in Norse, so Rhys and the other Welshmen could not understand, but Strian caught every smug word flung his way. When Grímr's hand attempted to travel lower, Gressa grasped his wrist.

"We come with information you might want to know."

"And why would you do that? Why would the man who sits at Jarl Ivar's table come to my aid?"

"We intend to make our home in Wales." Gressa responded.

"You act as though that explains everything." Grímr pinched her nipple. Gressa gritted her teeth to keep from wincing.

"It explains why we would look for the other Welshmen. If we are to travel back with them, then we must be of use to you first."

Grímr squinted at her as though narrowing his eyes would help him see better into her mind. Gressa had expected his skepticism, but she had failed during the march to devise a plan for overcoming it.

"A man who stood beside the jarl as a favored warrior and best friend to the heir doesn't come over to the enemy. What could be enough for that?"

"A woman," Strian interrupted. "A woman you are touching but doesn't belong to you."

Grímr cackled. It was the only way to describe the sound that choked free of his throat.

"You are not in much of a position to claim anything let alone the woman who has such a talented mouth."

"If you would like to keep your cock attached and not bitten off, then you would do well to treat your informant with some respect." Gressa hissed, ripping his hand from her breast.

"Leave Gressa alone, and I will tell you everything you wish to know."

"And how do I know you're not lying? Trying to fool me."

"You don't. But you do know I'll do anything to protect my wife."

"Including lie. I think not. I think we shall manage just fine without your help, and now we have a captive worth a hefty ransom."

"Is that how capturing Tyra and Bjorn worked out?" Strian's hushed tones had iron that rang out as more Norsemen congregated around the captives.

Grímr struck out his fist, aiming at Strian's face, at the reminder of his failed attempt to kidnap Tyra and Bjorn. Strian grasped his wrist and twisted until Grímr had no choice but to bend backward lest he suffer a broken arm. Strian pulled him close, so only Grímr could hear him. Not even Gressa knew what Strian said.

"Touch my wife again, even brush against her, and I will offer your arse to every Norseman here. I'll be sure to find a nice long stick for them to ram up your hole. Don't fool yourself into thinking any of these men are loyal to you. Not even those remaining from your tribe. Given half a chance, they will turn on you, and you'll turn up your arse." Strian released Grímr with a shove. "Now, what would you like to know?"

Gressa watched the exchange between Strian and Grímr with a mixture of pride and fear fighting to consume her. She had not wanted Strian to speak out against Grímr's mistreatment toward her, but she also wanted Grímr to know Strian would not stand

by and let him take advantage of her. She had not
wanted to anger Grímr, but she also wanted Grímr to
know he did not have the upper hand no matter how
she and Strian came to be in his camp. She needed
him to believe they were of more value alive than
dead. She desperately wondered what Strian said to
Grímr to make the older man go pale and nod when
Strian released him. Once more squarely on his feet
and with more distance between them, Grímr resumed his pompous stance as the leader of the
ragtag band of warriors.

"Take the man to one of the Norse warriors'
tents. Shackle him if you must. The woman comes
with me." Grímr barked his order and turned to
enter his tent, assuming they would follow his
commands.

Several of the men who gathered to observe the
exchange between their leader and his captives now
stared at Strian and Gressa. Three Norsemen
stepped forward to seize Strian, but he snarled. He
cocked an eyebrow, daring any of them to take him
on. He hoped they had been present when Grímr
made an error in judgement and captured Bjorn and
Tyra. Bjorn had fought a man while naked and
bashed his face in. The man died of a crushed windpipe. Tyra severed one warrior's manhood from his
body with a swipe of her knife. Strian relied on their
wariness of meeting the same end as their compatri-
ots. When the men did not reach for him, it reassured him that they had understood his silent
warning. He looked down at Gressa who watched the
interplay as the Norsemen whispered to one another,
casting looks at them.

"Gressa?" Strian kept his voice low now that they
no longer had a language barrier to guard their
privacy.

"Go with them. We don't have any other choice for now. I will find you when I can."

"I'm not leaving you alone with that fiend. Not in his tent, for damn sure."

"I saw the look on his face. Whatever you threatened rattled him enough that I saw genuine fear. What did you say?"

"I warned him that if he touched you, I'd make sure every Norseman here buggered him with a stick."

"Strian!" Gressa gasped as her eyes scanned the crowd.

"Do you think these men would turn down the opportunity? They bound themselves to Hakin, and their fealty passed to Grímr upon their jarl's death. The others pledged fealty thinking those bastards would reward them with the bounty from pillaging our homestead and Rangvald's. Look at them. They're half starved, filthy, and discontent. They only need a little nudge before they turn on him." Strian leaned over to whisper, "I'm that nudge."

"Just be careful. Please. I can't do this without you." Strian felt like he was drowning in the depths of her blue eyes as her gaze bore into his. He could read each of the emotions that passed through her mind as though she screamed them aloud. He could do this because he felt each one just as keenly as she did.

"I will. We have ten years to make up and a lifetime to plan. I'm not wasting our time together now that we've found each other. I'll be with you before nightfall. I promise."

Gressa swallowed as she nodded her head.

"Promise me you'll be careful, too. I trust you, but I don't trust him for a second. You know he will try to force you."

"I know. I will just use the same excuse that I did the last time."

"What was that?"

"I have the pox."

Strian's eyebrows shot to his hairline.

"And I got it from Rhys." Gressa sucked in her lips to hide her grin, but she winked at Strian, nonetheless. "At least that's what Grímr thinks. Between being disease ridden and belonging to one of the few men who scares Grímr, he did not force me into his bed."

"That's a dangerous game you played."

"Rhys believes Dafydd will lose the final payment if he angers Grímr by taking me."

"Gressa." Strian's voice was a mixture of disbelief, annoyance, and warning.

"What else was I supposed to do?" Gressa bit out.

Strian nodded but Gressa saw the skepticism in Strian's eyes.

"I know. I'll be careful. I promise, Strian. I didn't wait this long to find you to give in to another man's pressuring. I love you."

Strian's face softened, and Gressa was once more taken by how handsome her husband was. She never forgot and did not take it for granted, but there were some moments where his appearance took her breath away.

"Keep staring at me like that, and Rhys and Grímr will have no doubt which man you want."

Gressa did not bother trying to repress the smile that brightened her face. Strian's eyes twinkled as he ran his gaze over her body.

"You're horrible." She grinned. "Neither of us should smile at a time like this and you have me thinking about dragging you into the woods and having my way with you."

"I'm your humble captive."

Neither of them had a chance to say more. Their observers tired of waiting for the couple to finish flirting. The three Norsemen grabbed Strian and dragged him away while a Highland mercenary held back the flap of the tent, signaling Gressa could no longer avoid entering. She gritted her teeth once more and stepped forward.

EIGHTEEN

Gressa blinked several times as her eyes grew accustomed to the dimness in the tent after the bright sunlight outside. She sensed Grímr and turned to look at where he sat on a stool, chewing on a rabbit leg, the grease dripping from his chin. The sight made her stomach curdle. Grímr had tried to kiss her on more than one occasion, and she had worn the bruises on her cheek for refusing to yield.

"Why did you bring your man to me? Do you wish him dead, so you can finally move on?"

"I told you we want to make our home in Wales. We can't sail with a ship full of Norsemen. Ivar would never allow it, and Strian wouldn't be able to convince anyone to disobey Ivar. Our only choice is to travel back with the other Welshmen. The only way to do that was to come here."

Grímr once again squinted as though it would give him greater insight into her motives. He licked his lips before wiping them on his sleeve. He swiped his fingers against his tunic before standing. Gressa had never understood how Grímr could stomach being filthy when he could bathe and change his clothes. Every other Norseman she knew valued cleanliness and seized the opportunity to bathe even if it was in a half-frozen fjord. Even the Highlanders and Welsh had learned from their Norse counterparts and bathed frequently. It was only Grímr who seemed to wallow in his own filth.

Now he was prowling towards her as though she would be his next course. She stood rooted to the ground and did not flinch as he circled her just as a wolf would its prey. She stared straight ahead as though there was something of interest on the opposite side of the tent. Once again, Grímr reached out and squeezed her breast, his fingers biting into the tender flesh. Gressa held her breath, waiting for him to release her. He did but not before he squeezed them both. Grímr stepped back and ran his hand over his visible arousal. Gressa knew that while he was an unattractive man now, women once considered him good looking, and he was more than adequately endowed. Had she been interested, she did not doubt that she could have found pleasure with that part of his body. However, looking at the face that belonged to the same body as the large cock was enough to sour any thoughts of enjoyment. Her mouth grew dry and bile rose up her throat when she remembered having to take him into her mouth, his face hovering above her as he gripped her hair and thrust over and over. Gressa reminded herself that it had been to save Strian. She knew she could not trust Grímr's promises, but if it could even slightly increase the chance that Strian would survive, she would do anything to keep him safe. Dignity be damned.

"I don't believe you anymore this time you tell the tale than I did outside."

"Then why do you think we have come?"

"They captured you."

"On our way here."

"Why would you lure the man you love and were

willing to degrade yourself for, into the enemy's hands?"

"Because the price of going home is knowledge. Knowledge that Strian has that you want."

"Knowledge that I can get from you before or after he's dead."

"Kill him, and you will never see victory. You'll not even see the next morning."

"You make quite a lot of threats for someone with so little power. If you intended to kill me to save Strian, you would have done so before you ever sucked me to release." Grímr leaned forward, his putrid breath wafting across her face as his hand cupped her sheath. He rubbed as he pressed his fingers against her entrance. Gressa was grateful once more that she preferred her leather pants to any gown. "Perhaps you should offer more now that I have Strian in my camp. He's much closer to death than he was before."

"I am offering more. I'm offering you the chance to learn everything you need to know about Ivar's forces."

Grímr cackled like he had outside the tent. It grated against Gressa's nerves as their game of cat and mouse drew on. Grímr moved to stand behind her, not letting go of her mound but now grasping her breast while grinding his arousal against her backside. He pinned her against him as he kissed her neck. She held her breath, refusing to smell his stench nor react to his touch. His hold became more aggressive and his hand released her breast to clamp around her throat.

"You will warm my bed. You will do as I want. And you will fuck me. Or else your husband will die. After he's watched me defile you in every way imaginable. Then I will give you to my men."

"And you will still be none the wiser," Gressa choked out.

Grímr's grip tightened, and Gressa saw stars dance before her eyes, but just as quickly as he began to throttle her, he released her. He pushed her towards his bedroll, but she refused to move. He tried to drag her by wrapping her braid around his fist, but she twisted under his arm and lashed out with her foot to his groin.

Grímr doubled over but did not release her hair. He pulled her to the ground as he sank to his knees. She pushed her palm up against the underside of his chin until he lost his balance. She scrambled away and caught sight of his sword propped against the table. Had it been Strian's, she would have had little chance of lifting it let alone wielding it. But while Grímr's sword was too long for her, but it was not too heavy. It was cumbersome, but she soon found a grip that balanced its weight within her hands. She held it upright as she took her turn circling her prey.

"You're too impatient," she cajoled. "You want your pleasure before your work is done. As the leader of this army, you should be rejoicing that you have not one but two informants willing to trade secrets simply for a ride on someone else's ship. Come now, you've been waging this war against Ivar and Rangvald for several moons with little gained. You have the chance to gain all the information you could want and then some, but that can't happen if you kill one of your captives and the other wants to murder you in your sleep."

Gressa watched him come to his feet, the pain in his bollocks having subsided enough for him to stand.

"Tell me what you want to know, and I will tell you the answer. If it's something I don't know, Strian is bound to."

With his sword in her hands, Grímr knew she

had outmaneuvered him once more. He had seen her train both with a sword and a bow. He knew she was more than proficient with both weapons. He was more likely to die than recover his sword, so he backed down.

"I want to know Ivar and Rangvald's plans. But I doubt you are privy to that."

"I haven't been, but you know who has. I can tell you how many warriors they have, and how much food they have stocked for the approaching winter. I can tell you how many ships they will sail the next time you run, and I can tell you what Sigrid has foreseen."

Gressa threw in the last lie just for good measure. Grímr, like his brother Hakin before him, was a superstitious man who believed Sigrid, Leif's wife and a renowned seer, had the power to change the future. Hakin kidnapped Sigrid hoping her prophecies would empower them and that he could manipulate Sigrid into changing the outcome of the war he ignited with not just one neighboring jarl but two. Grímr was not as open about his reliance on rune readings, but Gressa had heard him discuss them with his sons more than once.

"Very well." He raised his hands to his sides and nodded his head. "What great knowledge do you have that will change the tides?"

"Food is running low with both Ivar and Rangvald's people living in the homestead. Rangvald cannot spare his ships to return to his land to retrieve supplies, and with the capture of your three spies, Ivar knows that sending out hunting parties would only make them the hunted. The only option is to fish, but Ivar is wary of sending out too many boats in case you set sail. They don't want you to get away, but you've trapped them. Rangvald's warriors want to return home to their families. They've been away for several moons, and there is no way for their families to join them. There's no safe passage, no room among Ivar's people, and now not enough food. There are grumblings within his tribe. Ivar is not faring much better. His people are tired of hosting the other tribe. There have been several fights over women, and both jarls are growing impatient."

Gressa watched Grímr's reactions to her news. He tried to keep his face impassive, but she saw each flair of hope and perverse pleasure as she spun her tale of falsehoods. Both tribes were living alongside one another with surprising ease. Ivar and Rangvald spent years cultivating the image that their good relations had fallen apart after Ivar's trial marriage to Rangvald's sister Inga resulted in her being returned home. He had refused to repudiate his relationship with Lena who had already been his companion for years, and the woman he insisted he would marry despite his father's demands otherwise. They allowed the rumors of ill will to grow and even helped spread them while their alliance grew stronger. Their supposed hostility made their neighbors wary of inciting conflict, not wanting to join in with crossed alliances, so they left both tribes alone. Hakin had grievously miscalculated when he attacked not one but both tribes.

"So, their friendship is ending. Rangvald's sister's betrayal wasn't enough to severe their alliance?"

"Why would it be? Your wife wronged Rangvald just as much as she did Ivar. She made you a cuckold while she carried on an affair with a man who never wanted her for more than the connection, she provided with Hakin. Inga whored herself to Einar, and they both ended up dead. She even fucked your brother, and the man's dead now, too."

The mention of his dead wife did not phase Grímr. Inga had served her purpose even if it had not been as a faithful wife. She bore Einar's children whom Grímr claimed. He felt no remorse when any of them died but enjoyed the benefits of having sons to fight for him and carry on his legacy. His brother was dead, so he no longer had to ignore Hakin bedding his wife. The only inconvenience he had suffered was with Inga's death went the income he had used to bribe the warriors Hakin hired. Inga's slave trade had been profitable, and the money earned enticed more than one Highland mercenary to join Hakin's forces. Grímr had bribed those same men to give their true allegiance to him rather than Hakin. With Hakin dead, no one stood in the way of his claim to Rangvald and Ivar's homestead once he captured them. However, Inga's death meant there was no more money to hire warriors. He had used the very last of what had been aboard his ship to wager the deal with Dafydd. Freya and Erik stole the rest of the bounty Inga gained through her trading and piracy ring.

"Ivar doesn't hold a grudge against Rangvald for Inga's part in Eindride's death, after all, it was Einar who killed his own brother to gain a position closer to Ivar. His killed his own brother to become captain of Ivar's warriors. Not to mention it was Rangvald who executed Inga for her crimes against her family and her people," Gressa explained. "Einar killed Eindride believing becoming captain of the warriors would impress Lena and give him more access to the women he truly coveted. He gained nothing since she never saw him as anything but her husband's vassal."

"What of Freya and Erik? Their marriage finally binds Ivar and Rangvald by the blood of the couple's future children. Not to mention Ivar's son married Rangvald's niece. I hear Sigrid is already breeding."

"What of those two? They're worse than rabbits. They'd rather hide away in their chamber than sail on another mission." Gressa told only a half truth. Freya and Erik disappeared as often as they could, but they were no worse than Tyra and Bjorn, Leif and Sigrid, or herself and Strian. They would all fight when duty called, but they were four couples who had almost lost their soulmate at one time or another.

"You would have me believe that Ivar and Rangvald's friendship is dissolving as their people grow weary of living together. Ivar's own daughter and Rangvald's son would rather fornicate than fight, and Eindride's son, your husband Strian, would come fight for the man who helped orchestrate his own father's death at the hands of his own uncle."

"Quite a twisted web, but that sums it up." Gressa nodded. "Tempers are short, and it's taking very little to spark arguments. With food growing scarce and no reliable way to gather more, people are hungry and angry."

Gressa waited. She would not offer more until she could be sure how Grímr interpreted her misinformation. There was more than ample food, and Rangvald's tribe sent food regularly from their homestead, and his warriors helped hunt as often as Ivar's did. Despite the homestead being crowded, the common enemy and mission had bonded the two tribes more than even Freya and Erik's or Leif and Sigrid's marriages could have.

Grímr seemed to mull over everything Gressa fabricated. Gressa watched him as he seemed to come to some conclusion. She forced herself not to speak just because the silence drew out. One of the many lessons in warfare Ivar taught his children and their friends was that silence spoke louder than words. A wise warrior would not need to fill the silence but would use it as a time to observe the enemy, listen to the sounds around them, and watch their surroundings. Silence afforded them time to control the situation. So she waited.

Grímr looked up at Gressa and peeled his lips back in a smile of sorts. He marched to the entrance to his tent and summoned a man to bring Strian. Gressa still held Grímr's sword, so he could not get close enough to hold her against her will. She was sure it frustrated him that he could not grope her in front of Strian.

Only a few minutes elapsed before a man shoved Strian through the flap and straightened to his full height. He was more than a head taller than Grímr and in much better physical condition. Strian's eyes darted to Gressa and the sword she clutched in both hands. He turned to Grímr and grunted.

"Your wife has been telling me quite a tale. I wonder if you are familiar with the story, too."

Strian and Gressa did not need to look at one another to know Grímr was testing them to see if they would tell the same lies or if their stories would not match.

"What is that you want to know? I imagine you are interested in how Ivar and Rangvald's friendship has suffered from this war your brother started. I would bet you're curious about how the jarls are keeping their people fed. I even think you're wondering why I would assist you when my traitorous uncle sold himself to your brother after he killed my father."

Strian crossed his arms and raised one eyebrow in challenge to Grímr. The men guarding him took him to the tent behind Grímr's, assuming he would summon the prisoner, and they did not want to keep Grímr waiting. His guards had been Highlanders who did not understand Norse. They had no way of knowing that by putting Strian so close to Grímr's tent, they had given him the opportunity to listen to every falsehood and exaggeration Gressa told Grímr. He had been prepared to stand in front of his enemy. His kept his back to Gressa, so Grímr could not accuse Gressa of giving Strian hints or codes. He also positioned himself between the foul man who had dared manhandle his wife and the woman he would die to protect.

Grímr once more seemed to size up Strian, as though he was both trying to gauge Strian's truthfulness and decide whether he stood any chance of defending himself if Strian attacked.

"Perhaps you are wont to know where you should position yourself during an attack on Ivar's homestead so you can oversee the battle but not dirty your hands. If you listen to me, you won't need to retreat, running and hiding like a little girl."

Strian needled Grímr, playing upon the two accusations that would most enrage a Norseman: accusing him of cowardice and effeminacy. Strian bit the inside of his cheek to keep from laughing as the color rose in Grímr's face and a vein throbbed in his temples. It was common knowledge that Grímr never fought in the battles if he could avoid it, especially after suffering a severe wound to this thigh that had not healed entirely and now caused him to limp and endure excruciating pain when it rained, a daily condition when in Scotland where he had spent much of his recent time. He would position himself in the back under the pretense of rallying the final waves of troops, but it was so he could beat a hasty retreat when the tide changed, and it was clear that once again he would lose. His brother Hakin had always led the charge, and it cost him his arm. Freya's sword severed the man's arm, leaving him with little chance of surviving the blood loss. That only strengthened Grímr's resolve to not enter the melee without a clear path to escape. Strian tapped his toes in faked impatience.

"These are all fascinating things you and your wife claim, but they do me little good with no way to enter the homestead. I doubt Ivar will fling open the gates to me."

"That may be true, but he will open them to us," Strian jerked his thumb over his shoulder to indicate they would welcome Gressa just as he would. "There are multiple ways to use that to your advantage."

Grímr waved his hand indicating he was impatient for Strian to continue.

"If you attack at night, we can arrive at the gates as though we escaped from your camp. When the gates open, you can flood through them and overrun the village. They won't be able to see your men lying in wait. Or we could show you the hidden gate in the wall that surrounds the village. We enter through the main gate to cheers that we returned in one piece while you invade from the back. Or you can use us to lure Leif, Freya, Tyra, and Bjorn from safety within the walls. Take one or all of them captive, and it will force both Rangvald and Ivar to negotiate or surrender."

"You make it sound so simple."

"It can be. Now that you have help from two people who no one would suspect of coming to your aid and know the inner workings of the village and the tribes."

Strian spoke with a straight face even though both he and Gressa wanted to laugh at how ridiculous their lies were. Grímr's greed and pride overcame the last shreds of his common sense. He nodded over and over as Strian spoke, some plan taking form in the man's warped mind.

"We shall use all of that. We will attack at night while you enter through the main gate of the homestead, we will invade through the gate in the wall. We will overrun the village while they all hail the return of their mighty warrior and his beautiful bride." Grímr looked over Strian's shoulder at Gressa. "We leave in two days' time. Until then, I shall collect my ransom for keeping you alive."

Strian shifted his weight to block Grímr's view of Gressa.

"If I don't succeed in killing you, she will run you through with that sword. Then she'll cut off your bollocks and shove them down your throat until you suffocate or bleed to death. Whichever comes first."

Grímr's gaze shifted between the two of them, and he appeared to decide that it was not the right time to force his will upon either of them. He barked a name, and a man entered followed by two more. Two of the men seized Strian while one inched towards Gressa, wary of the sword she brandished.

"Take them to a tent and guard them well. They will try to escape." Grímr stomped over to the table and snatched a mug of ale from the surface. He drank deeply from it as Gressa inched closer to Strian. Strian put up little fight as they pulled him towards the opening in the tent. Gressa followed and threw down the sword at the last minute before ducking out into the fading sunlight.

NINETEEN

arriors dragged Strian and Gressa to a tent further away from Grímr's. This time they had Norse guards who could understand anything they plotted. It was hours before anyone brought them a meager meal of Scottish bannocks, which were dry oatcakes, and two mugs of ale. Their jailors left with one water skein to share between the two of them. They appreciated small mercies: Grímr had allowed them to stay together. The couple huddled together, both for the security they felt in each other's arms and the opportunity to whisper.

"How much of our stories do you think Grímr believed?" Strian murmured near Gressa's ear.

"Most of it. His greed and ambition override most people's rational thoughts. He isn't stupid enough to rush forward with an attack because we told him how. He will send more spies. That's why he said we would wait two days. He will check to make sure we didn't lie." Gressa spoke in equally low tones. "I pray that our lies about relations deteriorating is enough to overlook the truth about ways to enter the homestead."

"They should be. How can he know that we've been doubling the guards at both gates? He won't be able to see the extra guards on the ground inside the wall. He'll only see the defenses Ivar wants him to see. We've expected spies the entire time."

"I suppose. I imagine the others noticed our absence by now, so they must have figured out someone took us. Do you think they've sent anyone to search for us?"

"Probably, but without a full army, they won't come close enough to risk being captured, too. I don't think this is where Ivar or Rangvald want to hold a battle. Grímr's too entrenched here. The tents offer too many places for hiding or ambushing our people. If anything, Ivar and Rangvald will lure Grímr away from the camp. He will take us with him as hostages. I don't think even he's arrogant enough to believe we will fight on his side."

"I wouldn't put anything past him, but I think you're right. As long as he doesn't separate us, we should make it through what he plans. I just hope we can get back to our people before they think we have switched allegiances."

"They won't." Strian reassured.

"I'm not so sure. They already believe I'm a spy. It won't take much for people to argue I bewitched you and forced you to turn against them." Gressa bit her bottom lip.

"The people who matter won't think that, and that's all that matters."

"Strian, you know that's about as true as the sky being green. Ivar and Rangvald can control people attacking us, but they can't control their thoughts or the small things they can do to lash out at us, at me."

"Then maybe when this is all over, you were right to say we want to travel back with the Welshmen."

"To be unwanted there, too? The only way that can happen is if Rhys is killed here, and that can't happen at either of our hands unless we can hide it from Dafydd. If Rhys lives, he will kill you to marry me, and if Dafydd discovers one of us has killed his brother, then we will both be dead."

"Then we send Tyra and Freya his direction. Neither of them will stand for any woman being forced to marry a man under such conditions."

Gressa could not repress her smile despite the dire circumstances.

"You are right," she chuckled.

Five men entering the tent cut their conversation short. None of them said a word, but three of them seized Strian before he could get to his feet. They pinned him down as the other two captured Gressa's arms and legs. She twisted and squirmed, making it difficult for them to hold on to her. The man attempting to hold her legs released them and stepped forward, driving his fist into her stomach, knocking the wind from her.

"Gressa!" Strian bellowed like an enraged bull. He fought loose of the three men, rampaging towards the men who struggled to carry Gressa through the tent flap. He dove at the man who had punched her, tackling him to the ground. Once more his need to protect Gressa consumed him, and before any of the other men could pull him off, he had choked the life from the man. Strian struck out the moment a guard pulled him to his feet. He kicked one man in the groin as he threw his head forward to headbutt another. He was prepared to move on to the next man when he heard Gressa's strangled voice call to him. Gressa stood with a man behind her, a beefy arm synching her arms to her side, and the other around her throat. Strian froze. The fight drained from him, and he put up little resistance when three more men rushed forward and forced him to the ground. He watched as a man dragged Gressa away at knife point; he saw the fear in her eyes as she cast one last look over her shoulder. He was not sure if the fear was for him or for herself. He knew his fear was for both.

Gressa was towed behind an enormous Highlander who blocked out any view of where they were going, though she suspected there were only three choices: Grímr's tent, Rhys's tent, or the center of the camp where all the men could watch whatever humiliation was planned for her.

She did not have long to wait until she learned it was the last option.

The man dragging her along thrust her forward, and she scrambled to keep her footing to prevent falling into a cook fire.

"You have been causing more trouble, I hear." Rhys looked up as though her arrival was of little consequence.

"No more than you should expect when you hold two people who offered help as captives."

"Help," Rhys's mirthless chuckle grated on Gressa's frayed nerves. He continued to look at the sword he sharpened. "And what help is that? And what do you demand in return?"

"You know the answer to both questions. We can provide the information and means needed to enter the settlement and overrun Ivar's forces." She remembered that Rhys had only spoken of Ivar while Grímr mentioned both Ivar and Rangvald. If Rhys and Grímr were not aligned in their ideas, mainly because they could barely communicate, she was not the one to correct them. "In return, we want safe passage back to Wales."

"So, you agree to marry me."

"I can't be married to two men at once. Your church doesn't allow it, and I refuse anyway."

"My church does not forbid me from marrying a widow," Rhys looked up, leering at her as his gaze settled on her breasts rather than her face.

"Then I would soon be a widow twice over." Gressa's voice had a steel edge no one missed even if they did not understand the Welsh conversation. "Don't doubt I'll kill you if you harm Strian."

"Why do you even want to return to Wales? You continue to refuse my offer of marriage, and you must have realized by now that Dafydd and Enfys sold you to Grímr."

"You know my reasons," she hissed.

"Yes. The dead babe that's already rotted in the ground. I suppose you've told that man about his dead son. He agrees to travel back to a foreign land, risk his own death, for a corpse?"

"*That man* is my husband, and he had a right to know."

"Your grief has carried on long enough. You'd return to a place you are now unwanted all for bones buried half a score of years ago."

"Those bones are my child's. You and your brother refused to grant him a proper burial. You have deprived him of his rightful resting place. I won't leave him there."

"He is in his rightful place. In heaven. You know we baptized him."

"You had no right," she spat at Rhys. "My gods will never recognize your white christ."

"You lived among us Christians. You even attended Mass."

"That doesn't mean I believed."

This made Rhys come to his feet. He stepped around the fire and attempted to use his height to intimidate her. It had never worked in the past, but with Strian as a casualty, it did now. She steeled herself for Rhys's outburst that she was sure would come. She was not disappointed.

"You pagan whore. You defiled our churches and the sanctity of communion by bringing your false gods and beliefs into the house of our Lord and savior."

Rhys lashed out, the back of his hand aiming for her cheek, but Gressa was just as quick. She ducked away and stepped back, forcing Rhys to step forward as the momentum pulled his body.

"I never claimed to believe in the white christ. I never said I renounced my gods. How could anyone have doubted that when I demanded a proper burial for my son? Or my anger when Dafydd and your priest insisted on a Christian burial. How about when I refused to leave for Scotland because I did not want to leave him with your heathenish people?"

Rhys's cheeks filled with color as spittle collected at the corner of his mouth. His other hand was quicker and wrapped around Gressa's braid. He tugged until she had no choice but to bend backward lest he break her neck. He leaned forward and glared at her.

"You ungrateful wench. My brother and his wife took pity on your worthless soul. They welcomed you into their home, fed you, clothed you. They allowed you near their children despite your heretical pagan gods. This how you repay them? Refusing a marriage to a man far above your station, denigrating our places of worship by pretending to accept the right faith, and parading your heathen lover in front the man you are to marry."

"Let go."

The two words were calm and clear above Rhys's vitriol. Gressa counted to five, giving Rhys the opportunity to release her. They were no longer in Wales.

They were in the camp of lawless men where survival of the fittest was the rule of the day. She had seen more than one argument settled by a knife fight where only one combatant walked away. If she had been a man, she would have been expected to fight. She had already defended herself more than once since joining this motley band of miscreants. They stripped both Strian and Gressa of their obvious weapons. They confiscated Strian's sword and Gressa's bow, but no one searched them for what they could not see. It had surprised the couple that no one investigated whether they had more weapons, especially the Highlanders, since they carried knives wherever they could fit them. Gressa reached into what looked like a loose pocket of her tunic, but it was the sheath to a very sharp and pointed knife. She pulled it free and spun towards Rhys before the man knew what was happening. The point of the knife entered him just below his sternum. Gressa thrust upward until she buried the knife to its hilt. As Rhys looked at her in shock, she spat in his face.

"You won't survive this. You should have ended your pursuit years ago when I told you I would not marry you. I don't have a heathen lover. I have a husband who I have remained faithful to since the day we wed. My time with Grímr was born of my devotion to keep Strian alive. You shouldn't have insulted him, and you shouldn't have besmirched the memory of my child. For that, you die." Gressa twisted the knife then ripped it away from his body. "You should have understood by now that I will always choose my family first. My son and my husband."

Gressa watched as the pain and sudden loss of blood clouded Rhys's vision. He was only moments away from death, but she was impatient to see one of her nemeses breathe his last. She drew the blade across his throat. Blood splattered across her face and her chest. She looked around at the crowd that had gathered. No one had attempted to intervene. Rhys was not a well-liked man by those who owed their fealty to his brother nor the ones who had met him through conscription to Grímr. Gressa swept her tongue over her lips as though she savored the taste of Grímr's blood. It made her want to retch, but it had the desired effect on the Highlanders and Welsh-men. They collectively took a large step backwards mortified to see a woman revel in wearing the blood of her enemy. The Norsemen turned their backs un-surprised and unimpressed. Gressa waited for men to rush forward and once again seize her, but no one appeared inclined to come near her. She looked around, trying to determine whether she was free to move about the camp or if someone would spring out to nab her.

When no one attempted to restrain her, she wiped her blade across Rhys's chest, sheathed the knife, and rushed forward. She wove through the camp looking for the tent where the men dumped Strian. He was not in the one where they had hud-dled together. She peeked into one tent after another, but to no avail. As she began to grow fearful that they had removed him from the camp, a Highlander she remembered from the battle at the Ross keep stepped from the shadows. She reached for her knife, but he shook his head. He placed his finger to his lips and gestured for her to follow him. He took her to one of the few tents she had not looked into. He pulled back the flap to let her enter but did not follow her in. He stood casually but was on alert as her self-appointed guard.

Strian turned towards the light as he heard someone enter the tent. The eye not swollen shut took in the sight of Gressa running towards him. At first, relief filled him to see her in one piece, but as she approached with blood covering the front of her, he struggled to pull himself onto his feet.

"Strian," Gressa moaned as she took in the damage done to his handsome face in the short time they had been apart. A part of her took a perverse pleasure in knowing Rhys was dead as she took in Strian's battered face. He held an arm around his ribs and limped forward. Gressa caught him as he tried to walk on unsteady legs.

"What did they do to you?" Strian pulled away to look at Gressa, his concern clear as he searched for the wound that could cause so much blood but still allow her to move about with apparent ease.

"Rhys is dead. He went too far and now will never make the mistake of insulting our family."

Strian took in what Gressa said, hearing her say Rhys was dead, but it was one of the few times she mentioned them as a family. The word lingered in his mind as she continued to speak. He was too fixated on her thinking of them as a family to follow along with the conversation.

"Strian?"

"Hmmm? I was just thinking about you calling us a family. You haven't done that often."

"Really? We are. We had a child together, and we've been married for years. Of course, we're a family."

Gressa watched the color drain from Strian's face as she mentioned the child they lost. She realized he had not even been thinking of their son. He had meant the two of them, perhaps even the family they might one day have. She wrapped both arms around him with care as she held him steady, one of the few times he had needed her strength to be his support. The only other time had been when his mother died. He had depended on her to get through his grief, but only a month later, he lost her and his father.

"We'll have more children, Strian. If we keep going the way we have been, it'll be sooner rather than later."

"You want more children?" Strian's hushed tones seemed to amplify his doubt.

"I want as many children as the gods bless us with. I understand now that my body was too battered and weak to grow a healthy babe the first time. I have no reason to doubt I can carry a healthy babe." Gressa cupped Strian's cheek. "There is nothing I want more than to be the mother of the children we create together, and there is no other man I would ever accept as the father of my children. I love you, Strian."

Gressa strained to reach his cheek, and he angled his battered face so she could give him a peck on the cheek. He turned toward her, and despite the blackened and swollen eye and the bruised jaw, he anchored her against him as she opened to him. The kiss held all the passion that always fired between them. Gressa welcomed his tongue into her mouth as it swept the velvet interior, and Strian groaned as he felt his body harden with a need he ignored since before they left the homestead. He was in a permanent state of semi-arousal whenever Gressa was near or he even thought of her. Now, with her body pressed against his, his body urged him to claim her. Relieved they were both alive and together, the soft mewling sounds that escaped her clearly reciprocated Strian's need to join with Gressa.

"I need you, Strian, but I'm scared that I'll make your injuries worse." Gressa murmured against his lips. "I'm even more scared that we might never have the chance to make love again. I haven't a clue what Grímr will do when he discovers I killed Rhys."

"Gressa, short of being dead, I will never turn down the chance to make love to you. My need is as strong as yours. Just be careful." Strian ended with a grin even though it tugged on his bruised cheeks.

Gressa looked around the tent for the first time and spotted a low table and stool along with a bedroll. She led Strian to the stool then pressed his shoulder down to indicate she wanted him to sit. Once he lowered himself on the carved down tree trunk, she sank to her knees and unlaced his trousers. She pulled the opening wide and eased his length free. She watched his eyes as she used lazy strokes. She recognized the expression as one he only ever wore for her. It was a mixture of love, need, reverence, and fascination. She always hoped that her face reflected the same feelings.

"I don't know that we have much time. I don't know that they won't catch us. But if this is the day we are to die, then I will go to my death knowing I didn't waste another moment with you," Gressa murmured.

"This might not be the place, but it is the time. Neither of us will meet Odin without sharing our love once more." Strian cupped her cheek. They both knew making love in their enemy's camp while awaiting their fate would seem ridiculous to most, but their need for one another had often overcome their common sense.

When a pearl of white viscous liquid formed on the tip of his cock, she licked it away with a long swipe of her tongue before continuing along the ridge until she reached the base. She ran her tongue along him until there was not a spot that had not received her ministrations. She lowered her mouth onto him, consuming all of it, the position giving her the opportunity to take all of him in. Her eyelids floated closed as she hummed, enjoying the taste and feel of her husband and the pleasure she knew she gave him. He combed his fingers through the hair that had come loose from her braid. His fingertips massaging her scalp as she continued to work his length. Strian groaned as his need swelled along with his cock. There were mere wisps of memories of what it had felt like with the women who came before Gressa, but he had known the first time she pleasured him with her mouth, there would never be another woman for him, and no woman had ever made the experience feel so earth shattering.

Gressa pulled away, needing a deep breath as her heart pounded and the ache in her belly made her shift in discomfort. She continued to stroke him as she blew cool air over the head of his sword. Once she was able, she resumed her task, using her hand to continue stroking what she did not suck or lick. She squealed when strong hands tightened around her waist, and she found herself being lifted off the ground. Strian stood with surprising ease and walked with Gressa to the bedroll.

"Put me down! You will hurt yourself even more." It amazed Gressa that Strian possessed such strength that despite injured ribs. He carried her as though she was little more than a feather.

"I will once we're at the bedroll."

Strian stepped next to the meager blanket that would serve as their only bedding. He lowered Gressa to the ground then attacked the lacing of her trousers. He pushed them down her hips before helping her to the ground. He stifled the groan that tried to escape him as he bent at the waist. He knew Gressa would argue with him about making love if she feared she would hurt him. Their protectiveness equaled their craving for one another's body. Strian kneeled beside her as he took in the taught belly and muscled thighs, a mere teaser of what he knew was hidden beneath her curves. He ran his fingers over the thin white lines that marked her belly just over the thatch of dark curls. He had not recognized them for what they were the first time he made love to her after their return from Scotland. Now he knew they were the evidence that she had once carried their babe.

Gressa watched Strian graze his fingers along the marks she had been nervous about him seeing then embarrassed. Before she had been ready to confess their origin, she had worried he would know what caused them. It still embarrassed her that they marred skin Strian had once claimed was perfect. She captured his fingers, making him stop, but Strian used his other hand to remove hers.

"Let me look. Please," he beseeched. "I wasn't there. This is all I have from a time stolen from us. From the time as a family we lost."

Strian lowered his lips to her stomach and smattered kisses over the scars. Gressa ran her fingers through his hair as it brushed against and tickled her skin. Strian pushed her vest and tunic higher until he could slide his hand up to her breast. He massaged the flesh that felt fuller and heavier as Gressa's need enveloped her. She became restless with a need to take his sword into her sheath.

"I know, my love. Soon." Strian reassured as his lips scorched a trail from her belly up to her breasts. He took his turn laving and suckling her heated flesh. He felt her nipple tighten to a dart as his tongue swirled around the darker skin surrounding her nipple. His other hand teased her as it drew circles around her other nipple, bringing that one to a puckered head. He blew cool air over the wet skin before he switched his attention to the neglected nipple. He lowered his body over hers. Her pants kept her from opening her legs wide, but her knees cradled his thighs as he thrust into her.

Their sounds of relief as their bodies fused together filled the tent, neither caring if everyone in the camp knew what husband and wife were doing. Strian used their limited ability to move, trapped by their clothes, to rock against Gressa, pressing as deeply as he could. Gressa gripped his backside, her nails biting into the taut skin. She marveled at how even his buttocks was chiseled muscle. She buried her face in his neck, muffling her moans. She nipped at the skin, unworried about leaving marks. Strian used one arm to brace himself as the other clenched around her hip.

"I'm scared I will hurt you," Gressa whispered. "It might feel good now, but what about later?"

"It feels a far sight better than just 'good.' My body, as well as my mind and heart, know what it needs. It needs you. It needs to be buried to the hilt, swallowed by your satin skin until I spill my seed into you and I feel as though Valhalla's doors are open to me."

Gressa moaned again, the sensations within her core colliding with the arousal his words fueled. She and Strian had discovered early in their relationship, even before they married, that they enjoyed hearing one another describe their need and what they wanted.

"Then don't stop. I'm so close. Always so close too soon." Gressa now panted as she felt the beginnings of her release blossom. She shifted and ground her mons against Strian's pelvis. With her head flung back, the cords of her throat called to Strian. He kissed along her neck until he came to the sensitive skin behind her ear.

"I will push you over the edge as I grind my cock into you. Gods, Gressa. You're so tight I can't wait much longer. I need to finish. I feel like my body is about to explode. All because of you. You do this for me."

"Then don't wait. I want to feel your release inside of me as my body clings to yours. You're so deep," A moan interrupted Gressa as it pushed its way out from deep within her chest. Her climax consuming her.

"So big," were the last words she managed as before his name spilled out on another long moan. Strian felt her inner muscles tighten around him, wringing the seed from him. He thrust as hard as he could thrice before going rigid. The extra force carried Gressa into a second release, the first ending moments before the next one seized her. Her back arched off the ground as she whimpered, frustrated that her ongoing pleasure beginning to wane.

Strian slid his arms beneath her, clutching her against him as he held her. He kissed her temple as he, too, came down from the high of their love making. Gressa clung to him, her inner muscles refusing to let go just as her arms pressed him chest to chest with her.

"Shh, my love. I feel the same. I never want to stop, never let you go," Strian soothed.

Gressa's belly and inner muscles contracted as she curled upward to kiss Strian's neck just as he had done to her moments before. Strian groaned as his cock twitched, demanding he continue moving within.

A long, languid kiss stole their words as they rocked together until each of them found pleasure once more. When they could no longer delay putting their clothes back in place, voices too close to their tent to keep their love making private, Strian withdrew.

"I hate that part," Strian grumbled.

"It's my least favorite, too," Gressa grinned. "We need to learn how to make it last longer. But I don't know that it's possible. It always feels so damn good; I can't keep my body from racing to the finish."

"You and me both." Strian kissed her nose as he rolled away to lace his pants as Gressa did the same.

They had not noticed that the sun had set, no light shining in under the tent. Strian pulled the blanket free then covered them. The bare ground their only mattress. They pressed against one another, this time for the warmth the meager blanket did not provide. With no idea what time it was, and exhausted from the day, they both drifted to sleep within a few heartbeats.

TWENTY

Strian awoke to the sound of rushing feet and bellowing voices. He looked down to see Gressa coming awake, too. He raised his eyebrows in questions, but Gressa only shrugged. They lay together as they tried to distinguish the sounds.

"They're only a couple hours out!" A Scottish voice filled the air.

"Who? Ivar? The others?" Gressa's lips moved still not risking making a sound.

"That's my guess." Strian's lips hardly moved as he responded.

They ripped the flap open as a swarm of Norsemen flooded the entrance. They yanked Strian and Gressa from the ground and shuffled them out of the tent. It was the middle of the night, the stars the scant light. Only a couple of cook fires still burned, but men were smothering them. Gressa recognized a bowman hurrying by. She called out to him asking him what was happening.

"Your friends will be here far too soon," the man threw back over his shoulder.

Strian and Gressa surveyed the surrounding scene them. It did not look like a warrior camp preparing for battle. Just the opposite. They scrambled to disassemble the camp to prepare for retreat.

"What's going on?" Gressa no longer tried to remain silent. "Why are they taking the time to break down camp if they're about to go into battle? If they don't fight here, which we already assumed, why not lead our forces away from here to a place where they might have a chance?"

Strian shook his head just as confused as Gressa. They had been left standing in the wide open.

"We should run," Gressa spoke aloud Strian's thoughts. "In this commotion, with no one guarding us, no one'll catch us. We could meet the others and prepare them for their attack."

Strian swept his eyes over the bedlam that had overtaken the mixture of Norsemen, Highlanders, and Welshmen. Grímr was nowhere in sight. He paused before shaking his head.

"Not yet. There is something really not right about this. I don't think they're just packing up to retreat further inland. I think they will make a run for their ships. They're tearing down the tents but not packing them. I don't see anyone even trying to gather the larger supplies. They will abandon them. I think they only lowered the tents to make the camp less visible perhaps to buy them a little more time."

Gressa stared at a group of men who had just yanked the stakes from the ground, and as the tent collapsed, they moved on to the next one.

"He's fleeing to their ships." Gressa realized. "He's going back to Wales."

"But why? He has no more money to recruit mercenaries, and he's back where the land he wants to steal lies."

"I don't know. I don't understand this at all. I can't imagine what is in Wales or even Scotland that would draw him back." Gressa spotted Grímr's son who bore an uncanny likeness to him from a distance even though he was Strian's uncle Einar's bastard. "Unless he wants to live more than he wants the land or vengeance. I'm sure he fled hours ago, but," she pointed to the young man, "he left his son behind. He's the one he uses as a decoy. He's going to let his son take the brunt of the fight, hoping that our forces will attack only seeing who they think is Grímr. He'll sacrifice the man for his own life."

"That part comes as little surprise. Do you think Dafydd will give him sanctuary?"

"As long as a battle doesn't show up at his door."

"Then we have no choice but to follow. We can't let Grímr live. It might take him years to rebuild an army, but he will be back. If nothing else, the man can be patient and holds a grudge with the best of Norsemen," Strian mused.

"Then we climb into the trees to watch a little longer. With Grímr gone, no one will follow us or even care whether we get left behind. Let's make sure they are traveling towards the coast."

Strian nodded, and they began to pick their way through the camp, trying not to draw attention to themselves. They made it to the edge of camp with no one questioning or detaining them. Gressa chose one tree and Strian moved to another a few trees down. They scrambled into the branches and watched the warriors tear apart the last of the camp. Men who had horses mounted, and the foot soldiers pulled their satchels with their few belongings over their head and shoulder. They jogged behind the horsemen until there was no one left. While they had made their camp at the base of a mountain, they were less than an hour from the coast. They would sail within the hour. Gressa and Strian needed to run to intercept their tribe and direct them back to their ships.

Strian looked over at Gressa, impressed that she was still running at a steady pace after an hour. The route had been flat most of the time, but they had covered several miles. Gressa halted, and Strian worried she was hurt or could go no further.

"Listen," Gressa turned her head as though she could hear better. "Horses. It must be them."

Strian heard it once they stopped. He nodded his head, and they took off again. It was only a quarter of an hour before the first horses came into sight. They jumped from the path and lay on the ground to observe the approaching riders until they were sure Bjorn was at the front of the group.

Strian and Gressa stood in the center of the path as Bjorn, Tyra, Freya, Erik, Leif, and even a very pregnant Sigrid who sat in front of her husband approached.

"About damn time we found you two," Bjorn snarled. "Do you have any idea how much you worried my aunt?"

Strian and Gressa both pulled their lips in to keep from smiling as Bjorn blamed Lena's concern for their breakneck ride to find them.

"You worried my wife, but what Bjorn is too proud to admit is you gave us all a scare." Strian and Gressa had not seen Ivar riding in the group.

"We're sorry," Gressa bowed her head to her jarl. "It wasn't our intention."

"We assumed as much, and Sigrid confirmed it when she had a vision. She was the one who alerted us that you were gone," Freya grinned. "We assumed you'd just gone home and were, um, otherwise occupied."

Gressa and Strian exchanged a glance, both of their cheeks reddening as they remembered what they had done earlier that night and why their friends' assumption was reasonable.

"Not quite." Strian smirked at Freya but turned a serious face to Ivar. "We had intended to see what we could discover. We were already in the woods when we stopped to talk, so we scouted. A group of bowmen sitting in the trees caught us. We spent the night as guests in Grímr's camp."

"Must have been lovely," Tyra added wryly.

"Very," Gressa once more joined the conversation after assessing each of their friends' reaction to finding them, to finding her. "We learned a few things."

Ivar dismounted and stepped forward.

"You can share all of that in a moment." He stared at the dried blood on Gressa's tunic. She had forgotten about it. Ivar did not hesitate to pull her into a tight embrace. He whispered near her ear, "You terrified not only Lena but me. We feared we had lost two more of our children."

Gressa squeezed Ivar before pulling back far enough to whisper, "I'm sorry, truly."

Ivar kissed her forehead and nodded before turning to Strian. His eyes swept over the bruises and still swollen shut eye.

"You're a mess," Ivar barked then pulled Strian into a manly embrace. "Don't scare years off my life like that again. You're not too old or too big for a good arse paddling."

Once Ivar released Strian, the younger man slung his arm around Gressa's waist and pulled her against his side as they exchanged a glance, both relishing Ivar's admission of love and affection to both orphans.

"Now that we have that straightened out, can we discuss things that are important?" Bjorn groused.

Tyra leaned over and pinched her husband's ribs none too gently.

"Stop being an ogre. Or sleep alone." Tyra's voice might have been a whisper if she had not intended for everyone to hear.

"It's a good thing I love you. You mistreat me so," Bjorn's eyes twinkled despite sounding beleaguered.

"I saw you fighting with a man who wasn't Grímr, Gressa. He had black hair and a slim build, but he was very strong. He spoke of a dead babe and you being his wife." Sigrid spoke up as she rubbed her belly at the mention of a babe. Leif's arms tightened around his wife.

Gressa's eyes widened as she looked at Strian in panic. She had not planned for anyone to find out about the child they lost, and she had not wanted to explain why a man assumed he would marry her when Strian's friends knew he had not moved on from her.

Strian tucked her head against his chest and answered for them.

"Gressa was carrying my child before we left for that raid. It was too early for us to know, and by the time she healed from her injuries, she couldn't travel. Never mind that no one would take her. Her injuries and illness left little for the babe, and he died upon birth. The Welsh wouldn't allow Gressa to bury our son, so she stayed rather than abandon him to a Christian grave." Strian realized he had been stroking Gressa's hair while he spoke. He dropped a kiss on her crown before carrying on. "Rhys was the prince's younger brother and pursued Gressa, demanding marriage. She refused him for years, and finally he went too far. He threatened my life and insulted our child's death. Gressa had no choice but to avenge us both."

"That makes what I saw more understandable. But I sensed people running from somewhere. It wasn't you. I could only see the shapes of men but no one clearly," Sigrid rubbed her temple as if that would make her vision clearer or strengthen her memory. "I felt like Grímr was escaping once again."

Gressa looked up from Strian's side and nodded.

"He is. They tore down the camp, so no one could see it from a distance, but they retreated to the coast. Strian and I believe they're sailing back to Wales. Grímr will seek safe harbor there until he can lick his wounds. He knows he's fighting a losing battle, over and over, but he refuses to give in. With Rhys dead and Rowan captured, there is little reason for Dafydd to allow him to stay. There's little chance Strian and I will be able to go there either." She finished in a whisper.

Sigrid opened her mouth but snapped it shut. Gressa stared at Sigrid wondering what the seer had just been about to say, but Sigrid gave a tiny shake of her head. Gressa was sure Sigrid knew of Strian's and her conundrum of where to live and what to do about their son's grave. She appreciated that Sigrid kept her thoughts to herself. By the looks on everyone's faces, the news that they had had a child was more than enough for the moment.

"How much of a head start do they have?" Leif asked.

"Two hours."

"It'll take us more than that to get back to the homestead and ready the ships. The best we can hope for is to sail with the morning tide," Erik looked behind them as if he could see all the way back to the village.

"Bjorn, ride with Tyra and let me ride with Gressa."

Bjorn grumbled, but no one missed his hand

roving over his wife's body. Strian mounted then helped Gressa onto the horse. Ivar had only brought mounted warriors with him, not wanting to slow their pace. They rode back to the settlement only stopping once to let the horses rest and drink.

TWENTY-ONE

While members of both Ivar's and Rangvald's tribes were happy to see them return, Gressa's welcome was lukewarm at best. Only Lena and Rangvald's wife Lorna seemed happy to see her.

"Why is she back?" Someone grumbled within the crowd as Strian dismounted and lifted Gressa from the saddle.

"Did Strian capture her again?"

"He can't see past fucking her to know she's a spy."

The last comment elicited a bellow from Strian that made everyone pause.

"Enough!" He roared. "She is my wife. She always has been, and there is no way she will ever be anything else. You will cease accusing her. You will cease taunting her. If I find anyone, *anyone*, does anything to run afoul of her, I will kill you. She is not a spy. If it wasn't for Gressa, we wouldn't know half of what we do about Grímr's plans and where he's headed."

"And if we hadn't had to chase after her, they would never have known we were prepared to attack. Now we have to chase after him again," an angry woman's voice came from the warriors still mounted.

Strian spun around, glaring at Magga, one of the two women who had attacked Gressa when she first arrived.

"Do not count on being a woman to spare you. Nor the mistake I made years ago taking a ride between your thighs. Get down."

Strian's voice sent chills running down Gressa's back. She stepped forward, willing to intervene on the woman's part to keep Strian from murdering her in front of the entire tribe. His glare swung to her, and she took a step back.

"She asked for it. She defied me and now she will die." Strian softened his gaze as he looked into Gressa's shocked eyes. He had not meant to direct his anger at her. "No one will mistreat you again."

Strian looked to Ivar and at the jarl's nod, he wrenched Magga from the saddle, driving a knife into her middle before she touched the ground. He threw her body from him, knowing she would be dead soon but not before she suffered a painful death.

"Who's next?" At his demand, many took a step back, shaking their heads. He looked to Gressa, and she understood the question in his eyes. She nodded. "You all want to know why Gressa didn't try harder to come home. She had her reasons. We had a son who did not survive his birth. He's buried there. In a Christian grave."

The last sentence drew gasps as understanding looks spread through the crowd.

"Why couldn't you have just told us that?" Leif asked.

"Because it was nobody's damn business but ours," Strian snapped. "Why would I make my wife relive that pain just to ease the gossips' nosiness? She's been a member of this tribe since birth. She's my wife. That should have been enough for everyone. If it had been anyone else, it would have. Instead you have attached a stigma to her for something she could never control."

Strian looked around before continuing.

"Yes, Gressa is half Sami. That will make our children part Sami, too. Accept my wife and my children, or we leave."

"Strian," Tyra gasped.

"Gressa and Strian aren't going anywhere. I will deal with anyone, personally, foolish enjoy to insult my sister or my nieces and nephews." Freya called out. "You know my parents have always welcomed Gressa in their home just as Leif and I have been. Speak against her, and you speak against the jarl's family. Your death will be your own fault."

Freya swung down from her horse and pulled Gressa from Strian. She squeezed, making Gressa cough.

"I'm so sorry. I should have protected you, too. You didn't deserve my censure." Freya's voice cracked as she confessed in Gressa's ear.

"You protected me. More than once."

Tyra joined the two women in their embrace then the three turned to face the crowd, united once more as they had been as children. With one dead body on the ground, and the jarl's extended family standing as one, no one dared voice any opposition to Gressa.

"What have you learned?" Rangvald stepped forward.

"Grímr knew someone was approaching. His spies warned him, but we never heard if he knew how many of you rode towards him. My guess is he thought there were far more of you since he abandoned their tents and many of their supplies. He is heading to the coast." Gressa spoke up, unwilling to fade into the background after Strian defended her.

"The man, Rowan, you still hold is Prince Dafydd's younger brother, but so was a man named Rhys. He was among the archers who captured us and took us to Grímr's camp. He made the mistake of speaking ill of the dead and threatening Strian. His body is near the embers of a fire, left for the carrion to pick apart. We think Grímr knows the Trondelag is no longer safe for him. There is no one who'll willing allow him to live on their land, and he has no home to return to since you burned the settlement. Besides, he has no real tribe left. I know most of the men are dead, and the women who escaped Inga's slave trade surely didn't return. He swore vengeance for his sons' deaths, but it was his pride not his heart that spoke. He needs to lick his wounds. I believe he'll impose upon Dafydd to host him as he stokes the anger Dafydd will undoubtedly feel once he knows one brother is dead, and the other is a prisoner. He'll try to convince Dafydd to give him more forces to return here, or he'll claim he has lured us there when we follow."

Gressa spoke as though their sailing to Wales was a foregone conclusion.

"How large an army could Dafydd raise against us?" Rangvald asked.

"That's complicated. The Welsh are a lot like us. Rather than jarls, they have princes. Each prince has a portion of the larger area known as Wales. The princes are all related one way or another, so it just depends on their family history whether they'll come to Dafydd's aide or will look at it as a chance to kill him in his sleep." Gressa shrugged. "I can think of at least three that'll come to Dafydd's side if he calls. With those three allies, Dafydd would have at least six hundred warriors."

Everyone took in the final piece of information, knowing their numbers paled compared to what this

Welsh prince could rally. Both Ivar's and Rangvald's tribes had lost too many lives in the ongoing war with Grímr to bring that many warriors with them. Lorna stepped forward.

"My clan will fight again," Lorna rested her hand on Rangvald's arm. "You know Alex will come to our aid. If the Mackays fight, the other clans will come, too. The MacLeods, Sutherlands, and Mackenzies lost men to Grímr, the Rosses, and the Munros. They will want their chance to end Grímr's alliances for stirring up trouble where there has been none in yonks."

Rangvald looked at his wife. Even thirty years after he brought her to live among the Norse, her Highland beauty outshone every other woman. Most people would argue Lorna was more beautiful than any woman in Scotland or the Trondelag, but she seemed unaware and disinterested in her appearance. Instead, she was as finely trained a warrior as any shield maiden, and despite bearing six children, she was still as strong as any woman half her age.

"Blood thirsty as ever," Rangvald grinned at Lorna.

"You always say that," Lorna harrumphed. "As though I'm the only one."

"If you believe Alex and the others will ride with us, then we set sail for Scotland first then on to Wales." Rangvald looked over Lorna's head to Ivar who nodded.

"This time, I sail with you. There is no great threat here as long as Grímr is so far away." Ivar's usually stern face broke into a wide smile. "This fight ends now, and I will not miss it by waiting like an old man before the fire. I still have a few more battles in me. Besides, we cannot leave Rangvald to think he's the greatest warrior in the land. He needs reminding I still best him every time."

The crowd scattered as people hurried to complete their duties to prepare for sailing in the morning. Tyra and Bjorn went to the docks to begin their inspection of the fleets. Tyra's innate ability to sail as though she was born to the waves had earned her a position as the captain of Ivar's entire fleet. Her skills were so well known that she led the entire mission while they were at sea last time. Bjorn refused to sail his own ship now that he was married. Instead he handed his longboat over to his first mate and gladly took a demotion to his wife's first mate. Tyra and Freya had the unusual luxury of a cabin on each of their boats because Ivar insisted that his daughter and her best friend have privacy. Bjorn intended to make use of the privacy every night, and Tyra did not complain when she could give her husband orders. Freya and Erik still maintained their own ships, but Erik usually slipped onto the Freya's boat each night.

Strian and Gressa finished talking to Strian's crew and were on their way back to their longhouse when they heard Leif and Sigrid arguing.

"I am going on this mission. I will be useful. And you are not convincing me otherwise," Sigrid's voice rose with each declaration.

"And I'm not taking my very pregnant wife into battle with me!" Leif's booming voice seemed to echo throughout the settlement.

"Fine. Figure it out on your own. But it won't be me they blame." Sigrid stood with her arms crossed over her belly as she tapped her foot.

"Oh no, you don't. You are not using your gift as leverage. I'm not watching them murder my wife and child all because you don't want to miss this saga's ending!"

"And I'm telling you, we will be fine."

"I'd ask how you know, but that would be a waste of time. However, we also know that fate can change. It takes only one person defying the gods, and everything you've seen could be for naught. I won't risk that, Sigrid. I'll stay behind if that's what it takes."

By the time Leif finished, there was real anguish in his voice. Sigrid took pity on him and stepped into his embrace. Strian and Gressa felt like intruders watching the couple, but they could not get to their home without passing them.

"Leif, you have to trust me on this. I have to be there. It's all part of the prophecy. We all have to be there."

Strian felt for Leif, understanding his friend's plight. He had not voiced it aloud, but he wished Gressa would stay behind, too. The last time they sailed on a mission together, he had lost her for ten years. It terrified him the same might happen again.

"She would have told me if I shouldn't go," Gressa whispered to Strian. She saw the sympathy in Strian's eyes as he watched Leif, and she knew what worried him. "We didn't know Sigrid then. There was no way for her to warn us if she had seen the battle. If she says she needs to go, then we have to support her."

Strian shook his head before looking down at Gressa.

"Then you understand how I feel about you going. I can't talk Leif out of his fear any more than I can myself, but you know we'll both give in to you and Sigrid."

Gressa pulled apart Strian's crossed arms and wrapped them around her. She rested her ear against his heart and listened to the steady rhythm. Strian stroked her hair as they stood embracing, no longer aware of the other couple or the people passing by.

"I can't lose you again." The words sounded as though something had ripped them from the very bottom of Strian's soul, his voice hoarse.

"I won't leave your side. No matter what."

Strian swallowed his argument, wanting to say she had promised the same thing the last time. Instead he leaned his cheek against her crown and nodded. They watched as Leif and Sigrid seemed to come to some understanding themselves, and the other couple walked arm in arm to the jarl's longhouse.

"I don't want to go to the jarl's house for the evening meal. Can't we just go home?" Gressa sounded as though she was thinking aloud rather than talking to Strian, but he was in agreement.

"We can eat and bathe in our own home. We will be around everyone else more than enough in the coming weeks. I crave one more night alone with my wife."

TWENTY-TWO

Gressa and Strian made the most of their final night alone. After a leisurely bath that involved more making love than it did cleaning, they fed one another before the fire until need once more consumed them. They joined throughout the night until exhaustion forced them to sleep to prepare for the long journey.

As the sun began to poke over the horizon, Strian and Gressa met the others on the dock. Strian took command of his crew, ordering them to load the last of the supplies and weapons into the compartments beneath the deck. Gressa consulted with Lorna and Tyra about the route from Scotland to Wales, explaining where the Welsh had anchored when they arrived in Scotland. Gressa guessed it would be a place Grímr would stop again in a final effort to recruit lawless Highlanders before arriving in Gwynedd, the territory where the prince and princess lived.

"Mama!" Heads turned as Freya ran towards her mother shaking her head. As a one, mouths dropped open to see their frú dressed for battle. Her hair was pulled back into tight braids, and she wore leather pants, a leather vest, and leather bracers on each wrist. Her shield rested against her forearm, and her sword was sheathed at her hip. Lena had once been a shield maiden, but that was before she became the lady of their tribe and a mother. She had fought alongside Ivar for years, but most people assumed she had not touched a weapon in at least two decades.

"Yes, daughter?" Lena raised an eyebrow at Freya. "You know my past. This may be our family's last stand or our most glorious victory. I won't let us go down without being a part of that fight, nor am I willing to miss the glory. It's my duty to fight just much as it's my duty to see everyone fed."

"But you haven't trained in years. Not since--" Freya trailed off not wanting to speak aloud of the babes her mother had miscarried or that had not survived their birth.

"You are not privy to everything that goes on between your father and me." Lena raised an eyebrow, and Freya flushed a deep red. "I'm more than able to keep up. Besides your father would have a fit if he thought I couldn't defend myself. Why do you think he has been willing to leave me behind to defend our homestead?"

Freya stood aghast to learn her mother had been training all along, obviously in private with Ivar.

"I never knew. I never imagined." Freya stumbled over her words.

"Just as Rangvald and Ivar kept their alliance a secret for years to trick other jarls into giving away their secrets, Ivar insisted we keep my skills a secret, hoping any jarl who set their sights on us while most of the tribe was away raiding would assume we were weak and not bring many warriors. Only a few have made the mistake of thinking our village can be over-run." Lena looked at Strian and Tyra before continuing. "You can imagine what made Ivar decide I had to keep training."

Lena referred to the last successful raid on their village ten years earlier that had killed Strian's mother and Tyra's as well. Lena had nearly died trying to protect the women and children of the village. It had led to the avenging battle that cost Strian his father and Gressa. His uncle took advantage of the melee to stab his brother in the back, and Gressa had been injured.

Gressa approached the women, looking at Lena with doubt clouding her eyes. Lena understood Gressa as any mother would and nodded her head in consent.

"Freya, there is one secret from our childhood that I've kept from you and Tyra. I didn't want to hurt you. It was your mother who convinced me to be a shield maiden alongside you and Tyra. I didn't think I'd be allowed because of who my parents were. Lena introduced me to sparring before you and Tyra began in the training fields. I've known all along that she trained. It's her sword I carry, the one Tyra recovered after I went missing." Gressa dipped her head, fearful Freya would be hurt that Lena passed her sword on to Gressa instead of saving it for her daughter.

"That was never a secret."

Gressa's head jerked up as she looked at Freya then swung her head to look at Tyra. Tyra shrugged and nodded.

"Ty and I knew Mama trained you. I just didn't know she still trained for battle. We used to spy on you and then pretend to fight like you did. I was peeking when Mama gave the sword to you. Why wouldn't she have? You are my adopted sister and older than me."

Gressa shook her head in disbelief, thinking all

these years that she was protecting her friends, her adoptive sisters really, from feeling slighted.

Lena stepped forward and wrapped both women in her embrace. She looked at Tyra and gestured with her hand for Tyra to join them.

"You three have always been my own. Tyra knows how much Ivar and I regret not bringing her to live with us when her parents died. We failed her by making her live with her aunt and uncle, but that didn't diminish the love Ivar and I have for her. Freya may be the daughter of my body, but you are all the daughters of my heart."

The four women squeezed one another before stepping back having shared more sentimentality in public than they each intended.

"Wife," the love in Ivar's eyes belied his gruff tone. "We have a ship to sail. Can we cease carrying on and be underway? We shall miss the tide."

"I thought to fill the time while I waited on you," Lena teased before dashing across the planks to Ivar's ship with him hot on her heels. He captured his wife as they stepped onto his longboat. He tossed her in the air before giving her sound kiss and a spank on her rear. With models like Ivar and Lena, and Rang-vald and Lorna, it was no surprise that the five friends could not keep their hands off their mates.

The fleet set sail just as the pinks and purples filled the morning sky. Strian stood at the tiller as Gressa took a seat at an oar, prepared to do her share. It struck Strian by how similar the scene was to a few weeks earlier but how different the circumstances were. As Gressa moved in time with the other oarsmen, he was thankful that they were speaking to one another on this voyage and that he did not have to disguise his looks at his beautiful wife. He had not been sure whether they could ever repair their marriage let alone fight for the same side. Their marriage had been tested over and over, yet their love continued to prevail despite how the gods interfered. Strian wanted to order one of the other crew members to take Gressa's place, so she could stand by him, but he knew she would be furious if he singled her out for better treatment than the others. He knew she would take her turn at the oar throughout the journey, even spending more time than anyone expected just to prove she was neither weak nor spoiled. She had done it when they sailed back to the Trondelag, but back then, it had also been to avoid Strian.

As the hours of the morning crept by, Strian controlled the tiller while watching for Tyra's signals. He had sailed with Tyra since they were children, and he still did not know how she understood the moods of the sea and the weather. It was as if one of their gods, probably Ran or Ægir, whispered to her secrets they shared with no one else. She had survived and led her friends to safety when others had floundered and sunk. The sun beat down as the day progressed, and Strian could feel the sweat sliding down between his shoulder blades. He called for a rest as the wind picked up. Once they needed the rowers again, they would switch with the next team.

Gressa pulled in her oar and stretched her back, appreciating the cracks and pops as her spine straightened once more. Her arms were tired and sore, but she counted her blessings that the callouses remained on her hands otherwise the wooden handles would have torn the skin with deep blisters. Gressa looked around, sensing someone watching her, and it was not Strian. Her eyes landed on a woman she remembered from years ago, but they had been little more than girls. The tribe was still large enough that she did not know everyone well, and she and Strian had spent as much time alone as they could. The woman watched her with open hostility. Gressa could not fathom what caused it. She guessed it might have been because they were on another mission when many believed they would end the fight with Grímr in their homeland.

Gressa turned when a gentle hand rested on her shoulder but not before she saw anger and malice fill the other woman's gaze. Gressa understood the cause now. Strian. She stood and Strian wrapped his arm around her middle, guiding her to the stern. He had given the helm to his first mate but still needed to be nearby. He pulled Gressa against his chest and lowered his mouth to hers.

"I've missed you," he murmured against her lips before sinking in for a kiss that made Gressa's toes curl. Using his own body as a shield, he ran his hands down Gressa's back until he cupped both globes of her backside. He squeezed and needed the flesh, eliciting a soft moan from Gressa who had lost feeling to her bottom from sitting for so long. The sound only encouraged Strian to massage deeper as he pressed his arousal against her mound. Strian pulled back when he knew he was on the verge of losing control, wanting to take his wife right there in front of his crew and every ship in their fleet. He repeated himself, "I missed you."

"How can you miss me when I was sitting only feet in front of you?" Gressa grinned.

"Easily. All of me missed you. Can't you tell?" He pressed his hips forward as he pressed hers against him. "I miss talking to you as much as I miss being hilt deep inside you."

Gressa buried her face against his chest to muffle her groan, but she rocked her hips against Strian, confirming her need for him equaled his need for her.

"Why must you tease me? We have days, if not weeks, before we can make love again."

"Why should I suffer alone?" Strian countered.

"Strian," she grumbled.

"I know, my love, but I can't help myself."

"No one will be in doubt of that." Gressa's brow furrowed. "There's at least one woman aboard this ship who would gladly ease your discomfort. And I don't mean me."

Gressa finished with a scowl, but Strian looked at her with genuine confusion.

"What are you talking about?"

"There's a woman who has been glaring at me since you called for a break. At first, I thought she was angry that it's my fault we have to chase Grímr, but when you stood next to me and touched me, I could feel as much as see her hatred. Who is she to you?"

Gressa steeled herself for Strian's answer, her stomach churning nonetheless. She thought they were past having doubts over each other's actions while they were apart, but now she questioned whether Strian had told her the truth.

"I don't know who you mean. Honestly, Gressa. You look as though you're questioning everything I told you about our time apart. You look like you don't believe me or trust me." Gressa turned her gaze back to Strian after looking at his shoulder, as though she could see through it to the other woman. She saw the hurt her doubt was causing him, and her own doubts quietened.

"Was there a woman who wanted you more than any of the others? One who tried to make you forget me?" Strian froze, and Gressa felt his body go rigid. Her fears flooded her. "There was."

It was Strian's turn to see hurt floating in Gressa's

eyes. He leaned forward so their foreheads touched, and they were nose to nose.

"There was one woman who was more persistent than the others." Strian knew he would regret the next thing he said. "Even after your return."

Gressa tried to pull away, but Strian's grip was like steel.

"Wait. You've asked, now you'll hear the truth. All of it. Her name is Betje, and she has pursued me. Ivar once tried to arrange a marriage to her when he thought a new wife would help me move past you. It was one of the few times I have ever yelled at our jarl, but I said vicious things about him and his part in leaving you behind. I refused to even consider it, but he had already spoken to her parents and arranged everything. I disappeared into the hills until after the wedding was supposed to take place. I humiliated her by not going through with the marriage. When I returned two weeks after we were to marry, Ivar insisted that I go through with it. He even forced me to the altar. The ceremony began, but I wouldn't speak. I turned my back on her in front of the entire village, once more shaming her. Gressa, I didn't want her because I never believed our marriage ended. I didn't want it to be over. Besides that, I didn't, don't, trust her. One of the few times we were alone together, she threatened to burn all of your belongings and anything that could remind me of you. The vile things she said about you was what finally convinced Ivar that she and I were ill suited for one another. It was the one and only time anyone tried to make me remarry."

"And she is still angry. How long ago was this?"

"About three years ago."

"That long? You know she will try to kill me. She may not want you anymore, or perhaps she does, but she won't want me to have you if she can't."

"I think you're exaggerating a bit. She must know of my warning. No one'll be foolish enough to touch a hair on your head."

"You don't understand women," she scoffed. "Her grudge, her need to avenge her honor, will have burned deeper in her than it could in any man."

"Then I'll order her from my crew."

Gressa did not speak. She knew that would provide her with safety while they sailed, but it would only insult the woman more.

"Gressa?"

"I don't know. Neither her going nor staying will make this go away. One will keep me alive for now while it only makes her anger fester, and the other makes me her victim sooner."

"Stay near me then. Sleep only beside me and don't walk around without me or my first mate with you."

"I can defend myself, Strian. That won't make this problem go away."

The days at sea were long and tiring, but the gods smiled in their favor with strong and continuous winds. There were only short periods when the rowers were needed. Strian was true to his word, despite Gressa's objections, and kept her close to his side. He witnessed the hostility Gressa described when he kissed Gressa in front of Betje. He had cracked one eye open as he devoured Gressa only to catch Betje clutching the hilt of her knife and baring her teeth. Despite Gressa's protests, Strian refused to allow the woman to remain on his ship. He arranged for Tyra and Bjorn to take the woman since she had both a brother and a sister sailing for the couple. Strian feared other members of his crew harbored a secret animosity to Gressa, and so he was her shadow.

It was on the ninth day that they caught their first sight of the Scottish Highland coast. Their longboats sailed into the Firth of Tongue until they anchored in the natural harbor below the Mackay keep, Castle Varrich. They received a warm welcome from Lorna's cousin, the laird.

Gressa watched as a handsome and charming man who resembled Erik but with darker hair greeted his extended family with warm embraces and hearty laughter. Erik's snarl was jovial when Alex Mackay turned his sights on Freya who returned the Highlander's flirting. Bjorn was not as gracious when Alex moved on to greeting Tyra. He stepped in front of his wife when Alex opened his arms for an embrace, but Alex clapped Bjorn on the back with a jest no one else but Tyra and Bjorn could hear. Gressa watched as Alex grew solemn for his introduction to Leif and Sigrid. The man had a clear respect for Sigrid, and Gressa was sure it was because the Highlanders appreciated the gift of second sight nearly as much as the Norse, even if they were more superstitious about it. When Alex finally turned towards Strian and her, his flirtatious grin was back in place.

"Another beautiful woman to meet. I think I may return with you to find a wife among your people. Unless you have brought one for me to meet already." Alex's smile was pleasant, but there was a sensuously wicked gleam in his eye. Strian wrapped his arm around Gressa possessively, and Alex's eyes widened in recognition then his brow furrowed. "So, you kept your slave."

Strian pushed Gressa behind him, but she tried to peer around his shoulder.

"That woman is my wife. She was when I found her. There is more to the story than I'm willing to share here but have no doubt that she is *not* available."

Alex's gaze hardened as he looked past Strian to Gressa who looked to be cowering behind Strian to anyone who did not know her.

"She doesn't seem as happily wed as the other wives in your group. I didn't know you called your slaves wives. I thought they were only concubines." Alex's toned had hardened to match his glare.

Gressa was not about to let Strian get into a fight with their host, nor was she going to allow the man to continue with his misconception of their relationship. She stepped around Strian, shooting him a dirty look when he tried to block her.

"Laird Mackay, I am Strian's wife and have been since well before you saw us together. We've been married for more than ten years. What you thought you understood is much more complicated than it seemed. Just to be clear, I am happy to be with my husband again, and I am too busy to look at anyone else. I don't need rescuing."

Gressa turned toward Strian, fisted a handful of his tunic and yanked until he bent over. The kiss they shared had several people turning away and clearing their throats. Strian grunted as he pulled away. He hefted Gressa over his shoulder and turned away from the group without a word. He carried Gressa until they reached the loch.

TWENTY-THREE

Gressa stared for a long moment at Betje's body before looking back at Strian, shaking her head.

"They'll never accept me. Your warning carries no weight." Gressa began pulling her clothes back on.

"That's not true. Betje had more reason than most to be hateful, even if she should have directed that hate at me. The rest of the tribe isn't like her."

Gressa felt her temper rising as she looked at Strian. She saw the concern in his eyes while she heard his conviction in his voice, but she knew he was being naïve. She shook her head.

"You are but the jarl's son's friend. You are neither the jarl nor his heir. Your words don't carry any real weight. You can't change the mind of people who have hated my people. Betje is just the first."

"Your people? I thought I was your people." Strian dragged his tunic over his head.

"Apparently not. I seem to be more than only half Sami to our tribe."

"She doesn't speak for everyone."

"No. Just those who aren't your friends. Which is everyone else in the tribe."

"My friends? So now they aren't yours? Your family?"

Gressa pushed hair from her eyes as she finished dressing.

"Strian, what are you and the others going to do? Put your lives on hold to be my nursemaid? Go with me everywhere, never leave me alone, because it's not safe for me? That's too much to ask. And it's ridiculous."

"Then I keep you alive long enough to get to Wales, and we make our home there, just as we talked about."

Gressa clamped her mouth shut. She knew they would only go around in circles since they were both right in their own way. Instead she looked at Betje.

"What about her?"

"She threatened you. You were well within your rights. If the Mackays want to offer her one of their Christian burials they can, otherwise, she can remain where she lies. It doesn't matter one way or another because Valhalla doesn't await her."

"And what do we say to Ivar?"

"He'll be the first to understand. He knows the wrongs he's done us both. He knows the error he made in trying to bind me to that hateful bitch. It won't come as a surprise since he's seen Betje try to seduce me since you returned."

Strian wanted to pull the boot from his mouth once the words were out.

"Just how many times was that? Just what happened between you two those few times you said you were alone?" Gressa demanded.

"We were alone three times while I was supposed to be courting her. She tried to kiss me each time and once succeeded. I kissed her back, wondering if I could move on. It took only a moment for me to realize how wrong it felt. I pushed her so hard she fell.

That's when she swore she would burn all of your belongings once I married her. Since we arrived home, I haven't been alone with her once. She has tried to flirt with me in front of Ivar, even hinted that my marriage to you was over when you didn't return and that her claim to marrying me stood. She tried to brush against me or flaunt her breasts, but she only became angry when I ignored her. Gressa, I never wanted her, and I can't say I regret she's dead. But I won't let a dead woman come between us."

"Then you should have told me all of this."

"Just like you told me all of your secrets?"

They stood staring at one another now that they were dressed, neither willing to say something they could not retract, but both furious at the other. Gressa dropped the hands from her hips and looked up at the sky, taking a deep breath to clear her anger. She was the first to capitulate as she leaned towards Strian. He did not pause and encircled her in his arms.

"I kept my secrets to protect you, Strian. I know you did the same. But it hurts to know another woman touched you, nearly had you."

"No woman has nearly had me. Never. We have to stop. We can't keep blaming one another nor questioning one another. The secrets end now. Betje is the only woman who kissed me, and I never attempted to kiss another woman. You know I let the others think I'd moved on, and I flirted with other women to make it seem convincing. There were feasts when I was drunk, and women offered themselves to me. Their hands were faster than mine, and they touched me. They tempted me to imagine they were you, to ease my loneliness with them, but they weren't you. It didn't feel right, and I saw what pretending did to Bjorn before Tyra gave in. Ten years is a long time to be alone, to avoid temptation, to refuse to let go of the past. But Gressa, there has been no one since the first time I noticed you were a woman. My heat, my mind, and my body refuse anyone else. They questioned my manhood more than once because my cock didn't stir. It couldn't, and I wondered if I was less of a man without you. But the moment I saw you at the Ross keep, there was no doubt in my mind that my body still worked. It just only works for you."

Gressa listened to everything Strian said. Parts had made her feel ill, parts had made her feel guilty, but most of it told her of a man devoted to her, who shared the same commitment she did.

"Strian, my story isn't that different from yours. Dafydd pursued me, but I couldn't imagine being with another man that soon after being taken from you. As the years progressed, other men approached me, some even tried to touch me. There were moments where it felt good to not be alone, but it was never you. It was never the same. I couldn't let it get past a brushing of the hand or a quick press of a body against mine before I grew so angry it tempted me to kill any man who thought to seduce me. I was angry that it wasn't you, I was angry that I couldn't move on, sentenced to a life alone, and I was angry that I couldn't have you. When Rhys started pursuing me, I wondered if I should put the past behind me and make the most of my life in Wales if that was where I would stay. He caught me one morning in the garden. Now I realize that Enfys most likely arranged it since he found me just after she left. He pressed me against a wall and kissed me. I wanted, needed, to know if I could move one. And for a heartbeat I thought I could, that at least my body could. But as he pressed himself against me, none of it felt right. None of it felt like you. I knew then that nothing would ever replace the feel of us together, and if it couldn't be you, then it would be no one.

My rejection only made Rhys more insistent. It was his pride that led him. He wanted to command me, to control me, and he wanted to brag that he was the man to tame me. But other than that, there was no one else. I swear to you, Strian. That is the last of my secrets. There is nothing left for me to keep from you, nothing else I want to protect you from."

Strian swept Gressa into his arms and started towards the keep.

"There is nothing left from our time apart to keep from you either. I won't stop trying to protect you, but the danger won't come from things I've hidden from you." Strian kissed her cheek, and Gressa turned her head to rest against his chest. They had finally put the past behind them, neither of them looking back at Betje's body but both remembering the love they shared.

TWENTY-FOUR

There was little time over the next week for any of the couples to slip off on their own. When the Norsemen were not in the lists training with their Highland allies, they were preparing supplies and making plans. Alex Mackay sent messengers to the Sutherlands, the MacLeods, and Mackenzies notifying them that the Norsemen had returned, and that the battle with Grímr would end one way or another before the weather turned for good. The days had already grown colder, and a few snow flurries hinted at the winter that was swiftly approaching. There was no time to waste otherwise it would trap the Norsemen in Scotland for the winter, and Grímr would continue on unpunished. Neither fate appealed to anyone, so they worked until the weak sunlight kept them from being able to see.

Alex was a hospitable host, and none of Rangvald's family or friends suffered discomfort. He gave Gressa and Strian a large chamber with a bed bigger than either had ever seen.

"I shall make one just like this for our chamber at home."

"But what if you lose me? It's so big, you shall spend more time searching and chasing me."

"Not at all. It just gives me more space for all the wicked things I intend to do," Strian covered Gressa's gasp with his mouth as he flung them onto the bed one evening and proceeded to show her many of those wicked things. By morning, exhaustion plagued them because Gressa had an idea to match each of his. They missed the morning meal, and the knowing looks when they arrived at training told them no one misunderstood what had kept them.

Neither could muster any guilt each morning when they appeared just as tired as they had when they retired. Their reunion appeared to make most of the Norsemen happy. Once the reason Gressa remained in Wales became known, much of the hostility had ended. Ivar understood the outcome of Gressa's showdown with Betje and even apologized for creating the problem. Only a few still turned their backs on her, but Ivar and Rangvald both echoed Strian's warning about mistreating Gressa. By the time they rode out with the Mackay forces, it seemed like they had fully accepted Gressa for the first time in her life. Still vigilant, Gressa no longer feared an attack from her rear as much as she did one from the front.

With such a large force of mounted and foot warriors, it took the Norsemen and Mackays several more days to reach the meeting point than it had in the past. The Sutherlands, MacLeods, and Mackenzies showed up with full contingents, having brought all the warriors they could without leaving their homes unprotected and having called upon their lesser septs to show their fealty.

Ivar and Rangvald charged Tyra and Bjorn will sailing their fleet around the north coast of Scotland until they reached the part of the coast the Macken-

zies controlled. Once the four clans and the
Norsemen reunited, they rode back to the Mackenzies' shore where the MacLeods had also docked
their fleet. With the full fighting force ready, the
Highlanders consulted Gressa about where Grímr
had anchored when she arrived in Scotland. She described the place and pointed to where she believed it
was when they showed her a map. It was still on
Mackenzie land, but the most southern portion.

The fleet left the harbor, and as they sailed south,
the horizon Scottish birlinns and Norse longboats
seemed to overtake the horizon. Gressa and Strian
stood at the bow of his boat and watched as Tyra
issued orders and the armada traveled with the
waves. They had shared a laugh when the MacLeod
captains initially refused to follow a Norsewoman's
commands, and Tyra had turned her nose up at their
smaller boats, but within a day at sea, they had come
to a truce. The Highlanders were in awe of Tyra's
sailing prowess, and she was willing to admit that
their smaller boats were nimble and just as seaworthy
as the Norse longboats.

The first leg of their voyage only took three days,
the wind dying at times, necessitating turns at the
oars. Strian's crew had taken note on their first
voyage with Gressa that she was more than willing
and able to sit her turn at the oar. Many had gained
respect for her before they landed at the homestead.
This mission had confirmed their feelings, and
without Betje present to poison the water, the crew
accepted Gressa. It was not long before the other
crews noticed that Gressa fit in with Strian's crew,
and that it had nothing to do with him interfering.
Betje's death had soured several until Freya and Leif
reminded them of the things Betje had said about
Gressa. Strian had not known the extent of Betje's
malice or how her words had instigated the early in-

cidents with Gressa upon her return to their homestead. It was Betje who had planted the seeds of violence in Magga and Soma.

Strian could feel how much more at ease Gressa was aboard his longboat and around the other crews. The tension seemed to have dissipated, and Strian noticed she did not look over her shoulder as often as she had. They had come to a new point in their relationship where neither wondered nor doubted what was being withheld. They had little privacy aboard the boat, but they continued their long talks well into the night. The past having firmly been put in its place, their conversations focused on their future. They avoided discussing where they would live, but focused upon the children they hoped to have one day, and what they wished for their family. Gressa experienced happiness without reservation for the first time since the fateful raid that turned her life upside down. Gressa marveled at how unguarded Strian was with her when they huddled together, whispering well into predawn hours. She would drift off against his shoulder as he held her in his snug embrace, the rhythm of his heartbeat even more powerful to lull her to sleep than the bobbing of the boat and the waves lapping against the wood.

Strian ordered the anchor be dropped as Gressa stood at the prow looking out at the coastline. She was certain this was the same place Grímr had stopped just before they had all gone ashore. Gressa had not been permitted to leave the boat, but she had seen the additional men who returned with Grímr's scouting party. Once more she was forced to remain with the ship, and she bristled at first until she realized only Rangvald, Lorna, Alex, and Tormod Mackenzie disembarked from their boats.

They even forced Erik to remain behind, his parents explaining that he and the others would only alert anyone lurking near the coast. They needed a small team, and they could not look too Norse lest they frighten away a potential informant.

It was nearing nightfall on the fourth day after the Norse and Highland fleets merged that the small scouting group rode toward the shore. Lorna's pleased expression gave everyone hope.

"They werenae that far from here," Lorna's brogue returned with ease each time she was around the other Highlanders. "They stopped for fresh meat the day before yesterday, and the farmer we met heard a few speaking Welsh. He hadnae kenned what language it was, but when Rangvald and I spoke Norse, he was adamant it wasna the same. We are hot on their heels."

"If we sail now before the tide changes, we won't be far behind them as they arrive in Gwynedd."

Gressa stepped forward once the leaders of the alliance gathered on the shore.

"Gwynedd is large. It's one of the largest areas of land owned by one prince. I think Grímr will want to arrive looking victorious rather than a dog with its tail between its legs. I don't think he'll sail into the harbor near Dafydd's home. I think he'll put ashore before Dafydd's sentries can spot him, and he'll march the men in while he rides. It's like how he arrived the first time. It made him seem like he had a much larger force than was there. It will also help hide the fact that neither Rhys nor Rowan are with him. Dafydd will not react well to losing his brothers. The men were very close. Enfys will seek her brothers for the truth and won't find them either. Our best bet is to sail past where Grímr anchors and go directly to Dafydd's home."

"And what do we say when we arrive? Excuse us,

we've killed one brother and keep the other a prisoner. Could we kill your friend?" Leif questioned. He threw his hands up in surrender as Strian growled at him for his tone. Gressa laid a hand on Strian's arm, making him pause.

"Yes. The second half of that is what we do. We let Dafydd know that Grímr is responsible for losing Dafydd's men in Scotland and in Wales, but we don't say who. We stoke the fire, and when Grímr arrives, the seeds of anger and distrust will have taken root already. Let Dafydd see the size of our fleet before he has a chance to call upon any allies. If we wait, and Grímr gets to him first, he will have time to summon the other princes to his side. We can't afford that," Gressa explained.

She looked around at the group of faces, a mixture of Norse and Highlander. She could see doubt in a few eyes, but many, and most importantly Ivar and Rangvald, supported her plan. She needed to see it through if she hoped she and Strian would have a chance to at least visit their child's grave. That was her motive. She did not care for the outcome of the ensuing battle except for how it would affect her husband's chance to meet their son, even if it was only a small marker in the ground. She was not sure how she would feel being back in Wales, the appeal not so great as it had been when she first stepped foot on Strian's boat.

"We should be on our way before the tide changes," Ivar called out.

It was a short time later that the flotilla was underway, leaving the Scottish coast and sailing much farther south than most of the Norsemen and any of the Highlanders had ever been.

TWENTY-FIVE

The sun beat down overhead as the armada sailed towards the natural harbor Gressa recognized as the major port and home of Dafydd and Enfys. Tyra continued to navigate, but Strian's boat pulled ahead, ensuring Gressa would be one of the first to step foot in Wales. She stood next to Strian as docks came into sight. The leaders had agreed that bringing all the ships into port would only set off warning bells and make their soon-to-be hosts assume the worst. They did not want to meet at sword point.

Gressa felt the tension rising within her as her shoulders crept closer to her ears. She threaded her arm through Strian's, in need of his comfort and relishing his size when he pulled her against his side. It was as if the mountain of a man next to her could block out any of the ensuing turmoil. As they drew nearer, Gressa recognized several of the warriors coming to greet them, and by that, their swords were drawn.

"I have to say something before they launch their own attack." Gressa murmured.

Gressa went to stand at the prow with Strian following her, a shield on his arm. He did not trust the renowned bowmen not to shoot first and ask questions later. He would protect Gressa at all costs. She attempted to climb onto the dragonhead, but Strian drew the limit at purposely making herself a target.

"They need to see and hear me," she argued.

"And I need my wife to stay alive." Strian's tone and hard stare told Gressa she would not have time to change his mind as his words sounded etched in stone.

"Fine," she huffed before taking a deep breath to prepare to yell.

"Rydyn ni yma i weld y tywysog. Dychwelaf mewn heddwch," she called out letting the people on the dock know that she wanted to see the prince and that she returned in peace.

"If you are returning and in peace, then why do you bring so many warriors to our shores?" a fisherman called out.

"These are the people of my homeland. The ones the Norseman pursues. We bring news to the prince and princess of their brothers." Gressa had not planned to share that piece of information so soon, but the hostility in the crowd forced her. It was one of the few things, short of saying she had married Rhys, that would guarantee her safe passage beyond the dock.

"What news have you?" called a booming voice that Gressa recognized. "You are on a boat that doesn't belong to the right man. That is not the right man who stands at your side."

"Prince Dafydd," Gressa dipped her head. "The right man stands at my side as he's my husband."

"The long lost one and the one to avoid the men you belong to?"

Gressa sucked in air and clenched her teeth to keep from saying the first words that came to mind.

Strian was watching her, feeling how her body tensed then went rigid at the last thing the man said.

"You made me a free woman. I belonged to neither of those men despite your bargaining me away. The only man I have ever belonged to stands beside me. He's the one they stole me from."

"And you thought to bring him here? You thought to return with an enemy I was paid to fight?" Dafydd's voice held the tone of command, and those on the dock recognized it as one that meant the man was on the verge of erupting.

"I brought you news of your brothers and those of the princess." Gressa prayed she was not giving up her hand too soon.

Dafydd approached the boats and cast a wary and assessing gaze over them. He took in the men, Ivar and Rangvald in particular, obvious that they were men in positions of authority. Then his gaze swept the women, his eyebrows rising as he noticed how many women travelled among the crews.

"I see now that you were not exaggerating when you said your people believe women should fight." Dafydd shielded his eyes from the sun as he tilted his head from side to side as he attempted to see the birlinns that floated beyond the longboats. "You brought Scots with you, too. You came prepared for a fight."

"I wouldn't call them Scots to their faces. They are Highlanders. And we came end this battle with Grímr. He has failed in his attempts to seize my jarl's land, he has failed to bring the glory and wealth he promised you, and he failed to protect your brothers as he swore." Gressa took a leap of faith and leaped to the dock with Strian following. He landed so close that the toes of his boots grazed the heels of Gressa's. He held the arm with his shield bent, ready to thrust it in front of Gressa if he felt they threatened her.

"Your man is awfully protective of a woman who has always claimed not to need a man."

"Can you blame him after waiting for ten years? Whether I need him doesn't matter since I want him."

"So you have decided after all these years to once more be a Norsewoman. You gave up trying to leave us early in your time here. Now suddenly, you abandon the people you claimed were yours?"

"You know why I stayed. You forced me."

"We did no such thing," came a woman's voice that set Gressa's nerves even more on edge. Enfys appeared from behind Dafydd, and her tone matched the one she had greeted Gressa with all those years ago. It was no longer the lilting one Gressa had heard so many times when she believed Enfys was her friend and greatest confidante. "We ensured your babe would not be trapped in the fires of hell as a heathen. We cared for your child's soul more than you did with your pagan ways."

Gressa opened her mouth, but a murder of crows squawked in a circle overhead. A collective gasp traveled among the Norse longboats.

"I would heed my warning, Princess. These crows are Odin's pets. The great god is near, and I doubt he appreciates your disparaging our ways in front of him." Gressa could not believe her good fortune that the All Father chose to leave Valhalla to watch over them. She glanced back at Strian who was just as much in awe as she was sure the others were. "Huginn and Muninn lead those ravens. Huginn, known as thought, and Muninn, thought of as memory, are Odin's favorites and bring him messages of those on Midgard."

"What is this Midgard?" Dafydd demanded as he

looked up to watch the black birds continue to circle above his and Enfys's heads.

"Where we are now. The land of people. He has left Valhalla and Asgard to grant us his favor. And to punish those who would go against us, to punish Grímr. You have only til sundown before they tell Odin how you greet his people."

"You spew blasphemy!" Enfys hissed. She pushed through the people until she reached Dafydd's side. "We took you in, healed you, then welcomed you among our people and in our church. This is how you thank us. You bring your pagan bastards to our shores."

"I sat in your church, but did you ever see me pray? Did you ever see me bow my head to your white christ? I refused baptism each time you demanded it. I was never one of you. My gods are the ones in my soul."

"You ungrateful bitch!" Enfys wailed. "Seize her!"

Enfys waved her arm, and guardsmen rushed forward. At the signs of an attack, the Norsemen began clamoring across benches and jumping from one boat to another. As the hoard of warriors grew larger and closer to the docks, it was clear the Norsemen far outnumbered the Welsh present.

Strian strained to catch what was being said around him, but he knew he would understand none of it. But he understood when Enfys screamed and ordered the men to rush forward. Strian grabbed Gressa and pulled her back against his chest as he wrapped his shield bearing arm around her and pulled a knife from his waist. He could not reach nor wield his sword with Gressa in front of him.

"Cease!" Dafydd roared, and the Welshmen came to an abrupt halt.

"Cease!" Ivar and Rangvald echoed once they

saw the prince ordered his men to cuit their attack. Both jarls were already on the dock and storming towards Gressa and Strian.

"Are you well, child?" Ivar inquired softly. "Did they threaten you?"

"Not specifically. Enfys isn't happy that I have once again renounced their god in favor of our true gods. She doesn't believe Muninn and Huginn are here to gather news to take to Odin."

"Then she is both a woman of conviction and a foolish one. Let her have her god. When the day comes of her death, she will learn the error of her ways." Rangvald kept his voice low. "What have they said about Grímr?"

"Not much. The arrival of the ravens shifted our conversation," Gressa explained. She pushed down on Strian's arm, and for a minute she thought he would refuse to budge.

"Gressa, just stay near me. Please," Strian beseeched. He wanted to lift Gressa back onto his boat and sail away to anywhere that would protect her.

She tapped her fingers against his arm before leaning further back against him.

"I'm not going anywhere without you in arms reach. My arms' reach." She murmured as she pushed the shield down.

Dafydd watched the petite dark-haired woman he had lusted after for years as she leaned against the giant blond man who kept her pressed against him. Dafydd felt anger and jealousy grow within him as he watched another man handle the woman he had coveted since he first saw her upon the dock they stood on now. He had only agreed that his brother could wed her understanding that they would share. Rhys had balked at first, but both men desired her to an unreasonable level. Dafydd had not wanted to trade her to Grímr, but Enfys insisted. He knew his wife knew of his desire for Gressa. In fact, it surprised him that she had not had Gressa killed already but instead pretended to be her friend. In the end, the information Enfys gathered had been useful when Grímr appeared. Trading Gressa had been the price of peace with Enfys, and Rhys had sworn to return with the Norsewoman tamed and ready to submit to either of them in bed. Now it seemed his brother had failed, and from the fleet's arrival, it appeared Grímr had, too. He turned his gaze to his livid wife and was once more reminded of the differences between the two. Enfys was a brilliant strategist, a manipulator, and a seductress who he loved and enjoyed bedding. He looked at her swollen belly, evidence of their fifth child. But his gaze swung back to Gressa, unattainable, independent, and sensuous. He wanted both. Dafydd looked back to the boats docked in his harbor and the three men who stood waiting for him to speak, guarding Gressa with undisguised determination.

"Why have you come here? It is clear you do not plan to return to your home." Dafydd demanded.

"My husband and I had thought to, but circumstances have changed. And our welcome hasn't been very warm. We came to inform you of Grímr's failures. Rhys is dead and Rowan, Afan, and Afon are captives."

Enfys screeched like a wounded animal and tried to lunge forward, but Dafydd whispered something in her ear, his hand resting on her belly. Once his wife calmed enough that he was sure he did not have to restrain her, he looked back at Gressa and the Norse warriors.

"How did that come to be?"

"Rowan and Enfys's brothers made poor spies. Rhys angered the wrong person in Grímr's camp." Gressa shrugged. "They lost many your men in the battle in Scotland. The one they assumed would be Grímr's certain victory. He underestimated the alliances the Highlanders held, and either he didn't know or underestimated one of the jarl's familial connections to one of those clans. They outnumbered us."

"You refer to yourself as part of that force, yet here you stand with our enemies."

"I was part of your band of archers, and they outnumbered us. But it was also where I found my husband."

"And you gave up your life here. After you've always sworn you wouldn't leave."

"I didn't go willingly at first. I admit that. There is something, or rather someone, who binds me to this land. But my husband knows of the child we lost. That's why we thought to make our home here, but that doesn't seem possible now that I understand the level of Enfys's betrayal."

"My betrayal!" Enfys once more pushed forward. "I would have had to care about you to betray you. You were a source of information and idle entertainment the way you carried on about your lost husband and dead babe. If I allowed you to follow me about, then it was less time you could spend in my husband's bed."

Gressa's head jerked back as she grimaced.

"I never once shared your husband's bed. I refused until he gave up and tried to pass me on to Rhys."

"You're a foolish twit if you think he gave up. He gave you to Rhys on the understanding that once you married, Dafydd would share you."

Gressa thought she would be ill. She glared at Dafydd then Enfys before her face transformed into a smirk.

"You are both very self-righteous to demand I

follow the teachings of your white christ when neither of you can do the same. Just because I don't believe in a god who allowed others to betray and
murder him doesn't mean I didn't listen to your tales.
Your false god spoke of turning the other cheek to
those who wrong you, but Enfys, you sold me to an
evil man when you thought I wronged you. Jealousy
consumed you. Dafydd, you're taught not to covet
another man's wife, but yet you did when you knew I
was already wed and planned to continue if I had
married your own brother. Neither of you are honest, and you both seem to live by the ways of your
angry god from before the white christ came. An eye
for an eye? That sounds more like our gods than
what you preach. Your white christ died for what?
For you to go to some place that no one knows of, no
one can tell you what awaits you. Our gods tell us of
the feasting and glory of Valhalla. Our god Odin
sacrificed his eye for greater wisdom, but yours gave
his life for what? You still sin, as you call it. Odin
does not need food to sustain him. Wine is both meat
and drink. Yours nearly sold his soul for food when
he fasted for forty days and night. Bah. What do I
need your gods for?"

Gressa took a deep breath. She had vented more
than she intended, but the betrayal still stung. She
had misplaced her trust, and for that she was sorry,
but she was not sorry for pointing out their faults and
hypocrisy.

"You would do well to fall on your knees and
pray now to your god because we are far stronger
than you, and you are stuck with no way to flee. We
can come to your table peacefully and await Grímr's
arrival. We can have our last fight and defeat him
with none of your people coming to harm. Or we
can pillage and plunder, ravage your homes and
fields, and leave you all for dead while we destroy

Grímr. Choose as I can sense my countrymen grow impatient."

"We are a well-fortified town, you know that. And I am not without allies." Dafydd pushed forward his chest, but he only elicited howls of laughter from the Norsemen and women who could see him.

"You won't make it off the dock alive. Dead men don't speak, so what allies will hear your call? We are already in the village." Gressa pointed behind Dafydd and Enfys to where she had spotted a band of Highlanders fighting their way through the village towards the dock. "I suppose they are even less patient than we are. They must have gone ashore while we carried on like old women. It seems they have already made your choice."

Gressa pushed back on Strian and turned to let Ivar and Rangvald pass. With the forward movement of the jarls, the entire Norse band surged forward once more. Ivar grabbed Dafydd and held a knife to his throat as the captured prince pulled a knife from his belt. A bolt of long blonde hair hurtled through the wave of Norse warriors. Lena's knife embedded itself in Dafydd's upper arm before he could strike with his own knife.

"Thank you, wife," Ivar grinned.

"I will be sure you thank me tonight, my love." Lena tossed back.

Lorna had run alongside Lena but continued on until she reached Enfys. While she was aware and careful of the pregnant woman's belly, she ensured Enfys could not summon any more guards nor bellow anymore orders.

With both the prince and princess captured with little effort, Tyra signaled for the birlinns to sail closer, and soon Highlanders swarmed the shore from both directions. Welsh men and women screamed and ran for shelter, but unlike a raiding party, the Norse were not interested in ransacking homes or overrunning the people. They would let the people live to tell the tale of the Norse invaders who battled their own people and prevailed on the foreign soil.

Gressa watched as Freya stepped forward to help Lorna maneuver Enfys towards the royal keep. The woman continued to fight despite her condition. Lorna and Freya attempted to control her without hurting her, but Enfys became so unruly that Freya slapped her hard across the face. The stunned princess became more compliant. Ivar and Rangvald each seized one of Dafydd's arms, showing the Welsh people that their prince was no longer in control and that his fate depended upon the two men who held him as their prisoner.

Leif helped Sigrid onto the dock as Tyra and Bjorn came to join them.

"Sigrid, did you summon the crows?" Tyra inquired.

Sigrid held her belly as she shook her head.

"I don't have that kind of power. All Father sent those on his own. I would like to cast my runes soon though. I foresaw this confrontation just before we arrived, and along with it, I saw spies leaving the village. I don't know whether they are Grímr's, one of the prince's enemies, or even an ally's men. But I feel a need to hurry."

"I want you to rest as soon as you're done." Leif whispered none too quietly.

"I won't break."

"But you might have our babe here." When Sigrid bit her lip and looked away, Leif exploded. "Damn it, Sigrid! I knew we shouldn't have come. How could you endanger yourself again?"

"Again? I don't recall ever voluntarily putting myself in danger. My gift put me in danger with Hakin

and then being your wife isn't without its own risks."
Sigrid stood toe to toe with her husband, her hands
on her belly as she leaned so far back, she looked like
she might topple, but it was the only way to see her
husband.

Leif put their debate to an end with a searing kiss
that had Sigrid clinging to his tunic and yanking him
back down when he tried to pull away. Leif swept
Sigrid into his arms and followed everyone else who
seemed to be following Dafydd and Enfys. Gressa
wondered how any of them knew where to go.

TWENTY-SIX

Gressa and Strian followed the others, and Gressa led the way to the prince and princess's home. The royal family lived in a large brick castle that sat upon a raised mound of earth towards the center of the village. A brick wall surrounded gardens and training fields Gressa had spent hours in. As she entered through the gate, she saw men sparring along with targets set up for the archers. After years on these grounds, she expected she would feel a sense of familiarity and comfort returning to them, but now they felt cold, austere, and repressive. A chill shimmied along her spine as she heard the familiar thwack of an arrow hitting the straw and wood target. She considered refusing to continue any further, rather wanting to return to Strian's boat. A sense of foreboding consumed her.

Strian sensed as much as saw Gressa trepidation as they entered the royal grounds. Gressa seemed even more on edge, if that was possible, than she did when she argued with Dafydd and Enfys. He lifted his arm, inviting her to walk closer. She needed little persuading. Gressa pressed against Strian's side, and he felt her tremors.

"What's wrong?" Strian murmured.

"Everything."

Strian had not heard Gressa sound so defeated since the day they returned to the homestead, and she burst into tears before collapsing.

"Gressa?" Strian's concern was clear as Gressa wrapped her arm around his waist and clung to the fabric near her hand.

"This doesn't feel right. Like something very horrible is about to go very wrong."

Gressa looked around and spotted Sigrid who had stopped near a tree. Leif whittled over her, and in turn, Sigrid was trying to shoo him away. Gressa pointed in their direction, and Strian led them to the other couple.

"Sigrid, you feel it too, don't you?"

"Yes," Sigrid panted. Her face was drawn and pale, and there were beads of perspiration on her forehead and temples. "I just don't know what it is."

"An omen, a harbinger of bad tidings. I don't know what it is either, but it makes me want to run back to Strian's boat and hide." Gressa's tone was hushed, careful not to let her fear filled words travel.

"I feel the same. I need to get somewhere I can cast the runes. It needs to be soon."

Gressa looked around, when she was fairly certain no one was paying attention to them, more interested in the larger group of Norse and Highland foreigners, she led them to a rarely used storage building. Part of the roof had caved in during the winter, and Dafydd did not order its repair. Gressa led them inside and felt around for the candles she was sure were still on a shelf near the door. She found the flint and struck it before lighting the candles. Once there was enough light for them to see, Sigrid moved to a large table in the center of the room. A fallen beam and rotted sod and thatch cluttered the far right, rodents scurrying at the sound of intruders. The table was still in good condition with stools around it.

Sigrid pulled the small sack of bones and pebbles from her waist and upended it on the table. She waited until the pieces found their resting place. She examined them as they lay then closed her eyes as she rolled each one in her hand. She was on the third pebble when her eyes snapped open, but they were glassy and unseeing. Leif reached out, but Strian pulled his friend's hands away and shook his head.

"You have to leave her alone. You know that," Strian whispered.

"Doesn't mean I like it."

"It's not a spirit walk. Let her concentrate," Strian reminded him then ignored Leif's glare for mentioning an experience Leif swore he would never allow Sigrid to repeat. Strian understood the man's fear for his wife when she entered another realm that existed between the living and the dead, but it was during that spirit walk that he learned the truth of his father's death, and his father's spirit found peace at last.

Sigrid rolled the pebble in her hand over and over before dropping it onto the table as though it scalded her. She yanked her hand away and made a fist as if to protect it. Her eyes drifted closed, then she blinked several times as she came back to them.

"No one can sleep inside the keep tonight. Dafydd and Enfys would rather burn their home down than allow us to remain here. They hope to kill us in our sleep or murder us as we flee the fire. Somehow, they know that Rhys didn't die because of Grímr. They need the wealth Grímr promised after he defeats us. Dafydd had debts to another prince, and he wants the coins and jewels to buy alliances. He has his sights set on unifying Wales under his banner. He thinks he is doing Grímr a favor."

"How do we tell the others without making Dafydd and Enfys aware that we know something is wrong?" Strian asked.

"Sigrid, I need you to find Lena and Lorna then the royal children. Take them to a small gate in the southwestern wall. The key sits under a patch of grass someone cut way to make a hidey-hole. Leif, you and Strian need to wait for them at the wall. Take them through and into the field to the west. Keep them there until I come for you. No one else unless it's from our immediate circle should tell you to come back."

"No." Strian crossed his arms and shook his head. "Send Erik or Bjorn. Even Freya or Tyra. I'm not getting separated from you again."

"But that's what I need. I need Dafydd and Enfys to see me away from you. They need to think you're not protecting me. They've seen me fight, but they don't understand what the other women can do. They still think I'm an oddity. I could tell from the way Dafydd looked at the women. He doesn't fear them but rather pictures joining with them. I need Tyra and Freya for this." Gressa faced Strian and rested her hands on his folded arms. "It won't be like before. I won't let it. I thought crawling into those trees would make me safe until you found me. I never imagined that I would be too weak to be loud enough for you to hear me. I'll be with Freya and Tyra the entire time."

"Doing what?" Strian's eyebrow seemed to disappear into his hairline.

Gressa shook her head. If she revealed that part, there was no way any of the husbands would agree.

"Please. I need you to trust me."

"Gressa, you promised no more secrets."

"It's not a secret. You just will not allow it if you know, but I know Enfys and Dafydd. This will work."

"You don't know them at all. If you did, they wouldn't have been able to manipulate you and betray you."

Gressa pulled back and set her shoulders, an edge creeping into her voice.

"That is true. But I lived with them for ten years. There are things about them I know that few others do. I intend to manipulate them just as they did me. I need their children safe. They aren't a part of their parents' machinations, but I will use them, or rather threaten them. We have to hide the children far enough away that the guards can't find them in the keep or the grounds. Strian, they can't see themselves become orphans."

Gressa's voice trailed off, knowing that she, Strian, Tyra, and Bjorn were all orphans, too. They had been part of loving families, even if she had not, and for all the prince and princess's faults, they loved their children. Gressa was an orphan, too, but she had never known what it was like to miss her parents. Ivar and Lena were the closest she had. She might not understand the feelings, but she could sympathize with her friends and the royal children.

"Leif will take Sigrid to find Lorna and Lena while I come with you to find Freya and Tyra. Only then will we consider leaving either of you." Gressa knew that was the only compromise they would offer her.

Both husbands pulled their wives in for searing kisses that held promises of love making but also included an element of goodbye. All four knew there were no guarantees to their safe returns.

Gressa watched Strian walk away, looking back over his shoulder often. It had been easy to find Freya and Tyra, but it had been difficult to convince their husbands to let the women go with Gressa. They sent Bjorn and Erik grumbling to oversee the Norse warriors who milled about in the courtyard and to prepare for the second half of her plan. Gressa, Tyra, and Freya joined Ivar and Rangvald who held Dafydd a captive in his own solar. The women shared Gressa's plan with the jarls, and both Rangvald and Ivar laughed as they looked down at Dafydd who had been firmly placed in a chair. Lorna and Lena entered soon after with a hissing and swearing Enfys. The Norsemen and women left the solar but not before Ivar locked the door and handed the key to Gressa.

Gressa had already told Freya and Tyra the plan, and Lorna and Lena were wise enough to be patient until their husbands could share the details. The two frús knew they were to help Sigrid gather the four royal children, so left in search of Sigrid.

The three women stood in the passageway listening to the squabbling that came from within the solar. Gressa quietly interpreted the argument between the royal couple while they stripped off their vests and tunics only putting the vests back on. She had a hard time keeping a straight face as she told Freya and Tyra some of the more colorful insults Enfys fired at her husband and his manhood. When the arguing seemed to end, Gressa counted to one hundred, then she unlocked the door and ushered Freya and Tyra in. It relieved the three women to see the others had bound both Dafydd and Enfys to the chairs they occupied.

Dafydd's eyes followed the three young women who entered his solar. He noticed they had removed their tunics and not because it was warm. All three of the women had their bosoms on display, and while he knew they were attempting to seduce him, his mouth watered. He shut out his wife's curses that they were whores and gorged his eyes on what he wished to feast upon. Freya approached him first, leaning far forward as she inspected the knots that bound his wrists together. Dafydd reached for Freya, but she was too quick. She wagged a finger at him. Tyra came next, squatting between his legs, checking that each of his calves was bound to a chair leg. Dafydd tried to lean forward to touch the amble flesh he could see beneath the neckline of Tyra's vest, but the rope around his middle yanked him back. Once Gressa was convinced Dafydd could only look, she walked over and straddled his lap. Freya and Tyra pulled the man's arms over his head, so he could not touch Gressa. Instead she rested her hands on his thighs beside his very noticeable arousal. She rocked forward, bringing her breast a hairsbreadth from his chest. He grunted as he tried to thrust his hips below her.

"Uh-uh-uh," Gressa purred. "Not yet. Soon enough you will finally have me."

Dafydd scowled.

"What about your husband? The one you were so adamant that you wanted. The one you brought here."

"We Norse have a different idea of marriage than you do. Now that we are together again, he is free to keep concubines, and I can have whichever men I want as long as it's not their bastards I bear." Gressa wanted to retch as she told her lies. She could not look at Freya or Tyra while she spun their story. "Not only will you have me, but you will have all three of us. I know that's what you want. I saw the way you looked at them on the dock."

Gressa looked over at Enfys who continued to spew vile words at them while forced to watch the three women seduce her womanizing husband since they bound her to her chair, too.

Gressa slid from Dafydd's lap and began to unbutton her vest. Tyra and Freya joined her and began to undress as well. Gressa had not been untruthful. The Norse did not view nudity as something fearful or shameful, so while none of their husbands would be pleased to learn that they had bared their breasts for another man, the confines of Norse marriage did not forbid it. The three women took up places near Dafydd's chair. Close enough to tease but not close enough for him to touch. All three of them had boundaries they refused to cross even if their culture did not frown upon nudity.

"I know what you want, Dafydd. I've heard the way you talk to your women when Enfys is pregnant, the way you tell them what to do. We can do all of those things for you. Is that what you're imagining?" Gressa once more used a sultry tone that surprised even her. She would tuck the memory away until she could use it with Strian for a very different purpose.

"Perhaps," Dafydd's gaze spoke of his cynicism and suspicion even if the hardened rod in his pants declared his arousal.

"Why would you help Grímr when we have arrived with enough warriors to defeat your enemies without you having to spend coin or jewels? Why help him when you know we would never lay with a man who supports our enemy? Renounce Grímr, and we'll defeat your enemies, so you can strengthen your claim to Wales."

Dafydd was quick enough to grasp Gressa's waistband and pull her forward, tipping her onto his lap, his mouth aiming for her breast. She pushed his chin up at a painful angle.

"We shall play soon enough. You will have your feast but not until we have what we want, too."

"Don't tell the bitch anything, Dafydd." Enfys's voice held a warning that Dafydd ignored.

"Would you like to make your wife watch us? Watch you with all three of us?" Gressa purred.

"Yes," Dafydd ground out as his hands yanked on Gressa waistband again, but this time she did not budge.

"Then you must play our little game. You answer my questions, then you will receive your reward."

Tyra and Freya embraced each other; their breasts pressed together made Dafydd's eyes widen. Gressa returned her hands to each side of his cock and squeezed his thighs.

"I'm waiting." She pushed back off his lap and stepped away.

"You would ally with us if I no longer support Grímr? Why should I believe you?"

"If we didn't want the agreement, why would be here with you now?" Gressa countered.

"I already have what Grímr promised me. It is more than enough to buy the allies I want. Once you leave, what happens? My allies renege on their agreements with no threat of force to uphold them. If I pay them, they have reason to remain."

"And when the money runs out? You will look weak if the only way you can control them is with a purse. A show of force will make them understand why you are the prince who will lead this country."

"I'm not worried about that. Grímr brought more than enough to last until I have secured my power."

"There isn't a chamber in this keep large enough to store what you would need to accomplish this. You must have some other way."

Gressa looked over at Enfys as she continued speaking to Dafydd.

"Which of the children have you promised in marriage? How old are the men now that you wed your daughters to? Will you wait until they are thirteen or send them as soon as their courses begin?"

Enfys screamed when she registered the look of surprise on Dafydd's face. It was the look of being caught.

"You sold our children?" Enfys was so irate she tried to stand from her chair, forgetting they bound her to it.

"I began the complicated work of forming allies."

"You whored your daughters," his wife wailed.

"And what do you think your father did with you? Our marriage formed an alliance. You were just fortunate that you possessed beauty and like to fuck." Dafydd snarled at his wife.

Tyra, Freya, and Gressa backed away as the argument overshadowed their playacting.

"You will not send my daughters away."

"They are mine, and I shall decide their future."

"Bah. You think they're yours. I've been bedding Rhys since the second night after we married. I only waited long enough for you to know I was a maiden."

"What?" Dafydd exploded.

It even shocked Gressa that Enfys confess a secret that Gressa had suspected for years but had never confirmed.

"That's right. At least three of our children are his, and this one might be, too. I don't know since I was with you both on the same day for several moons."

"Enfys, I thought you would never tell Dafydd this secret," Gressa interjected, goading both of them.

"It's just as well she has since her lover is dead, and we already sold their bastards to my allies."

"Just what did you receive besides an agreement

to come to your aid if you summoned them?" Gressa wondered aloud.

"The gold and silver I shall use to build the other alliances."

"Have you seen that, Enfys? Didn't you wonder where it came from?" Gressa continued to insinuate herself into the conversation as Freya and Tyra slipped behind the couple to replace their clothes.

"No, I haven't. It seems my husband has been hiding as much from me as I have from him. I can guess where it is though."

"Enfys," Dafydd threatened.

"Are you daft enough to think we are coming out of this alive? What does it matter now?" Enfys glared at Gressa. "The ruins of the monastery at Angelsey. He had it all taken there. He assumed that since your people had already raided and sacked the monastery, leaving nothing but rubble behind, no one would think to look there."

"Our people? They were Danes. We are Norse. We are no more alike than you are the Saxons or Britons. Perhaps, if you had learned the difference, neither the Norse nor the Danes would have sacked your shores so many times." Gressa taunted.

"Angelsey is not your land, Dafydd." Gressa pointed out. "How could you be so sure no one would find your treasure?"

Enfys cut in before Dafydd could answer, "Because he once again thought with his cock rather than his head. The prince of Angelsey has a wife who spreads her legs for Dafydd each time we visit."

Gressa rapidly translated the conversations for the other two women now that they role in the seduction was over.

"And they call us heathens. I thought their vows of marriage pledged forsaking others," Tyra looked askance at the royal couple. "They are little better than farm animals, rutting anything in heat."

Gressa shrugged. There were a few more pieces of information she needed.

"You took the bride prices paid for your daughters to Angelsey, but what of the riches Grímr gave you? He bought your archers and me. I know you didn't give the archers for free," Gressa wry expression matched her last comment.

"No, they weren't though you were," Enfys turned on Gressa. "I gave you to him to get you away from Dafydd and Rhys, but my husband wanted Rhys to take you. Do you not see, they wanted to share both of us?"

"But I thought Dafydd didn't know of your affair with Rhys. No, you sent me away to keep Dafydd from forcing himself on me. You didn't do it to protect me but to mark your territory." Gressa turned back to Dafydd. "Where did you hide Grímr's payment? Tell me, and perhaps I will stop questioning you and finally give you what you have desired. And your wife, who tried to keep us apart, can watch."

Gressa placed one hand on each side of the back of the chair and allowed her breasts to sway before Dafydd's face. The man was predictable to a fault. The arousal that had waned during his exchange with his wife returned, and his pupils dilated.

"It wasn't that much, but rather the first installment. I lied that he'd given me everything. I didn't want you to know there would be more. He was to return with more once he ransacked and pillaged Ivar's and Rangvald's homesteads. That riches are gone already, gifted as incentives to the other princes to join with me."

"There's nothing left?" Enfys snapped. "You are too stupid to rule. You thought to do this without consulting me and see where we are now."

"I consulted you about Gressa." Dafydd barked.

"A lot of good that did. The bitch is standing before us."

Gressa looked at Tyra and Freya, and both women nodded. Gressa whipped a knife from her boot and sliced the blade across Dafydd's throat, blood splattering her chest, belly, and arms. Enfys screamed and tried to pull away.

"We aren't going to kill you, you bellowing sow," Freya hissed. "Shut up."

Gressa was sure to translate each of Freya's words.

"You're not?" Enfys whined.

"Not until after you have your babe." Tyra reassured.

Enfys looked to Gressa, but Gressa cocked an eyebrow, challenging Enfys to ask any favor from her. Tyra cut Enfys loose and pulled her from her chair. She and Freya dragged her from the room before Gressa took a log from the fire and brushed the flames along any surface that would spark. She left the log burning at Dafydd's feet, his blood dripping into the flames and making them hiss and leap.

TWENTY-SEVEN

"Do you think baring our breasts made that much of a difference? Bjorn will have a fit when he finds out."

"You can reassure him it made all the difference. Dafydd had odd predilections, and if my devotion to Strian hadn't been enough to keep me away, the rumors were. He liked pain. The men could have tortured him, but he would not have broken. He has a high tolerance for it. I heard his father abused him and his brothers. Rhys grew up to enjoy inflicting it on others, while Rowan avoids it at all cost, and Dafydd finds, found, it arousing. More so than even seeing our breasts. He would have confessed nothing to them, but then found a woman or even his own hand to pleasure himself as soon as the men abandoned their torture. I knew the type of arousal we would offer and the chance for immediate pleasure would get us what we needed to know. And I wanted the satisfaction of killing him myself."

The women paused in the passageway, Enfys still with them, as they rushed to put their clothes back to rights, the smell of smoke wafting from beneath the solar door. Once they covered themselves, they shuffled Enfys through the keep and out of a side door that Gressa pointed out. She guided them to the gate they found unlocked. They dragged the pregnant woman, stopping often as she stumbled, until they reached the field where Strian and the others waited. She whistled a loud bird call that she knew would carry back to the keep. It was only a few minutes later that the first plumes of smoke began to rise above the wall.

Gressa stood with her husband and friends as people raced out of the main gate with horses and livestock squealing. Enfys huddled with her children as Ivar and Rangvald led a group of their warriors to corral the people and separate the guardsmen and Welsh warriors from the others. Erik dragged a young boy who looked about the same age as Freya's barrel man, Freund, who was only twelve. Freund bounded after them, chattering away despite the terrified look on the boy's face.

"Wonderful," Freya griped. "Another cabin boy, only this one won't understand a single order I give."

"I'll take him then," Tyra offered and laughed when her friend huffed. Freya's gruff exterior guarded a fragile heart that was much larger than she acknowledged.

Erik, Bjorn, Ivar, and Rangvald joined them, and when everyone got a closer look at the boy, they knew they had found a spy. His blond hair and fair skin declared his Norse heritage before he opened his mouth.

"Who is this?" Leif asked.

"We found him hiding in the stables. It seems Grímr sent him to spy on the prince's household."

When Freya stepped forward, the boy stood eye to eye with her. She smiled, and the boy's eyes widened in surprise. Freya was a breath-taking at her worst, but she stole the boy's breath when she smiled.

"Grímr must trust you a great deal to give you such a vital task. You must have proven yourself to be very brave and very intelligent." Freya forced awe into her voice but was careful not to overdo it. She knew from Freund that a boy that age was transitioning into a skeptical phase where false praise would get her nowhere. Tyra stepped next to Freya, and the boy looked as though he might collapse. Tyra's hair was a shade darker than Freya's platinum locks, but the contrast only showed off both women's unusual beauty.

"Were you with us in Scotland?" Gressa asked, stepping up to the other women.

Strian looked at his wife and friends, Gressa's dark waves an even starker contrast against Freya and Tyra's blonde heads. The women he and his friends had married were more than uncommonly attractive. Even pregnant, Sigrid was striking, but she hung back with Lorna and Lena. He forced himself to return his attention to the questions Gressa asked the boy.

"Yes, I was with you. I saw you with the other archers. You were amazing. After I saw you and the other archers, I wanted to come here to learn. When Grímr wanted one of us younger men to serve as a spy, I jumped at the chance."

The group bit back their smiles when the boy referred to himself as a younger man. They had all been that age once, eager to prove themselves as warriors of merit.

"Then you must have proven yourself. Where are you from?" Strian asked.

"I'm one of the few from Hakin and Grímr's tribe who have survived. I'm Inga's son."

Strian lifted the boy's chin and his hair fell away. He was looking at a younger version of himself.

"You're my cousin," Strian offered, unsure of what the boy knew.

"Then you are Einar's nephew."

"You know that Grímr isn't your father?" Strian was tentative, but he had to know.

"Everyone knows Einar was my father, but Grímr had no choice but to claim me since he and my mother were married."

"You should have been raised in our tribe," Ivar announced. "What's your name?"

The boy backed away from the imposing figure and looked cautiously at the man who was clearly a jarl.

"Brynjar Grímrson." The boy grimaced as he spoke his surname.

"Would you rather live with our tribe?" Ivar softened his tone "Your father was once one of my warriors, and your cousin is among my most trusted. He is like a son to me. His father was my closest friend. That makes you practically family."

"Family to a jarl? A real one?"

Rangvald clapped the boy on the shoulder, and the Brynjar had to take a step forward to keep from being knocked to the ground.

"That will make you family to two jarls. Two real ones."

Brynjar looked up at Rangvald and gasped.

"Yes, boy. I'm your Uncle Rangvald, your mother's brother. If you would like to live with me, you are welcome. If you would rather live with Ivar's clan, you are always welcome to visit."

Brynjar looked back and forth between Strian and Rangvald, fearful of making the wrong choice.

"I—I— don't know," he stammered.

Lorna joined them, and once more Brynjar's eyes became the size of saucers. Lorna made the other women, despite their own beauty, pale in comparison.

"This is your Aunt Lorna," Rangvald leaned near his ear but did not lower his voice. "Get used to it, boy. The women in our family are more beautiful than any you will find in this land or ours. I have sailed around much of the Christian world and into a warm sea known as the Mediterranean where the women have brown skin and dark eyes. But none have the beauty of your aunt or the women you see here. We are a blessed lot of men."

Brynjar could only nod.

"Dafydd confessed that he hid his wealth among the ruins of the Angelsey monastery," Gressa spoke up. "We found out that's where he hid what he collected over the years for his daughters' hands in marriage. He has already spent what Grímr gave him. He tried to buy his allies, and Grímr promised him more once they defeated us. Dafydd allowed his political ambitions and greed that matched Grímr's to lead him to his downfall."

"Angelsey is where Grímr said he would meet me. He plans to stop there to search for that treasure. Grímr learned of it somehow, I think when he drank with Rhys. He thought to pay Dafydd with Dafydd's own coins to avoid having to find more when he used the last of my mother's money," Brynjar spoke up.

"How do we know you are telling us the truth? You are a spy, after all," Bjorn questioned.

"Because what have I to gain from being loyal to Grímr? I carry his name, but he's rejected me as the youngest and because he knows I'm a bastard. My older brothers can fight for him and have died for him, but he says I'm too small. He hated my mother and said horrible things about her in front of me and my brothers. He sent me here alone most likely hoping I would die despite the information he hoped

I would gather. I owe him nothing." Brynjar spat on the ground.

"Then our final battle shall be on Angelsey." Rangvald pulled the boy against his side. "And you shall lead the way."

TWENTY-EIGHT

The Highlanders had occupied themselves with arranging the villagers into those they would leave behind and those who agreed to fight against Grímr. They also aided the villagers from letting the fire that destroyed the keep spread to the homes of the innocent.

"Let her stay here with her children," Gressa jutted her chin towards Enfys. "Her son inherits the land his father ruled, but he is too young to lead. She will do it, and she will end up having to marry one of the princes Dafydd intended to subjugate. She will become the wife of a lesser prince. Losing status will be its own punishment."

The Highland lairds and the jarls' families stood together as they watched Welsh warriors being loaded into the longboats. The Welsh language was so far from the Highlanders' Gaelic and Norse that the only effective communication were hand signals and various grunts.

"We shall have the fight we have waited for," Tormod Mackenzie spoke up.

"The morning tide will carry us out of the harbor, but we will need our oarsmen to do much of the work crossing the strait to Angelsey," Andrew Mac-

Leod looked at Tyra, almost challenging her to speak against the word of a MacLeod, the Highland's best sailors. Tyra shrugged and looked to Bjorn.

"If you have a plan in place, then you don't need us," Tyra tossed over her·shoulder as she pushed Bjorn toward their boat. It was not long before the newlyweds were running to Tyra's longboat. Their laughter floating back to the group as they ducked into their cabin.

"Tyra seems content to relinquish her title as Queen of the Sea now that she is the queen of Bjorn's heart," Erik laughed.

"How romantic you can be. Perhaps you should remind me." Freya stood on her toes to whisper something else in Erik's ear. He lifted his wife over his shoulder and marched to their own cabin.

"Is tupping all ye people think of before a battle? Lusty for blood and bedding," Kenneth Sutherland looked about, his eyes lingering on several Norse women.

"Aye, we are," Lorna chimed in. "Ye lads find yerselves a way to stay warm tonight. Tomorrow shall show us our fate."

It was rare that Lorna spoke of life and death like a Norsewoman would. Similar to Gressa who had not relinquished her pagan gods for the Christian one despite the years spent living among Christians, Lorna had never relinquished her Christian god despite more than thirty years among the Norse. She simply did not talk about it, but she understood the faith of her husband's and children's people. She could see the truth in some of their beliefs.

The night was too brief for everyone. Couples found places to bed down, privacy was limited but enough, so they could make love one last time before the next day's battle. Strian and Gressa found a storeroom where hay was being stored, but they offered it to Leif and Sigrid, so their expecting friend could try to find some comfort. However, Leif and Sigrid had already claimed a cottage within the keep walls that seemed to no longer have occupants. Gressa spread Strian's cloak over the hay, trying to prevent the itchy stalks from scratching them throughout the night. Strian returned from his ship with a blanket and some provisions. They sat cross legged as they ate in silence.

"Strian, the sun won't set for a while longer. I want to take you there now. There may not be time in the morning, and we may never return here." Gressa forced the words around the lump in her throat.

Strian looked up and gazed at Gressa for a long moment before nodding. Gressa led them through the same small gate that they had used earlier in the day. She was not sure how Strian would react, nervous that he would shut her out, but he held her hand as they walked towards a Christian cemetery. Gressa walked towards a small headstone that stood on its own, in a corner far from the others.

Gressa had spent so many hours laying along the grave, that the earth had become compacted and the grass did not grow as tall as in other parts. She dropped to her knees and ran her hand over the small mound, just as she had done thousands of times during the ten years she had visited the cemetery. She knew nothing about the other graves, having no interest in them. She knew her tiny corner where the Welsh laid her son against her wishes. Gressa looked up when Strian did not come closer. She almost wished she had not. Strian's stricken face would haunt her nightmares just like the day fate separated her from Strian and the day their son was born and died. She reached out a hand, but Strian did not seem to see it. Gressa rose to her feet and was about to step next to him, but Strian shook his head, backing away. He rushed to the tree that grew near the tiny grave. He heaved over and over as the contents of his stomach sprayed across the exposed roots. Gressa did not know what to do. She was torn between giving him his space and trying to comfort him. For the first time since she could remember, she did not know how Strian felt or what to do for him. She was unprepared for the accusation that filled his eyes when he lifted his head to look at her.

"You haven't bled since I found you. When were you going to tell me?" Strian's voice clawed open wounds Gressa thought had healed. She had not allowed herself to think about having more children with Strian, at least not beyond the most general of terms.

"I hadn't thought about it. I hadn't realized how long it had been. After," she waved her hand in the grave's direction, "my courses were never the same. They are not predictable."

"You were willing to enter another battle carrying our child," Strian accused. "You would have us lose another babe."

Gressa gasped and stumbled backwards. She shook her head as she looked at Strian as though he were a stranger.

"How could you say that," no sound escaping her moving lips.

"Because you could die this time!" Strian bellowed. "You could both die this time."

Gressa felt as if he had knocked the wind from her. She watched as the strongest man she had ever known, the only man she had ever loved, the only man she had ever desired, seemed to deflate in front of her. He returned to the grave and sank to his knees, his shoulders shaking as they had when she first told him of the child they lost. Gressa understood his fear and understood it drove the words that struck her like blades piercing her heart and mind, but that understanding did not diminish the pain.

"I can't live without you, Gressa. I don't want to. What if this time, I not only lose a child but you, too? What then? What's left for me? What if I can't find you in Valhalla?" Strian choked out the words that voiced his deepest fears since the first time he feared Gressa had died.

Gressa lowered herself next to Strian. She pried one of his hands free and wove her fingers through his.

"I don't know that I am carrying yet, my love. It's far too soon for me to know. My courses don't always come every month or sometimes they last far longer than the sennight they should. The midwife here told me it was from the deep wound that cut through my back. She said it may have nicked my womb. Strian, I don't even know for sure that I can have any more children." Gressa swallowed. "What if I can't? You deserve sons. You deserve a home filled with your children, your legacy."

Strian looked at Gressa and saw his fears mirrored in her eyes, but it was there for a very different reason.

"What are you saying, Gressa? Do you think I will set you aside? Will you push me towards another woman who could bear me children? How can you think these things? I can't overcome my fear of living without you again, and you think I won't want you if you can't have more children. Gressa, don't you understand? I don't want to live if it's without you. I've been at best half a man while you were gone."

"Do you not want me to fight? Do you want me to remain aboard your boat? Stay with Sigrid?"

Strian shook his head then nodded before shaking it again.

"I don't know, Gressa. I know you have as much right to see Grímr breathe his last as any of us, perhaps more than most of us, but I'm afraid."

Gressa rested her head against Strian's shoulder. There was nothing more to say. They knew they shared the same fear and the same uncertainty of what the following day would bring. As the sun set, Strian stretched out along the tiny mound where Gressa had so many times before. He had brought his cloak when they left the storeroom, so he wrapped it around them, and Gressa nestled into his embrace. They fell asleep with their fingers once more entwined, resting on the tiny mound that completed their family.

Strian and Gressa awoke feeling as though they had only just shut their eyes. They stared at the grave until there was little time left for them to meet the others at the boats.

"Gressa, go ahead. I will be there in a moment. I need some time here. I need to speak to my son."

Gressa nodded before walking towards the docks. She looked back once to see Strian kneeling exactly as she had countless times.

"Son, little Strian, I'm sorry I did not protect you and your mama better. I'm sorry that I wasn't there on the day of your birth. I'm sure your mama has told you how much she loves you; I know she even told you how much I would have loved you. I would have you hear it from me. I love you, son. You will always be my first born. Know that I wanted you as much as I know your mama wanted you." Strian looked around before he began to dig with his bare hands and a rock he found nearby. "I pray your mama understands what I'm doing, why I'm disturbing you. Your mama and I dreamed of the day you would join our family. You belong with us."

Strian dug until his fingers brushed against a swath of fabric that had thinned over the years in the ground. He pushed the last of the dirt away until a tiny shroud lay before him. He pulled his cloak from his shoulders before lifting the form from the grave. He wrapped it in his cloak, leaving a gap just as he would for a living baby who would need to draw a breath. He stood and kicked some dirt back in place.

"They had no right to disobey your mama's wishes, to ignore our gods. We will see your spirit set free, but you may need to wait a little longer, baby Strian."

Strian choked on a sob as he spoke his son's name aloud, the name they shared.

Gressa awaited him when he arrived at his ship. She looked at the bundle he carried, and tears streamed down her cheeks, she nodded once before spinning around and stepping onto the deck. She waited for Strian by the tiller. When he joined her, she raised her arms, and he placed the cloak and its precious cargo in her embrace. He tucked Gressa against his chest, and the couple stood together, grieving, as the fleet of boats pushed away from the shore. Both Gressa and Strian knew they would never return. They no longer had a reason to.

Dawn passed into morning as they neared the coast of Angelsey. Gressa had already informed Tyra about where the ruins lay and of the land surrounding it. She had traveled on pilgrimages with Enfys to the ruins many times over the years. She explained to Tyra the most likely place for Grímr to anchor, guided by the remaining Welshmen even if they had no way to speak to one another. When their captors took her and Strian to Grímr's camp, she had noticed that they seemed to have managed without her.

Tyra navigated them into a natural cover where many of the boats could hide. Only a few had to sail further down the coast to find a safe place to weigh anchor. There were no signs that Grímr was on Angelsey, but they had not passed him either. They went ashore, scouting the best place to ambush Grímr.

"He hasn't arrived yet, so that means he must have found Highlanders to come back with him. He told me that would be the only thing that would delay him. I was to meet him here with news from the royal home." Brynjar explained as he stood with Gressa and Strian. The boy had sensed not to ask about what looked like a babe that Gressa held but never moved.

"Is he expecting you to be waiting for him?" Skepticism filled Strian's voice.

"I think so," Brynjar looked towards the shore.

"You're not going to the meeting point alone," Strian's voice left no room for the boy to argue.

"He's not going at all," Gressa broke in. "It's not safe, and you are not yet ready to fight in a battle like this. You must help Freund and the other barrel men guard the boats. Several of the warriors will stay with you. Brynjar, your job is among the most important. If anything happens to the fleet, we will be trapped here. And there is one more thing that I need you to guard."

Gressa looked down at the cloak that filled her arms before she looked at Strian. His hand ran over her hair and along her back, encouraging her to continue. "Brynjar, this is the son Strian and I lost all those years ago. They denied him his proper burial instead placed in a Christian grave. We are taking him home, so his spirit can rest at last."

The boy looked at the bundle Gressa settled on the seat beside the rudder. He looked at the couple, seeing the pain they shared, and despite his young age, he understood their grief.

"I shall guard my cousin. No one will come near him and live. I will be the guardian of his body and his soul." Brynjar seemed to grow with those few words, and his voice deepened with the sense of duty that filled him.

"Thank you," the couple murmured before they both took one last look at the small form on the bench then stepped onto the shore.

In less than an hour, they scattered the entire combined forces throughout the ruins, hidden in the tall grass and the remaining rubble. Little was said, and no one moved as the time ticked by. It was early evening when at last the signal was given that ships had been spotted. Gressa and Strian lay next to one another not far from Ivar and Lena. Freya and Erik lay near his parents on another stretch of earth that faced the approaching boats, and Bjorn and Tyra had climbed into the trees with the other archers. Several of the Welsh bowmen had scrambled over the rubble and found elevated places from which to shoot. Gressa was uncertain whether these Welshmen would fire upon their fellow countrymen who would arrive with Grímr, but she was confident they would shoot Grímr or any of the foreigners they resented arriving on their shores to disrupt their homes and their lives. Sigrid remained hidden in Freya's cabin while Leif lay on the far side of Ivar and Lena.

The first sounds of boats coming to a halt floated up the hillside then the splashes of men wading ashore followed. Voices carried through the still air, and Grímr's voice rose above the others.

"Find the boy and find the chests. We gather those before we continue to Gwynedd. I'll have that fool's hidden stash and will pay him with his own goods. Then we'll put an end to Ivar and Rangvald. They cannot be far behind us now."

Ivar raised his hand and made a slicing signal forward. The Norsemen and Highlanders rose to their feet.

"We are not that far in front of you!" Ivar roared.

The Highlanders beat their sword hilts against their targes, dark blue woad covering their faces, leaving only the whites of their eyes to gleam as the sunlight softened towards dusk. The Norse formed their shield wall, and the Highlanders found their places among it, having learned from fighting more than one battle alongside people they thought once to call their enemy.

"Grímr!" Rangvald taunted. "There is nothing left to make us think your cock is bigger than your pinky. We have your gold and coins. We have killed or captured your sons. You have no home to go back to. And your ally in Gwynedd is dead. You are a man who has been cut down at the knees. You are but half a man, a half the Valkyries will fly right past. The rest will shit on your remains. Your place shall be to wallow in Helheim, left in darkness and agony, while all who live know you as a níðingr, a man with no honor. A man no other will respect nor revere. Nornar has chosen this place, this moment for your death. Will you accept it as a man or pish yourself like a child?"

Rangvald's laughter echoed behind the shield wall, but his taunts did what he intended. Grímr roared and ordered his men forward. Rangvald and Ivar ordered their shield wall remain. They waited as Grímr's forces advanced up the hill while Rangvald and Ivar called for them to hold. When Gressa could see their enemy was halfway up the rise, she tapped Strian's shoulder. He moved his shield aside enough for her to aim her bow through the gap. She awaited Ivar's order, and when she heard it, she released her arrow, lodging in a man's belly. It was the signal the other archers had been awaiting. Arrows flew from every direction and rained down on Grímr's forces. As they continued to push their way uphill, they left their backs open to the archers they had not noticed passing. Grímr's shield wall shifted and rippled as a mixture of Norsemen, Highlanders, and Welshmen attempted to remain a unified force with no one to communicate among them all.

"For Valhalla!" Ivar's order rang across the field of battle as the Norse and Highlanders charged forward, using their elevation to their advantage. They barreled into Grímr's warriors, knocking them backwards, many falling then rolling as arrows whizzed by and found flesh to embed in. Gressa used her bow until her quiver was almost empty. She stayed beside Strian, part of her always touching him, reassuring them both that she did not fall behind. As the two shield walls collided, the melee began in full force. It was each warrior for themselves, and Strian fought back to back with Gressa. They had trained together to fight like this long ago but had never had the chance. Now they moved as a beast with two bodies but one mind. Their movements were synchronized and in tandem as they cut through one enemy after another.

Gressa spun in time to see an archer aim for Strian. She lunged and tackled him around the waist, pushing him to the ground. His body absorbed most of the brunt, but he pinned Gressa's hands beneath them.

"Gressa?"

"Arrow," she panted. "You eat too much."

She fought to free her trapped hands and shook them before picking up her sword and shield. Strian followed her, using his shield to protect them both as they picked a position near Freya and Erik. The battle waged on, and more of Grímr's forces fell, but never him. He evaded each warrior who set their sights on killing him. Gressa caught sight of him several times from the corner of her eye, her rage growing each time she realized he was still alive. She fought one enemy after another, indiscriminate of their origin only with the singular goal in mind to defeat Grímr. Strian slayed a man who dared leer at Gressa before charging at her. She spun around and found herself face to face with Grímr.

"You have come to me yet again." Grímr tried to reach out to grab Gressa's arm, but she was quicker, her knife slashing across his forearm. "Bitch, I will kill you for that. After you suck my cock once more. What you can do with that pretty mouth of yours."

Gressa hurled a wad of spit onto his face.

"That is what my mouth can do for you."

Grímr roared as he launched his attack. He fought with no finesse and no plan. Gressa could easily read his next movement before Grímr even seemed to decide what to do. She ran her sword blade into the flesh and bone beneath his collarbone. Blood geysered from the large puncture wound. As it splattered her face, Gressa licked around her mouth.

"Your blood tastes far better than your seed. Perhaps that is what I shall drink tonight."

She lunged again and sliced her sword across the thigh that still bore a wound received many months earlier. Grímr sank to the ground no longer able to bear his weight. Gressa moved around him, and kicked his back, forcing him flat onto the ground.

"I would run you through, kill you right here and now, but I have a better idea for you. Perhaps Jarl

Ivar and Jarl Rangvald will even allow me to do the honors."

Gressa brought the hilt of her sword down on Grímr's temple, turning his world to black. Once his eyes slid shut, and she was sure he would not be moving again, she looked up to see Strian watching her. He had been guarding her as she fought Grímr. He had once told her he would give her the chance to kill Grímr if he could.

"I have a better way to make him suffer than a clean, quick death. I will hear his screams ring through the air as mine did in my head each and every time he forced me near him."

Strian nodded and whistled a call to signal that they defeated the enemy. The Norsemen and women killed the last of their opponents while the Highlanders rounded up their injured and dead. Ivar and Rangvald made their way to where Gressa continued to stand with her foot on Grímr's back.

"He's dead?" Rangvald narrowed his eyes as he looked at his former brother-in-law.

"No. Not yet." Gressa answered.

"You had the chance, and you didn't take it? You had the right," Ivar questioned.

"Blood eagle." Gressa's two words brought everything to a halt. They considered the form of execution barbaric even among their tribes and one they reserved for the most heinous of enemies. Gressa raised an eyebrow at the two jarls.

"He lives," Ivar grunted. "That is the only requirement at this point."

"Very well," Rangvald shrugged.

"Who has he wronged the most?" Gressa asked.

"Who hasn't he wronged?" Erik returned her question with his own. "He was complicit in Hakin's plans, taking them several steps further. He helped orchestrate Sigrid's kidnapping not once but twice.

He captured Tyra and Bjorn and you and Strian. He led Freya and me on a merry chase that nearly got us killed more than once. He swore to kill all of us and steal my father's and Ivar's land. But you are the only one he's touched. You are the only one who has suffered the most at his hand."

Gressa looked around the group and saw several heads nod. She looked at Strian, fearful of what she would see. While Erik may have been accurate that she had suffered most directly from Grímr's evil, it also pointed out a part of her past she wished never happened, or at least that no one knew of. She was embarrassed to meet Strian's gaze, but he stepped forward and raised her chin. He brushed his lips against hers before kissing her in front of everyone, their friends, family, and tribe members along with the others present. Strian once more pronounced her as his wife with a kiss that left no one doubting his devotion to his wife.

"Kill him, so we can go home and make those babies," he murmured against her lips.

TWENTY-NINE

The moon rose over the treetops as the last of Grímr's most loyal men hanged from a tree limb. Their bodies no longer writhed or twitched. They swayed in the light breeze. They had waited until Grímr awoke before binding and gagging him then forcing him to watch. The antipathy showed Grímr had never cared for anyone but himself. Perhaps once he had loved Inga, but his wife destroyed that with her affairs. He never loved his brother nor the children who carried his name. Once the last of his men were dead, it was his turn to die. He would die alone, befitting his life and his legacy.

Leif and Bjorn rushed to stretch him prone against the ground, his arms tied to stakes they hammered into the dirt. They pulled his legs apart to leave him spread eagle. Gressa looked to Strian who passed her an axe he had spent the past two hours sharpening to a fine edge that could split a hair.

Gressa looked around at those who watched. Lorna had explained to the four Highland lairds what would happen. They had each insisted they would watch, but the Norse warriors wagered how long they would last before they looked away, vomited, or collapsed. Her eyes came to rest on Ivar and

Lena, the only parents she had known. She looked at the man who had tried to steal their home and end the lives the couple had spent decades building together and for their people. She glanced at Rangvald and Lorna who had proven to be the best of allies. She even looked at the Highlanders who valiantly fought alongside people they did not trust nor understood. They had formed their own alliances within the group of extended family and friends. Finally, Gressa looked once more at Grímr. Someone had removed the gag, so all could hear the howls of his pain.

Gressa raised the axe over her head, prepared for the first cut when two ravens cawed and landed on a stump nearby. The Norsemen and women went silent as the two birds turned to watch Gressa.

"See," she lowered her axe and pulled a fistful of Grímr's hair to raise his head enough to see the two blackbirds. "Odin is here. He is here to be sure that no one confuses you for anything but an honorless pile of shite. No Valkyrie shall look for you. The goddess Freya will not be looking for you in Folkvang. The doors of Valhalla will remain locked to you, and you will never see the inside of the great feasting hall. Instead, you shall rot until the end of days in Helheim. Not with the ordinary people who die a less than valiant death. No, you shall reside with the other cowards and weaklings. You will live in fear of the cold and dark until there is nothing left of you. But first, you shall soar like an eagle, or at least your bones will."

Gressa swung the axe, making the first cut along his spin, splintering several ribs from his spine. She brought the axe down again on the same side, shattering the connecting fibers between Grímr's ribs and spine. She repeated the process on the other side, cutting through meat and bone in between his howls of pain. She paused again when the sound of two wolves echoed his wails.

"Do you hear that? Geri and Freki call to Odin. They tell him that your death is only moments away. They laugh along with your screams of pain. You cannot even die with pride and dignity. Even in death you show your weakness and cowardice. A real man would bear the pain and praise Odin for the chance to feast with him. But you know," Gressa's laugh was harsh. "You know you are nothing. A níðingr."

Gressa swung twice more, releasing the last rib from its bindings to the man's spine. Gressa dropped the axe and plunged her hand beneath his right ribs. She pulled several times before she withdrew his lung. She held it above her head as Grímr's blood dripped down her arm. His cries of agony grew louder when his own lung landed beside his head, but the last of the air that filled his single remaining lung escaped, and he could not make more than a whimper, a gurgle in the back of his throat. Gressa reached beneath his left ribs, but this lung did not want to break free. She drew her knife and sawed through the connective tissue until she felt it give way. She speared the second lung and pulled it out, sitting upon the tip of her blade. She raised it for all to see before dropping it next to the other. With both hands, she pried Grímr's ribcage open, making it look as though his ribs were a set of eagle's wings.

Leif and Bjorn whipped away the rope binding his legs to the ground, then they pulled the stakes free that pinned his arms to the ground. Both men tugged on the ropes wrapped over tree limbs, lifting Grímr's body from the ground. Suspended in midair, Grímr's body swung and twisted as his lifeblood drained from his body, and the last of his life slipped away.

Strian took Gressa's hand and weaved through the crowd until they came to the shore. He had thought ahead and brought a bar of soap from his own belongings to the execution. He guided Gressa into the lapping water until they were far enough out that the waves crashed against their knees. He pressed her hands under the water then lifted them and began scrubbing. He watched her face for any clue to what she felt. She seemed dazed, not from battle lust nor shock. She appeared to be both deep in thought and without a thought in her head.

"He's really dead. It's really over," Gressa looked at Strian as though it surprised her to find she was not alone. She watched him continue to scrub the blood from her hands and arms. The water was frigid, but Strian pressed her down until she dipped below the surface. He was quick to scrub her hair, her chest and clothes, then her face before easing her beneath the water again. She was too tired to say the saltwater would only make her hair worse. She had an overwhelming need to curl up next to Strian and go to sleep.

"As soon as we get you dry. Then you can sleep. I won't move from beside you."

Gressa nodded, vaguely aware that she must have spoken aloud.

"Gressa?" Strian watched as she turned towards him, her eyes growing more focused each time he spoke to her. "Do you regret being the one?"

"No," she was emphatic and shook her head to reaffirm her point. "He deserved it. It just seems an-ticlimactic now that he is dead. We have been through so much, and now it is all over."

"Do you fear that now there's no danger, there will be nothing pushing us together?" Strian was slow to speak and watched Gressa even though he tried to sound casual.

Gressa was sure a wave had just crashed into her

face as Strian's words sank in. Whatever cloud she had been floating upon gave way.

"There will always be something pushing us together. Fate decided long ago, and our love reaffirms it. We are meant to be together. And if it's not fate, then is will be me wrapping my legs around your waist with you deep inside me that pushes us together."

Strian let go of the soap as he pulled Gressa against him. His mouth devoured hers as their need overcame them. It had been days since they had made love, but it felt like yet another eternity. Strian lifted Gressa into his arms then marched to his boat.

"Off!" He demanded.

His crew looked at him, most getting ready to settle in for the night.

"I said off. All of you. Find somewhere else for the night."

His crew came to their feet, looking at him with annoyance until he lowered a soaking wet Gressa to her feet. His crew hastened to jump to the sandy shore. Even Brynjar seemed to understand the urgency. Strian turned them so his back was to the shore before he helped Gressa peel off her sodden clothes. He pulled a blanket from a pile near the starboard rail and draped it around her. He peeled off his tunic, but when he began to untie the laces to his pants, Gressa gasped. She looked around him, and there were plenty of people on the beach near the boats. More than a few were watching them but turned away when they realized Gressa caught them staring. She opened her arms and waited for Strian to step within the blanket. He pushed his pants free and stepped out of them. His hands found Gressa's waist as he kissed her, wrapped within the wool. He lifted her until her legs coiled around him, and he slid into her. His strong legs lowered them to the deck where Strian sat with Gressa straddling him. Their bodies warmed as much by the blanket as the growing heat between them. Strian guided Gressa's hips as she rocked against them. Their kisses were slow and languid as they took their time, drawing out one another's pleasure. They remained joined as the camp grew quiet, and only the soft sounds of other couples floated to them over the sound of the waves.

Strian's hands roamed over Gressa's body as she clutched his shoulders. He kneaded her breasts before lifting one to his mouth. He suckled as his hands found her backside again. His fingers spread wide as the firm flesh filled his hands. His groan vibrated through his chest as Gressa's hands glided over the muscles until her nails raked over the ridges of his abdomen. The slight bobbing of the boat added to the rhythm of their love making until their need could no longer coincide with their leisurely pleasure. Strian lowered Gressa's body to the deck before stretching out over her. She arched her back as his thrusts grew stronger. He drew her arm over her head as their fingers laced together. His other hand gripping her hip, his fingers surely leaving marks. Gressa sank her teeth along his shoulder, leaving her own marks. Neither of them had relinquished their possessiveness while both of them reveled in feeling so loved and desired.

It was late into the night before they grew too tired to continue. They looked up at the stars as they had done many nights while Strian courted her then through their chamber window. Strian's arms held Gressa against him, but once more, they joined their hands. The boat listed, and it drew their attention to the cloak that still held their newborn son's body.

"Once we are home, we will give him the burial he deserved."

"Do you think the gods will still accept him?

After so long? After where he has been?" Gressa wondered.

"They are capricious and unpredictable at times, but they do not punish the innocent."

Gressa turned to look at Strian, and something shifted within her belly. She could not describe the feeling, but she placed her hand over it, sure of what she prayed for over and over.

"I don't know if it happened this eve or if it was one of our many times over the past weeks, but Strian, I'm almost certain now that I am carrying. Something---" She trailed off, shaking her head. At his gentle kiss upon her forehead, she felt encouraged to continue. "It was like a flutter then like whatever it was landed and can't be pulled away."

"Then I shall pray that you are right and give thanks to the gods when we know for sure."

"It will be weeks before a midwife will know, but I could ask Sigrid."

"No," Strian shook his head. "Let the gods tell us when your body is ready. We don't need to know everything about the future."

They drifted to sleep in one another's arms, enjoying the last bit of intimacy before they traveled back to Scotland.

THIRTY

S trian placed her on her feet, and it was only a
heartbeat later that they once more came together in a cataclysmic kiss, both frustrated and
needy after so many days of forced abstinence. They
tore at one another's clothing, shedding them in a
pile at their feet. Strian pressed Gressa back against a
boulder as she tangled her fingers in his hair and
held his head as she wanted it while her tongue invaded his mouth. There was little finesse as Gressa
wrapped her legs around Strian's waist, and he thrust
into her. Their coupling was rough as fingers bit into
flesh and nails raked across skin, each marking the
other as possessiveness and love tangled into inextricable need. A voice in Strian's mind emerged from
the fog long enough to warn him that he would hurt
Gressa by being so rough with her against a rock, but
when he tried to slow and shift them, Gressa's teeth
tugged at his lip and her heels dug into the base of
his spine.

Gressa gasped with pleasure that coursed
through her each time Strian surged into her.
Nothing permeated the cloud she floated upon as she
clung to the only man she had ever been with. She
knew the Valkyries could claim her now, and she

would go to Valhalla without having missed anything by not having more partners. She could not imagine any man could make her feel what Strian did. The hunger for Strian that gnawed at her throughout their voyage, ravaging her each time he was near, now controlled her every move and thought. His breath tickled her ear as his tongue brushed against the whorl of her ear. He nipped then sucked her lobe into the warmth of his mouth, scalding her wherever his lips touched. His whispered words eliciting moans she did not try to stifle.

"Do you have any idea how much I've wanted to thrust into you over and over until I can no longer say my name? How many times I nearly took you against the rail of the ship, crew be damned? Gods Gressa, I want to fuck you as much as I want to make love to you. I just want to be bollocks deep in you and hear you scream my name."

Gressa felt her nipples tighten into painful peaks as his words pushed her closer to the edge.

"Then fuck me, Strian. Don't hold back. My whole body aches for you. I need you. Show me I'm not alone in how much I need you inside me."

Gressa's last words shredded Strian's final vestiges of control. He could no longer hold back. He would feel guilty later for being so rough, but as Gressa's moans filled his ears, and her soft chanting for more released his last threads of reason, he plunged his cock into her over and over. Each time he thought he was as deep as he could go, he pushed just a little further. Gressa's feet pressed against the rock as she lifted her hips to meet each thrust, her nails biting into the flesh of his backside as she held him within her for an extra moment while the muscles of her core contracted around him. Their movements driving one another closer to the brink; the pressure building within them both. Strian saw stars dancing behind his clenched eyelids each time he felt Gressa's inner muscles tighten around him, holding him deep within her.

"Gressa, let go. I need you to find your release because I can't hold on much longer. I need to spill, but I refuse to finish until I've pleasured you and you scream my name. Fuck, Gressa. Hurry."

Gressa bit into Strian's shoulder as she ground her mound against him, the burning ache within her belly giving way to her climax. She moaned as the feel of Strian's body grinding against hers tipped her over the edge.

"Strian!" she did not care that her scream scared the birds from the trees and was surely heard all the way to the keep.

"Gressa!" Strian's responding bellow only confirmed to anyone who could hear that they both found their release.

Gressa's knees cradled Strian's hips, as they lay panting, Strian's chest pressing against Gressa's. Her fingers drew lazy circles over the sweat drenched skin, and Strian continued to press kisses along the column of her neck and behind her ears. They were content to remain joined as they struggled to regain control of their breathing. The physical need satisfied, their emotional need demanded they remain connected as tenderness overtook them.

"I wish it could be only the two of us. At least until our family grows. Then I wish we could live without the demands of others interfering," Strian murmured as his hand cupped Gressa's neck and she nuzzled against him.

"You would have us live like hermits? Wouldn't you miss our friends?" Gressa's toes ran along the length of Strian's calf before winding around his leg.

"You forget that I go into the mountains at least once a year for longer than a moon." Strian felt

Gressa suck in air, surprised he knew that she knew. "I figured Freya told you that morning she pulled you off to the side. Your face went so gray, I feared you'd pass out."

Gressa's mind flooded with guilt and doubt about her decision to stay in Wales. She had been so sure that it was what was best for their child, that Strian would understand, but once again the harm her absence caused Strian confronted her.

"Stop, Gressa." Strian pushed up on his forearm to look at her. "I would have stayed with him, too."

Gressa's eyes filled with tears as she stroked Strian's jaw, his beard grown in after days at sea.

"I should have told you that sooner, Gressa. I'm still angry and bitter about the years stolen from us, but I should have said something before I now. I've thought about it countless times since you told me your reasons, and I would have done the same thing. Gressa, I think about him all the time now that I know. I can't stop wondering what he looked like, what he would be like now. He'd be old enough to train with us. I would have already given him his first wooden sword. I want to know if he would have been fair like me or had your dark hair. I can't stop wanting to get to him faster and being frustrated at having to wait. I want him to know that his father loves him."

Strian's voice caught on the last sentence, and he hung his head. Gressa's cool hands lifted his chin, and she curled up to brush a kiss against the corner of his lips. Her thumbs swiped away the tears that fell from Strian's misty eyes. She wrapped her arms around his back and nudged him to lie against her again. She stroked his hair as he rested his head against her shoulder.

"I told him every day that you loved him. I had no way of knowing if you had moved on, found another wife and had a family, but I knew that you would have loved our son no matter what. I didn't want to think about you being with another woman, creating a life with her that we had promised each other, but I knew I was gone too long to expect you to not continue your life. I even sat at his graveside and wondered aloud what your new family would be like. I told him of the brothers and sisters I assumed he had, and how you would have gladly included him as you played with and taught each of them. He knows, Strian. No matter where his spirit rests now, he knows you would have loved him just as much I love him."

"But you saw him. Were you able to hold him?"

Gressa nodded, unable to force words around the lump in her throat. Strian tilted his head to see Gressa's face. Tears leaked from her eyes, too. Their shared pain still looking for ways out.

"I did. Strian, he looked so much like you." Gressa's hoarse whisper came with a feeling of gravel traveling along her throat.

Strian rolled onto his side and covered her belly with his hand as though he might feel whether a new life already grew inside.

"No child can take the place of our son, but I pray more children will join our family one day." Strian infused his with tenderness, and Gressa welcomed the love they exchanged. When Strian pulled away, she offered him a watery smile.

"We've certainly been trying enough that something should take sooner rather than later."

Gressa's smile withered as a look of horror crossed Strian's face. It was not the reaction she had expected when she tried to lighten their mood.

"Do you think you're already with child?" Strian croaked. "You're not leaving the boat, Gressa. I'm serious. Once we're there, you're staying on the boat. I'm not risking losing you or our child."

Gressa shook her head, understanding Strian's protectiveness.

"It's too soon to know. And I can't hide just in case something might go wrong. Strian, we both have a duty to fight, and I need to. I need to avenge what Grímr forced me to do and the threats he made against you."

"But what if you're carrying already? And if you're injured again? You could lose another child."

"And you could die with me left wondering where you are." Gressa pushed against Strian and sat up. She stormed into the water until it was knee deep before turning around. Strian could see the red staining her cheeks and the cords of her throat straining as she bit out, "You're not leaving me behind again."

Gressa continued to wade in as Strian stalked into the water behind her. She did not try to get away when he pulled her to a stop. His chest felt twice as broad as hers when he held her against him. His hand once more resting on her belly.

"Do you think we'll ever stop being so protective of one another?"

"I pray that we don't even if it makes life complicated."

Gressa leaned her head back against Strian's chest and pulled his other arm around her. She placed his hand over her breast, and she arched as he massaged the flesh. She swayed her hips as she felt him harden. The hand on her belly traveled down to the apex of her thighs, and she widened her stance, granting his entrance.

"Why can't I get enough of you?" she murmured.

"Because you are as much a drug to me as I am to you."

"How can my body crave you, feel so empty without you, when we joined only minutes ago?"

"Because we aren't joined anymore."

Gressa took Strian's hand and pulled him back to the shore. Neither spoke another word as Gressa pressed her front against the boulder, lifting one leg and tilting her hips back. Strian slid into her, teasing her as much as himself. She pushed back so that her sheath engulfed his sword, and they were once more a single entity. They rocked together, their movements slow and drawn out. Strian draped his body over hers, lacing their fingers together. Gressa reveled at his much larger form covering hers, his size dominating her while her body controlled his need.

"You're mine, Gressa." His possessive words eliciting a moan from her.

"Show me." She looked back over her shoulder. "Show me, and I'll do anything you ask."

Strian's eyes slid shut, overwhelmed by the feelings Gressa created in him. Her resilience and tenacity to overcome any challenge drew his respect and his pride, but her willingness to concede control to him in moments like this made him feel stronger and more manly than any battle ever had. It was her implicit trust and his conviction to protect it, and to nurture their love that gave him strength.

His fingers found the hidden button that controlled her pleasure. He rubbed slowly and firmly until he felt her urgency grow as she sought release. He pulled his hand away, eliciting a whimper from Gressa. His other hand found her nipple, and he pinched until he knew she felt pain, but the way her hips thrust back told him she also felt pleasure. He released her nipple. Her mewls of need along with the faster rocking of her hips told him she understood the game they played. He once more toyed with her nub, bringing her close to release then pulling away, this time with a shark spank to her backside. They continued this pattern until they both were insensate. When she was certain she could support her own weight, Gressa pushed back from the rock and turned to face him. She dropped to her knees, cupping her breasts around his cock as she sucked his tip. With her eyes closed, Strian watched the happiness at pleasuring him blossom across her face. When he could feel himself leaking onto her tongue and saw his seed on her breast, he lifted her and turned her to face the boulder. He gripped her hips and thrust into her as hard as he could, seating himself to the hilt. He gave her a sharp spank before pinching both her nipple and her nub. She exploded around him, words and curses tumbling from her lips as she demanded more. Strian was only too happy to oblige as his hips continued to pound into her until she once again climaxed and squeezed the seed from his cock.

Strian slid his hands along her body and arms until they interlaced their fingers again, and he dropped kisses on her shoulder. With his body draped over her, only her legs and fingers were visible. Strian paused, sensing they were not alone. His eyes scanned their surroundings as he tried not to alert Gressa to his concern.

"Who's there?" her voice barely loud enough for him to hear.

"I don't know," he exhaled. He would not move until her was sure there was no danger to Gressa, his body shielding her from anyone's sight or their weapon.

Gressa looked around, too, as best as her position pinned against the rock allowed.

"There," she murmured as she squeezed his fingers and adjusted them to point to their left. "Betje."

Strian began to pull away, thinking Betje posed little harm, but the threats she hissed at him as he forced her onto Tyra's longboat came back to him. He had underestimated her as Gressa predicted. The venom of her words had shocked him as she stepped across the plank joining his boat to Tyra's. She had threatened to kill Gressa, to rip any unborn babe from Gressa's womb, and to trick him into coupling with her while Gressa watched. Now he saw the calculating look on the woman's face as she continued to stare at the couple. Strian leaned close to Gressa's face so they could whisper.

"She watched us," Gressa whispered. "I wonder for how long."

"Too long," Strian hissed.

"Now what? Do we just wait her out?"

"I'm not moving and making you a target."

"And I'm not remaining here forever waiting for her to tire of spying on us."

Gressa pushed Strian from her, her body unhappy as he slid from her and causing her to moan. She slipped from beneath him and stood gloriously naked before the woman who coveted her husband.

"I know you saw everything," Gressa called out. "You can't believe he wants you or anyone else after what you saw, what you heard. Leave now, and we will pretend like we never saw you."

"You have an answer for everything, Sami," Betje called back. "But he cannot be everywhere at once. He can't watch you every second during battle, not if you want him to live. No one wants you alive, but everyone wants you dead. If it's not a Welshman, then it'll be one of Grímr's men. If not one of them, then a Norseman, or woman, will do it. You don't belong with us, Sami. You won't breed with our men and bring your filth into our village, our tribe. But I will bear your man's child one day, and you will be dead and unable to stop me."

"Dead women don't fuck." Gressa called back as Betje turned away.

Betje whipped around with a knife in her hand, but Gressa had expected it and was quicker. She had already snatched a knife from the pile of clothes. As Betje raised her arm, Gressa released the blade, hurtling it toward her newest nemesis. It embedded in the other woman's throat, and Betje collapsed with a soft gurgle and sightless eyes.

THIRTY-ONE

The armada sailed back to the Mackenzie land where the clans departed ways with old and somewhat flimsy alliances now forged into partnerships that would last for several generations. The Mackays sailed alongside the Norse until they docked below Castle Varrich once more. Alex Mackay convinced his family to spend a few days resting before setting out to once more cross the North Sea. It was during those days that Gressa began to feel unusually sleepy and restless. She lost her appetite and turned away most foods. Strian watched as Gressa withdrew only seeming interested in being with him or sleeping.

Their second day crossing the North Sea led them into choppy water that forced the oarsmen to strain to keep their boats on the right course. Strian sat at the tiller while Gressa took her turn to row. She had seemed to perk up with the sea air and insisted she was well enough to do her share. As the boat listed from one side to another, Strian watched Gressa pull her oar in before leaning her head over the side. He called to his first mate who was already rushing to take the tiller. Strian leaped across the benches until he got to Gressa's side. She heaved over and over, but the little food in her stomach had already washed away. Strian pulled her into his arms and carried her with his cloak shielding her from the wind and spray. He huddled in the bow, trying to protect Gressa from the elements as she slept in his arms. Strian was beside him with worry and fear as the day progressed into night and the sun rose once more before Gressa's eyes opened. She blinked several times and looked around, confused at how she ended up in Strian's lap. Her husband was snoring and most of the crew was just awakening. She looked at the man who held the tiller, but he shrugged before looking away.

Gressa was about to shake Strian awake when the wave of nausea threatened to capsize her. She scrambled from Strian's lap and managed to wretch over the side rather than on the deck. She heard Strian's panicked voice call her name. She lifted one hand behind her in some sort of wave. He was beside her in an instant.

"That's it. No more. Lena needs to examine you."

"There's nothing wrong with me."

"Nothing wrong?" Strian exploded. He threw his hands into the air, curses flowing from his mouth as he looked to the heavens then to his wife before dropping to his knee and leaning his head against her middle. "How can you say nothing is wrong? You can't stop sleeping, and your violently ill any time you're awake. You've never been seasick a day in your life."

Gressa stroked his hair away from his face before cupping his jaw.

"That's because I'm not seasick, silly man. I didn't realize what it was either because I didn't experience this last time. Maybe because I was much younger, or maybe because I had other illnesses to disguise it."

"Gressa, you're not making sense. You've never been ill except for when you were wounded."

"Exactly. Strian, I didn't know I was pregnant then, and I was ill for two moons after the battle. Perhaps some of it was morning sickness, too. Maybe not. But this time I'm certain that it's morning sickness that is rude enough to stick around all day."

"Morning sickness?"

"I told you the night before we left Anglesey that I was sure we had made a babe. Now I know."

"Were you going to tell me?"

"I assumed you would remember our conversation." Gressa shrugged. "Besides when I was awake, I was vomiting. The rest of the time I've been asleep. It hasn't given us much time to talk."

Strian looked at his wife as though she spoke a foreign tongue. She patted his head as though he were a loyal hound before she stepped back.

"I'm starving. Where is the pickled herring stored?"

"To break your fast? You hate it."

"I know," she shrugged once again. "But it's the only thing that sounds good right now."

The rest of their voyage was a mixture of Gressa trying to reassure and calm Strian, who worried over everything, along with Gressa needing naps and discovering what food she had an aversion to and what she could not have enough of. The fortnight of sailing felt as though it rushed by for the couple, but Strian's crew would have described it as interminable. There was an audible sigh as they sailed into their harbor.

Gressa and Strian hung back, allowing Strian's crew and their families to reunite. They waved to their friends and nodded as the others looked to see if they would follow. Strian picked up the bundle that remained enshrouded in his cloak. He passed it to Gressa before lifting her into his arms to protect all three of his precious cargo as he waded to shore. When he was on solid ground, he lowered Gressa to her feet. They stood looking at the homestead, and at last it felt like home to them both. Strian had dreaded it each time he sailed into the harbor without Gressa. Gressa had feared for her life when she returned weeks earlier. Now they felt as though they were where they belonged.

Strian had spoken to Freya and Erik during the voyage when their ships floated close enough for the three of them to stand at the rails of their boats and not have their words shared with everyone. Strian shared what he and Gressa wanted once they arrived home, and Erik and Freya promised to see to the arrangements.

Standing together as the sun sank below the horizon, Strian and Gressa looked at the remains of their son nestled in Gressa's arms. Strian wrapped his arms around her and rested his hands over the new life that grew within her belly. They stood together in silence, both lost in thought but savoring the time together as a family. It was not long before Leif and Sigrid, Freya and Erik, Tyra and Bjorn, Lena and Ivar, and Rangvald and Lorna joined them. The men carried a small hollowed log that had a fur pelt resting within. Gressa recognized it was a log that would have been part of the fencing, but the men were preparing it as a funeral pyre. Lena came to stand at Gressa's side with a blanket Gressa recognized as one she had made many years ago for a baby that Lena never bore. Gressa swallowed back tears as she nodded to Lena. The two women walked to where the men had lowered the log. Gressa unwrapped Strian's cloak until the shroud appeared.

Then she placed the infant's body upon the pelt and Lena covered it with the blanket. There was not much to send with a babe to the afterlife, but each of their friends found something to include. Tyra and Freya each included an arrow with their unique fletching. Bjorn added a small knife. Ivar and Lena had offered the pelt and the blanket while Rangvald and Lorna placed a torque and a Thor's hammer medallion beside the remains. Leif and Sigrid were the last to come forward. Sigrid closed her eyes and passed her hand over the crib dug into the log. Her lips moved but no one could hear what she said or make out the sounds her lips formed. They knew she was ensuring baby Strian would find safe passage to the afterlife. Leif placed a fealty ring as the last gift. One day, Gressa's and Strian's children would grow old enough to pledge their fealty to their jarl, and by then, Leif would likely be the jarl. Leif's gift symbolized that the babe was a member of the tribe and ensured his manhood.

The men carried the log to the water's edge, and Strian and Gressa each grasped a side, the rings neither had ever taken off since the day they wed flashed in the moonlight as they pushed their son towards the waves and his afterlife. As the miniature funeral barge caught the tide, Sigrid's haunting voice floated with the melody of a mourning song. Tyra and Freya dipped their arrows into a small fire Bjorn has built then launched them onto the log as it drifted further out to sea. It was only a moment after they landed that the fire sparked in the twigs and branches that filled the opening.

Strian held Gressa as they said their final goodbye to the babe they had lost, the time stolen from them, and the life they nearly missed. Strian did not hide the tears that fell from his eyes, remembering that Ivar had never hid his when he and Lena ost a babe. Gressa gripped his arm as she leaned against her husband, counting on him to hold her up as much as she supported him. As the pyre floated out through the fjord, the others slipped away, leaving Gressa and Strian alone.

"For so long, I refused to let myself dream that one day we would be together again." Strian whispered. "But the dreams came, anyway. Over and over. I thought it was the gods punishing me, torturing me. I understand now that they were trying to tell me to be patient."

"We'll never be able to recapture those years, but we have so very many more ahead of us. They will far outnumber the ones we missed."

The couple looked out at the water as they watched their past disappear. It was gone from the earth but not from their memories or their hearts. Strian once more covered Gressa's belly with his hands, and she covered his with her own. Their present and their future were bound in the life that grew within Gressa.

As the aurora borealis began its dazzling nightly show, they cuddled together in their bed and watched through their window as the lights dazzled between the stars, falling asleep as they had always dreamed they would.

EPILOGUE

"Gressa! Gressa! What do you think you are doing?" Gressa turned to see her husband storming through Bjorn and Tyra's front door. "You're not supposed to be on your feet right now. You promised."

"I said it so you would leave me alone. How am I supposed to stay off my feet with two children under two and another on the way with a friend just as ready to give birth as I' am? Stop bellowing before you wake Tyra." Gressa snapped at her husband.

Everyone was tired, their nerves frazzled after a tense fortnight of long labors and births. Sigrid and Leif's daughter had joined their son two weeks ago, and Freya delivered her first babe the same night even though she was early. Erik came close to killing the midwife for suggesting that he leave the room. He was beside himself that they were far from their home with Rangvald and Lorna, but Freya reminded him they were home with her family. Tyra and Gressa were both past due and miserable in the summer heat. One of the village women who had been helping Tyra since she passed her due date had to visit her elderly mother. Gressa's two young children were asleep with Leif and Sigrid's son, so she slipped out to check on Tyra.

Apparently, she had not been stealthy enough because her overprotective ogre of a husband had chased her down.

"You needn't worry. I can't get comfortable, anyway. I'll just finish here, and Bjorn should be back from the fields soon." Tyra put away the clothes Gressa had helped fold.

"Gressa, you're supposed to be resting when the children are."

Gressa refused to budge, knowing her husband was too terrified to manhandle her.

"And when am I supposed to get anything done if I don't do it while they sleep?"

Strian opened his mouth, but the color leached from it as he watched her belly twist and shift as the babe turned over. Gressa rubbed one hand over her belly as the other tried to support some of its weight.

"That's it. You're going to bed. Now." Strian lifted Gressa as though she weighed as little as a feather. He turned to Tyra and nodded. "I'm sorry. I know Bjorn will be livid, but I'm taking my wife home."

Tyra waved them away as she closed the door behind the still bickering couple. Gressa waited until they were within their home before she began blistering Strian's ears. He ignored her and moved towards the chamber they had claimed after their first son was born. With a growing family, Gressa and Strian braved the raw emotions that came with opening Strian's parents' chamber and moved in. They had since made it their own, but a few of Strian's parents' belongings lingered as fond reminders of happier times when the four of them had lived there.

Gressa gave up when Strian just started talking

over her. She allowed him to pull her boots from her feet and peel down her wool stockings. He helped her settle on the bed with the pillows arranged as he knew she preferred. She stopped her own thoughts to watch her husband move about their chamber ensuring she had everything she could need within reach. It reminded her of the many ways Strian cared for her. The next time he walked past, she snagged his hand.

"Thank you for always taking care of me."

Strian sat on the side of the bed as he leaned in for a kiss. As it always did, the most innocent kiss roared their passion to life. Gressa's desire did not diminish with the advancements in her pregnancies, and Strian marveled at every change in Gressa's body whether before, during, or after having a child. Neither could keep their hands off one another. This time a sharp kick that they both felt made Strian pull back.

"That's why you need to rest. You are growing our child within you."

"And this is how we ended up with three babes one after another. You need only look in my direction and I seem to find myself with child."

"It that's the case, we shall have babes until we are old and white haired because I have no intention of stopping looking at you."

Gressa had a retort ready, but a pain seized her middle. She bit back the moan and tried to relax her face, but she knew she already alarmed Strian.

"Gressa, please just stay in bed this afternoon. This pregnancy isn't like the other two. We both know that. This one has been much harder since the beginning. If you won't do it for my sake, or even your own, then for the babe. Please."

Gressa nodded and tried to smile, but another pain seized her.

"Damn it," she muttered.

"What? What is it? What's wrong?"

"Nothing. I'd just hoped to have supper cooking before this started."

"Before what star-- Damn it, Gressa! Are you in labor?"

She scrunched her eyes closed as she nodded.

"For how long?" Strian pulled Gressa to lean against him as he rubbed her lower back.

"Last night," she whimpered.

"Gressa," he moaned. "When did the pains get worse?"

"A few hours ago, but I thought I had plenty of time. They were far apart and not very regular. But now—ugh," Gressa could not finish as a contraction stole her breath.

Strian eased her back against the pillow once the pain subsided. He ran to the door of their longhouse and almost wrenched it from its hinges. He scanned the passersby and thanked the goddess Freya when he saw Leif and Erik heading towards the jarl's longhouse.

"Leif! Erik! Get your mothers. It's Gressa's time."

"I can't! My mother's gone to attend Tyra!" Leif called back, but Erik was already running towards the home where his parents were also staying, having come to visit with Freya and Erik in anticipation of Sigrid's delivery and staying on through Freya's and now both Tyra's and Gressa's.

"Strian!"

Strian crashed through their living space not caring what he pushed aside as he ran back to Gressa's side.

"This is happening too fast. It all seemed fine when I walked over to Tyra's, but now I feel like I need to push already. It's too soon. My waters haven't even broken." Gressa froze as she felt a puddle surround her hips. She leaned her head back and cried. "I'm all wet now."

Strian understood what she meant after sitting with her through the last two deliveries. He also knew she was right that things were moving far faster than in the past.

"What do you need me to do, Gressa?"

She shook her head.

"I don't know. I can't think right now. Oh gods, Strian, it hurts. I'm not doing this again. I'll take pennyroyal like Tyra and Freya did. I won't stop bedding you, but I'm not doing this again either. It hurts too much."

Strian pulled the sheet from the bed and pushed Gressa's gown up over her knees before sliding behind her.

"Lorna will be here soon, my love."

"I'm here now." The woman who had become like a second adoptive mother to the two of them over the past two and a half years entered their chamber and examined Gressa. "You're ready to push. It'll all be over soon."

The next two hours were a whirlwind as Strian supported Gressa through each contraction. Her labor was not as swift as they thought, or as Gressa hoped. But after two hours of pushing, Gressa held their daughter while Strian held their son. They did not notice when Lorna slipped away.

"A little sister for our three boys," Gressa crooned.

"And she will be in charge just like her mama," Strian kissed his son's downy scalp before placing a kiss on his daughter's forehead. "She will be just as beautiful as her mama."

The dark locks their daughter possessed fascinated Strian. Their three sons were fair like Strian.

"What shall we name them?"

They had agreed without saying it aloud that they would name none of their sons Strian since they already had one by that name. They named their oldest living son Eindride after Strian's father, and they named their second son Ivar after the man who had been much like a father to them both.

"Geir?" Gressa suggested.

Strian rolled it around in his mind before smiling. "What made you think of that?" he wondered.

"I don't know. I just rather like it."

"Very well. What about our daughter?"

"I picked our son's name. You should pick hers."

"Risten," Strian whispered.

Gressa's smile dropped, and she shook her head.

"We've named our children for my father and our jarl. Why not name our daughter after your mother?"

"No. We are not giving her a Sami name. People may have accepted me now, but your memory must have faded if you don't remember what it was like for me as a child. I won't do that to her." Gressa shook her head again. "Kari. After your mother. Strian, I have no memory of my mother. It's not that I don't want to honor her or that I'm ashamed of who I am, but I won't set our daughter up for ridicule. Kari is a beautiful name."

Strian nodded. His heart hurting that after three years of living among her tribe again and after their victory against Grímr coming at her hands, she still knew not everyone accepted her. He looked into her earnest blue eyes and knew he could not tell her no.

"Kari and Geir. You've chosen well, Gressa." Strian moved to sit on his side of the bed and inched closer as they exchanged children so she could nurse Geir.

"What do you think we shall call the next one?" Gressa brushed her lips over Geir's few wisps of hair.

"Next one? I thought you swore we wouldn't have anymore." Strian was incredulous.

"You can't believe what a woman in labor says. How do you not know that by now?"

Gressa smothered whatever Strian was going to say next as her lips pressed against his, and her tongue flicked against his teeth, demanding entry. With their newborns in their arms, the couple kissed as though there were newlyweds.

"And this is why our children are so close in age," Strian muttered as he kissed his wife again. Gressa rested her head against Strian's shoulder as they both cooed at their babies and listened to them gurgle in their sleep.

"I love you," they whispered to one another as they once more looked at the stars through their window.

Discover how the saga began with Lena and Ivar's tale of unstoppable love in *Lena & Ivar*.

THANK YOU FOR READING STRIAN

Celeste Barclay, a nom de plume, lives near the Southern California coast with her husband and sons. Growing up in the Midwest, Celeste enjoyed spending as much time in and on the water as she could. Now she lives near the beach. She's an avid swimmer, a hopeful future surfer, and a former rower. When she's not writing, she's working or being a mom.

Visit Celeste's website, www.celestebarclay.com, for regular updates on works in progress, new releases, and her blog where she features posts about her experiences as an author and recommendations of her favorite reads.

Are you an author who would like to guest blog or be featured in her recommendations? Visit her website for an opportunity to share your insights and experiences.

Have you read *The Highland Ladies Guide?* Learn all the behind the scenes details from my flagship series! This **FREE** book is available to all new subscribers to Celeste's monthly newsletter. Subscribe on her website.

Get Celeste's freebie

Join the fun and get exclusive insider giveaways, sneak peeks, and new release announcements in

Celeste Barclay's Facebook Ladies of Yore Group

Leif **BOOK 1 SNEAK PEEK**

Leif looked around his chambers within his father's longhouse and breathed a sigh of relief. He noticed the large fur rugs spread throughout the chamber. His two favorites placed strategically before the fire and the bedside he preferred. He looked at his shield that hung on the wall near the door in a symbolic position but waiting at the ready. The chests that held his clothes and some of his finer acquisitions from voyages near and far sat beside his bed and along the far wall. And in the center was his most favorite possession. His oversized bed was one of the few that could accommodate his long and broad frame. He shook his head at his longing to climb under the pile of furs and on the stuffed mattress that beckoned him. He took in the chair placed before the fire where he longed to sit now with a cup of warm mead. It had been two months since he slept in his own bed, and he looked forward to nothing more than pulling the furs over his head and sleeping until he could no longer ignore his hunger. Alas, he would not be crawling into his bed again for several more hours. A feast awaited him to celebrate his and his crew's return from their latest expedition to explore the isle of Britannia. He bathed and wore fresh clothes, so he had no excuse for lingering other than a bone weariness that set in during the last storm at sea. He was eager to spend time at home no matter how much he loved sailing. Their last expedition had been profitable with several raids of monasteries that yielded jewels and both silver and gold, but he was ready for respite.

Leif left his chambers and knocked on the door next to his. He heard movement on the other side, but it was only moments before his sister, Freya, opened her door. She, too, looked tired but clean. A few pieces of jewelry she confiscated from the holy houses that allegedly swore to a life of poverty and deprivation adorned her trim frame.

"That armband suits you well. It compliments your muscles," Leif smirked and dodged a strike from one of those muscular arms.

Only a year younger than he, his sister was a well-known and feared shield maiden. Her lithe form was strong and agile making her a ferocious and competent opponent to any man. Freya's beauty was stunning, but Leif had taken every opportunity since they were children to tease her about her unusual strength even among the female warriors.

"At least one of us inherited our father's prowess. Such a shame it wasn't you."

Freya

Tyra & Bjorn

Strian

Lena & Ivar

A Spinster at the Highland Court

BOOK 1 SNEAK PEEK

Elizabeth Fraser looked around the royal chapel within
Stirling Castle. The ornate candlestick holders on the altar
glistened and reflected the light from the ones in the wall
sconces as the priest intoned the holy prayers of the
Advent season. Elizabeth kept her head bowed as though
in prayer, but her green eyes swept the congregation. She
watched the other ladies-in-waiting, many of whom were
doing the same thing. She caught the eye of Allyson Elliott.
Elizabeth raised one eyebrow as Allyson's lips twitched.
Both women had been there enough times to accept they'd
be kneeling for at least the next hour as the Latin service
carried on. Elizabeth understood the Mass thanks to her
cousin Deirdre Fraser, or rather now Deirdre Sinclair.
Elizabeth's mind flashed to the recent struggle her cousin
faced as she reunited with her husband Magnus after a
seven-year separation. Her aunt and uncle's choice to keep
Deirdre hidden from her husband simply because they
didn't think the Sinclairs were an advantageous enough
match, and the resulting scandal, still humiliated the other
Fraser clan members at court. She admired Deirdre's
husband Magnus's pledge to remain faithful despite not
knowing if he'd ever see Deirdre again.

Elizabeth suddenly snapped her attention; while everyone
else intoned the twelfth—or was it thirteenth—amen of
the Mass, the hairs on the back of her neck stood up. She
had the strongest feeling that someone was watching her.
Her eyes scanned to her right, where her parents sat
further down the pew. Her mother and father had their
heads bowed and eyes closed. While she was convinced her
mother was in devout prayer, she wondered if her father
had fallen asleep during the Mass. Again. With nothing
seeming out of the ordinary and no one visibly paying

attention to her, her eyes swung to the left. She took in the
king and queen as they kneeled together at their prie-dieu.
The queen's lips moved as she recited the liturgy in silence.
The king was as still as a statue. Years of leading warriors
showed, both in his stature and his ability to control his
body into absolute stillness. Elizabeth peered past the royal
couple and found herself looking into the astute hazel eyes
of Edward Bruce, Lord of Badenoch and Lochaber. His
gaze gave her the sense that he peered into her thoughts, as
though he were assessing her. She tried to keep her face
neutral as heat surged up her neck. She prayed her face
didn't redden as much as her neck must have, but at a
twenty-one, she still hadn't mastered how to control her
blushing. Her nape burned like it was on fire. She canted
her head slightly before looking up at the crucifix hanging
over the altar. She closed her eyes and tried to invoke the
image of the Lord that usually centered her when her
mind wandered during Mass.

Elizabeth sensed Edward's gaze remained on her. She
didn't understand how she was so sure that he was looking
at her. She didn't have any special gifts of perception or
sight, but her intuition screamed that he was still looking.

THE HIGHLAND LADIES ALWAYS

BOOK 1 SNEAK PEEK

I hate him. I hate him. I hate him. How can he do this to me? How could he pick her over me? That fat sow. Kieran will regret this till the day he dies. He and she both. This is her fault. All her fault. I hate her too.

Madeline MacLeod felt the four walls of her tiny convent cell closing in upon her. Her brother, Kieran, had dragged her from Robert the Bruce's royal court at Stirling Castle and dumped her at Inchcailleoch Priory earlier that week. She refused to accept that any of her words or actions had caused her fall from grace. She'd only spoken the truth each time she told Maude Sutherland how unconventionally curvaceous she was. Why her brother wanted to marry a woman who looked more like a tavern wench than a lady was beyond Madeline.

He just wants a good rut. He'll realize what a dreadful mistake he's made when he takes her home to Stornoway. He will realize that tupping her won't be worth the humiliation of having such a plain-faced, round as a barrel, heifer for a wife. He could have had Laurel Ross!

As Madeline listened to the bells toll for yet another Mass, she grimaced. All she seemed to do was pray these days, but God certainly wasn't listening because she remained at the priory despite her fervent appeals. She kneeled among the other novices, postulants, and nuns eight times throughout the day and night as they followed the Liturgy of Hours. The bells in the background signaled Prime, so she knew it was still very early. She'd already attended Matins in the middle of the night and Lauds at sunrise.

Madeline glanced out the narrow window set high in the wall, thinking that the masons must have designed it so the women couldn't escape. The sunlight, weak and dismal, matched Madeline's mood. When she lived at court, six o'clock in the morning was an hour she'd never seen. Now that she lived at the convent, she'd already been awake for an hour and a half.

Madeline dragged herself from her cot and her introspection. She could feel her anger simmering below the surface, and if she wanted to avoid another outburst— which would result in two days of wearing a hair shirt for penance — she would do well to calm herself. She splashed freezing water from the washbasin onto her face. It was refreshing, but it only reminded her of the austerity she now faced daily. Already dressed in her postulant's dark gray gown, she'd tucked her roughly shorn hair beneath her wimple, and a large wooden cross hung around her neck. The undyed wool of the dress made her skin itch, and it chafed the open cuts upon her back. But it was far better than the hair shirt they forced her to wear the third day she arrived. She'd lashed out at another postulant who bumped into her as they entered their pew. The postulant was formerly a lesser noble, and Madeline reminded her that she, Madeline, was the sister of a laird and a former lady-in-waiting to Queen Elizabeth de Burgh. Madeline's voice carried, but the other woman was more discreet in her own set-down, as she pointed out that Madeline's brother was the one to banish her from court.

A Hellion at the Highland Court

An Angel at the Highland Court

A Harlot at the Highland Court

A Friend at the Highland Court

An Outsider at the Highland Court

A Devil at the Highland Court

His Highland Lass **BOOK 1 SNEAK PEEK**

She entered the great hall like a strong spring storm in the northern most Highlands. Tristan Mackay felt like he had been blown hither and yon. As the storm settled, she left him with the sweet scents of heather and lavender wafting towards him as she approached. She was not a classic beauty, tall and willowy like the women at court. Her face and form were not what legends were made of. But she held a unique appeal unlike any he had seen before. He could not take his eyes off of her long chestnut hair that had strands of fire and burnt copper running through them. Unlike the waves or curls he was used to, her hair was unusually straight and fine. It looked like a waterfall cascading down her back. While she was not tall, neither was she short. She had a figure that was meant for a man to grasp and hold onto, whether from the front or from behind. She had an aura of confidence and charm, but not arrogance or conceit like many good looking women he had met. She did not seem to know her own appeal. He could tell that she was many things, but one thing she was not was his.

His Bonnie Highland Temptation

His Highland Prize

His Highland Pledge

His Highland Surprise

Their Highland Beginning

Highland Lion **BOOK 1 SNEAK PEEK**

Liam Mackay gazed at the bustling Orcadian village of Skaill, on the isle of Rousay. He thought of how it reminded him of his clan's village, outside the walls of Castle Varrich in the Scottish Highlands. As he crossed the dock, he noticed the massive longboats that Norse traders sailed to conduct trade on the island. With his father's jet-black hair and emerald eyes, few would believe Liam had Nordic heritage, but it had connected his family to Orkney for ten generations. He swept his eyes over the crofts nearest the marina of sorts. He watched as a tall blonde woman stormed out of a house and slammed the door shut. The fury on the woman's face made him think of his mother when she was angry with Liam and his younger brothers and sister. But the woman before him, statuesque and voluptuous, couldn't resemble his petite brunette mother any less. Her tall stature belied her curves until she leaned forward to fill a bucket at the well.

"Elene, come back here. We are not through speaking," an older woman called from the doorway to the croft Elene Isbister left. The younger woman continued to fill the bucket as though no one spoke to her, but Liam watched her face grow red, and it wasn't from exertion. His path carried him toward the well, but he could have continued past to reach his destination. Instead, intrigued by the stunning blonde and the scene playing out before him, he stopped at the well as the woman finished raising the bucket. She poured the contents in her own pail before letting it drop back into the cavernous pit. Unaware of Liam, she jumped when he stepped forward and grasped the crank.

Liam's emerald eyes met deep sapphire, the shade of the Highland sky in autumn. Liam observed the surprise, then wariness, in her gaze as she stepped away. He drew the full bucket to the ledge and dipped the community ladle into the cool water. As he sipped, Elene took two steps back before turning away, disconcerted by the handsome stranger. However, her feet grew roots as the older woman stormed toward her. Liam kept his head down as he lowered the bucket, chiding himself for his nosiness but unwilling to move away. The older woman glanced at him dismissively before settling her attention on Elene.

In Norn, the language of Orkney, the woman continued her chastisement. "I didn't tell you that you could leave. We were in the middle of talking."

"No, Mother. You were in the middle of talking, and I was in the middle of not wanting to hear any more. I cannot believe you're considering marrying him."

"Not considering. I've already decided. When Gunter returns in a sennight, we will wed. Then we will all move home with him."

"Home?" Elene scoffed. "Norway hasn't been our people's home in ten generations. And you are a fool if you believe he will allow me to remain."

"You're old enough to marry."

"Getting married is a far sight different from being sold!" Elene made to step around her mother, but the older woman was just as quick.

"You exaggerate."

"And you believe a slave trader over your own daughter."

"Gunter is not a slave trader. You would smear his name because you aren't getting what you want, you selfish child."

Clearly not a child, Elene stood to her full height as she gazed at her mother, who was at least two inches shorter than her daughter. "Selfish," she repeated her mother. "I hadn't realized Katryne and Johan raised themselves."

"I am their mother."

"But I raised my brother and sister. I lost my chance to marry while you lost yourself in barrels of mead." Elene swung her glare at Liam, who'd remained near the arguing women while he spoke to his two ship captains. Despite speaking Gaelic, Liam sensed Elene knew he understood her conversation with her mother. It explained her accusatory glare.

"That was my grief."

Elene released a dismissive puff of air. "That was your habit. You haven't missed Father in years. You welcomed Petyre into our home almost every night, and Father hadn't been dead two moons."

"We need a man to provide for us," the older woman sniffed defensively.

Elene gawked at her mother before she laughed. "We do not need a man to provide for us. You might need one because you can't stand to be alone for more than a day. But I work our fields and hunt out supper. Petyre, and now Gunter, come into our home and eat the food I provide. I should have accepted Duncan's offer before he grew fed up with waiting."

"You didn't love him."

"You mean like you love Gunter?"

"I do love him," Elene's mother insisted.

"More fool are you," Elene muttered.

"Come inside. You're causing a scene."

"I'm not the one yelling. And I can't. I must bring Bess this water, feed the chickens, muck out the stalls, then milk Bess. I haven't time to argue when I know you refuse to believe me."

"He is not going to sell you!"

"He will. Or he'll force me to bed him. He will not feed and clothe another adult without getting something in return. He told me."

Highland Bear

Highland Jewel

Highland Rose
Highland Strength

The Blond Devil of the Sea **BOOK 1 SNEAK PEEK**

Caragh lifted her torch into the air as she made her way down the precarious Cornish cliffside. She made out the hulking shape of a ship, but the dead of night made it impossible to see who was there. She and the fishermen of Bedruthan Steps weren't expecting any shipments that night. But her younger brother Eddie, who stood watch at the entrance to their hiding place, had spotted the ship and signaled up to the village watchman, who alerted Caragh.

As her boot slid along the dirt and sand, she cursed having to carry the torch and wished she could have sunlight to guide her. She knew these cliffs well, and it was for that reason it was better that she moved slowly than stop moving once and for all. Caragh feared the light from her torch would carry out to the boat. Despite her efforts to keep the flame small, the solitary light would be a beacon.

When Caragh came to the final twist in the path before the sand, she snuffed out her torch and started to run to the cave where the main source of the village's income lay in hiding. She heard movement along the trail above her head and knew the local fishermen would soon join her on the beach. These men, both young and old, were strong from days spent pulling in the full trawling nets and hoisting the larger catches onto their boats. However, these men weren't well-trained swordsmen, and the fear of pirate raids was ever-present. Caragh feared that was who the villagers would face that night.

The Dark Heart of the Sea

The Red Drifter of the Sea

The Scarlet Blade of the Sea